T0354315

HEAT SEEKERS

by
Joseph M. Pujals

Order this book online at www.trafford.com
or email orders@trafford.com

Most Trafford titles are also available at major online book retailers.

Printed in the United States of America.

ISBN: 978-1-4269-9314-5 (sc)
ISBN: 978-1-4269-9316-9 (hc)
ISBN: 978-1-4269-9315-2 (e)

Library of Congress Control Number: 2011915657

Trafford rev. 09/30/2011

 www.trafford.com

North America & international
toll-free: 1 888 232 4444 (USA & Canada)
phone: 250 383 6864 ♦ fax: 812 355 4082

Also by Joseph M. Pujals

Islam's Fire

For my wife Sherron without whose help and patience
this book would not have been possible.

CHAPTER 1

An Unforgettable Voyage to Exotic Ports of Call That You'll Remember the Rest of Your Life.

The passengers who read that advertisement couldn't possibly know how prophetic that statement was. The Sea Traveler had left the port of Valencia, Spain the previous morning and had reached Port Said, Egypt where the passengers had a chance to disembark for a few hours of sightseeing. Once underway again the ship joined a south bound convoy of ten other ships entering the Suez Canal. The eleven hour transit of the Canal was somewhat boring because there was little of interest to see. Someone viewing the convoy of ships from the shore of the Canal would see what appeared to be the ship's super structure, seemingly gliding across the desert. From the ship the passengers and crew would not be able to see any of the fabled wonders of Egypt on the shore, only the endless expanse of dull brown desert sand.

After exiting the Suez Canal they were too far away from land to see anything except the distant outline of the shoreline, and the occasional dhow, or flicker of light made by some distant cooking fire.

The itinerary for a sixteen day cruise carried them through the Suez Canal, into the Red Sea and the Gulf of Aden, with ports of call in Egypt, Yemen, India, and Pakistan. On the return leg, Sea Traveler would pass through the Straits of Hormuz into the Persian Gulf stopping in Kuwait, Qatar, Saudi Arabia, United Arab Emirates, and Oman before again going through the Suez Canal and stopping in Tel Aviv, Israel. On leaving Tel Aviv the Sea traveler would end her journey at Athens, Greece.

The Sea Traveler was a medium sized cruise ship that was ideal for sailing to the more out of the way and exotic ports of North Africa and the Middle East. She weighed in at 35,000 tons and was designed to carry 536 passengers. Although not as lavish as some larger cruise ships, she was well appointed and fast for her size.

The trip would take them through waters where a number of ships had been taken by pirates in recent years. International law precludes the carrying of weapons aboard a cruise or merchant ship despite the real threat of being attacked by armed pirates. However, new technology provided a defensive non-lethal alternative. The owners took the added precaution of installing a LRAD (Long Range Acoustical Device) unit. Originally designed for the military and law enforcement, the LRAD could be used for crowd control and in any situation where a means of nonlethal crowd control was needed. The LRAD is designed to issue voice commands in an emergency, or emit a narrowly focused loud beam of highly irritating noises which could disorient a crowd or inflict pain. Sounds, such as fingernails scraping across a black board, or the continuous beep of a smoke alarm, could be generated with enough intensity to create pain to anyone within a range of 1500 feet and within the focused area. The LRAD provides a means of protecting the ship by inflicting such intense pain that the pirates would be incapacitated if they entered the effective range. Since the LRAD was not lethal it was not in violation of maritime law.

There had been a brief stop in Yemen before the long run to Mumbai, India. The passengers had a few hours of daylight to relax and take in some sun before dinner, but for the crew, being on the Gulf of Aden brought a heightened degree of alertness. They knew that the Gulf of Aden had become a more dangerous place.

Within the past few years a large number of cargo ships, including a super tanker, a Russian freighter carrying a cargo of arms and ammunition, and a passenger ship, in addition to many other large and small vessels, had been taken and held for ransom by Somali pirates. Even though the Sea Traveler was cruising over 150 miles from shore, there was always the threat of an attack.

The Sea Traveler's Captain, Mason Larken, had retired from the British navy three years earlier. At fifty-two years of age he was a handsome man, he was tall, with a slender build. He had a full head of dark brown hair betrayed by just a touch of gray at the temples, giving him a distinguished look. The male passengers on the ship quickly learned to respect his naturally reassuring manner. The ship's female passengers simply considered him a very attractive man. Some would even call him a hunk. The combination of his experience and his confident bearing made him the perfect choice as a cruise ship captain.

As every Friday evening, Captain Larken had hosted a dinner for special guests, after which he attended the entertainment in the ship's theater. This particular night the entertainment consisted of a comic who provided the lead in to a quartet from Poland that could play classical and popular music which often included comedy routines that caused the audience to erupt in laughter. When the entertainment ended the Captain made is way to the bridge for a final check on the ships operation before going to his cabin.

Earlier in the evening, Captain Larken had noted that his First Officer, Jack Muldoon, had been engaged in a lively conversation with a gorgeous and shapely blond. In the crowd of mostly gray haired, middle aged, and overweight passengers typically found on cruise ships, the woman stood out, particularly because she seemed to be traveling alone, which was unusual for an attractive young woman. For his Officer's sake the Captain hoped that she was traveling with her grandmother and not her husband.

Captain Mason made his way to the elevators that would take him to the ship's bridge. As he stepped onto the elevator his First Officer joined him. "Good evening Jack. I saw you entertaining that rather attractive blond at dinner. She seemed to be enjoining your company."

"Yes sir, I dare say she did. I am supposed to meet her later for a drink."

As they stepped onto the bridge they were greeted by the Third Officer, "Good evening Sir, everything is in fine shape, the weather is perfect, just a very light breeze out of the East, the sea is as smooth as glass, and the engines are purring like kittens."

"Thank you, Mr. Kellum."

The Captain looked at the First Officer saying, "It looks like this will be an excellent cruise. I think I'll go out for a smoke before turning in. Care to join me?"

Thank you Captain I believe I will. Muldoon had been the executive officer aboard the last ship that Captain Larken had commanded before retiring from the Navy. They had worked well together while in the Navy and had formed a close personal friendship. When Captain Larken retired and joined the cruise line he had talked Muldoon into leaving the Navy and joining him as first officer on the Sea Traveler. A move that Muldoon never regretted, the pay was better and there was a never ending supply of women to entertain.

As they stepped out onto the starboard bridge deck they felt the wind created by the ship's movement. The moonlight was so bright that stars in that quadrant of the sky seemed to disappear. It was a peaceful, quiet and calm night that could easily lull a person into believing that all was well with the world. Stepping to the rail they could look down and see the light green luminescent glow emitted by microscopic sea life after being disturbed by the ship's prow. The green phosphorescence would gradually fade as it passed along the length of the ship, only to reappear in the turbulence created by the ship's propellers. Viewed from an aircraft overhead, it would look like a light green line that pointing directly at the ship before fading back into the dark sea.

The Captain and Muldoon lit their cigarettes and stared out to sea enjoying the evening. There was not much need for conversation. After a few minutes Captain Larking noticed what looked like four white lines in the water. Instantly he knew that he was looking at the moonlight reflecting off of the wake of four fast moving boats, "Jack, take a look at that!"

"Yes sir. I see them, they are moving pretty fast. Those aren't fishing boats. At the rate they're moving they'll be here in just a couple of minutes."

"The only boats out here that move like that are pirate boats, you had better get on the LRAD unit, it looks like there's going to be trouble."

The Captain stepped back onto the bridge and told the helmsman to turn 30 degrees to port. He then reached the control panel and pushed the throttle to "Ahead Full," there was an immediate increase in the throbbing sensation felt throughout the ship.

He grabbed the intercom and pushed the button for the radio room. "This is the Captain. Send a message that we are under attack by pirates and give our position. Keep on sending."

"Yes Sir, right away."

He then pushed the button for the crew quarters and the alarm button. When the klaxon stopped ringing he said, "This is not a drill; prepare to repel boarders. This is not a drill; prepare to repel boarders."

He next turned on the announcement system for the passenger area and said, "This is the Captain. The ship will be conducting safety drills in the deck area. We ask that all passengers stay in the inner passenger areas. For your safety, doors to the deck area will be locked to insure that no one inadvertently steps outside while the drill is being conducted. We will announce when the drill has been concluded."

Crew members that were in bed, reading, or playing cards immediately leaped to their feet, jumped into their pants, stepped into their shoes, and pulled on a shirt. They grabbed their life preservers and darted from their cabins, heading for the passenger deck. Their response was urgent but orderly. Captain Larkin had drilled his crew until every man instinctively knew his responsibility and assigned station. Some crew prepared fire hoses that would be used to repel any pirates should they try to climb over the railing. Other crew members headed to the various doors leading to the passenger deck. They checked to see that there were no passengers on the deck then closed the doors and locked them. If passengers tried to go on deck the crewman politely told them that it was dangerous to go on deck while the drill was being conducted. If asked what kind of drill was being conducted they were told that it was a fire suppression drill and that there were high pressure fire hoses on deck that could be dangerous if they inadvertently hit a passenger. The drill would probably last an hour or longer and after it ended passengers would be free to roam the decks.

Minutes later the radioman called the bridge. "This is radio Sir, I just heard from a British cruiser about 60 miles east of our position. They said they're coming to assist but it will be about two hours before they can get here."

"Thank them and tell them we'll keep them informed." The Captain's calm voice did not betray the urgency of the situation.

The four small boats were coming up fast, each appeared to be about 30 feet in length and looked to be carrying about ten people. A number of men had what looked to be rifles slung across their backs. A man near the bow had a grappling hook ready to throw while another man held a scaling ladder that had a hook on one end that could be placed over the ships railing.

The boats continued to move in fast. Suddenly, the boats separated so that two boats could approach each side of the ship. At the rate of speed they were traveling they would be alongside the Sea Traveler in less than a minute despite the fact that she was now moving near her top speed. Boarding her from a small boat traveling at high speed would be extremely difficult and dangerous. Even so, the pirates were getting ready to lift scaling ladders.

In an effort to get the ship to slow down, some of the pirates fired their AK-47's. Most of the bullets ricocheted off the hull taking bits of paint with them but not doing any damage. It was by pure chance that one bullet hit a window on the bridge. It went through the glass then ricocheted around the bridge. By the time it hit Mr. Kellum in the chest it had lost most of its energy but retained enough force to penetrate his chest and sever his aorta. The Captain called for the Medical Officer to come to the bridge immediately, then began applying pressure to the wound. Within less than a minute Mr. Kellum was unconscious. The Medical Officer and two assistants removed Mr. Kellum from the bridge to attend to him in sick bay.

In the meantime the pirates had realized that the bouncing of their small boats made the gun fire ineffective and they stopped shooting.

The First Officer and two crewmen reached the LRAD units mounted above the bridge. They immediately put on ear protectors, uncovered the sound generating equipment, and switched on the power. They swung one parabolic audio lens toward the boats on the port side of the ship while the second parabolic audio lens was aimed at the boats on the starboard. The First Officer flipped the transmit switch and instantly a very loud screeching sound was emitted. The men in boats dropped their scaling ladders, grappling hooks, and weapons as they clapped their hands over their ears. This proved ineffective in stopping the pain. They dropped to the bottom of the boat and writhed in pain. The piercing sound seemed to come from every part of their skull.

The boats fell back and pulled away from the ship. Several times the boats tried to return to the ship but each time were turned back by the loud high pitched sound of fingernails on a blackboard.

The loud screeching noise forced the pirates to stay away a distance of at least 1500 feet from the Sea Traveler. It didn't take long for the pirates to realize they were not going to be able to board this ship and they reduced their speed.

Although the LRAD units were not directed at the bridge the unpleasant noise was still loud enough to be very uncomfortable but not intense enough to be painful to those on the deck of Sea Traveler. The Captain left the open deck and returned to the enclosed space of the bridge. Within the ship passengers were barely aware of the sound being generated.

The Sea traveler was almost a half mile ahead of the pirates and the LRAD units had been turned off when a helicopter from the British naval cruiser approached. The Captain had just returned to the bridge deck to see what was happening, when he saw the helicopter come in low, passing directly over the pirates before they realized it was there. As the helicopter came around for another look, a streak of light shot up from one of the boats, hitting the helicopter, there was an immediate explosion. The helicopter instantly disintegrated in a fire ball and fell into the Sea

"Damn, they shot it down with a missile!"

The Captain ran back onto the bridge and reached for the intercom, pushing the button for the radio room. "This is the Captain. Inform that cruiser that their helicopter was shot down with a missile a mile directly northwest of our current position."

"Yes Sir, right away Sir."

Stepping out to the bridge deck, the Captain watched as a second missile was launched. This time it was directed at the Sea Traveler. The missile obviously had a heat seeking guidance system that zeroed in on the dining room, the warmest spot on the Sea Traveler. The missile exploded when it struck a huge plate glass window, showering the dining area with shrapnel and glass shards killing two stewards that were cleaning up.

The blast ignited several small fires but the automatic fire suppression system was able to extinguish them quickly. The dining room sustained a good deal of damage from the explosion and even more damage from the overhead sprinklers. Water continued to cascade into the dining room until the fire suppression system was turned off by a member of the ship's damage control team. There was no structural damage to the ship and it was not in any danger of sinking or burning.

The Captain re-entered the bridge and called the radio man. "Send a message to all ships in the area with our position and tell them we have been attacked by pirates. When they could not board us they fired a missile. We sustained some damage but we are in no immediate danger."

At the same time, the First Officer returned to the bridge. "Shouldn't we go back to see if there are any survivors from the Helicopter?"

"I doubt anyone survived that explosion and the fall into the sea. Besides, we can't endanger the passengers. We've taken one missile hit already and they probably have more. No, we'll let the Navy handle this problem." Although he didn't like to turn his back on the helicopter, or what was left of it, his first obligation was towards his own ship and passengers, and he took this obligation seriously. "Check on the damage. Your girlfriend is just going to have to wait till later. Meanwhile I'll try and calm the passengers."

"Yes Sir, right away." The First Officer saluted and left the bridge in a calm hurry, almost bumping into the Medical Officer who returned to the bridge to report Mr. Kellum's death to the Captain.

No one said anything for a few seconds, until the Captain broke the silence. "Thank you, doctor."

Then he took a deep breath and, checking the charts, gave the helmsman a new heading that would take them directly to Mumbai, where the Sea Traveler could be repaired so the voyage could continue.

The passengers had heard the explosion and fire alarms. Many of them left their staterooms and started to run to the lifeboats but the doors to the decks were locked. The corridors leading to the dining room were closed by fire doors. Since there was no order to move to the lifeboats the only alternative was to move to the main salon. Within a few minutes of the missile strike, the public address system announced that there was no danger and that the Captain would be in the salon in a few minutes to explain what had happened. Some passengers returned to their staterooms to put away their life jackets, others continued to wear them. By the time the Captain reached the salon all the passengers had assembled.

There were not enough chairs in the salon to accommodate everyone, some were sitting on the grand staircase, others were standing along the wall, others sat on the floor. Two passengers had been moved to the infirmary with suspected heart problems. The few children on board sat wide eyed clutching their parent's hands. A few of the passengers were crying.

When the Captain stepped into the room several of the passengers yelled questions at him. The Captain held up his hand. "I'll tell you what has happened and answer all of your questions. But first let me tell you that we are in absolutely no danger. About twenty minutes ago we were attacked by Somali pirates. The noise that you heard was the ship's defense system. It is a system that creates a non-lethal intense focused sound. The sound was aimed at the pirates who were trying to board us and it can generate extreme pain if you are in the focused beam. For those of us outside of the focused beam the sound would be uncomfortable but not painful. For those within the ship the sound was barely noticeable.

"The pirates did fire on the ship with rifles and my third officer was hit by a ricochet bullet that came through a window on the bridge. In their frustration at not being able to stop or board the ship the pirates fired what appeared to be a rocket at us. It hit the dining area killing two crew members who were cleaning. The explosion set a few small fires that were quickly extinguished by the automatic fire control system. As a result of the explosion and water damage the dining room will be out of commission until it can be repaired.

"We are sailing directly to Mumbai, India for repairs and should be there by late tomorrow afternoon. I'll have more information for you about our stay in India before we reach Mumbai.

"The kitchens were not damaged and we will serve all meals in the cafeteria. I know it is not as luxurious as our dining room but if you will bear with us I assure you that you'll continue to receive the delicious meals that you have come to expect. In the meantime the bar will continue to be open to serve you and the drinks will be free."

Several passengers asked how long would they be in Mumbai for repairs. Other asked if they would be staying on the ship while repairs were made. The Captain answered each question, when he didn't know the answer he said he would find out the information for them before they reached Mumbai."

After about thirty minutes the Captain excused himself and the passengers returned to their cabins or headed for the Bar. The Captain would not have an opportunity for sleep until late the next morning. He spent the remaining of the night examining the damage and then writing reports for the authorities in Mumbai and the cruise line company headquarters.

When the Sea Traveler sailed into the port city of Mumbai, the authorities were there in full force. Three Naval officers representing the Indian Navy, two officers from the National Police, a five man team of forensic experts, and two military officers attached to the British embassy were all waiting on the dock.

Although the Captain had made a full report over the radio he was required to describe the attack and the crew's reaction again. Following his presentation, the Captain and the First Officer, as well as the radio man and other bridge crew were interviewed separately and in great detail.

The bodies of the three dead crewmen killed by the missile and gunfire were picked up by the Mumbai Medical Examiner to certify cause of death. After the bodies were removed from the ship, members of the forensic team went through the dining room collecting every piece of metal, glass or other debris in order to determine its origin.

Twenty-two hours later the ship was released for repairs and moved to a local shipyard where workmen advanced on the dining area like a swarm of ants.

At the expense of the cruise ship company the passengers had been moved to local hotels for the duration of the repairs, which were estimated to take three days. Although the passengers got an unexpected extension to their cruise, they were not happy. A few made airline connections to return home then sat down with a telephone to call their lawyers to begin lawsuit against the shipping company for placing them in danger by taking them through water they knew to be plagued by Somali pirates. Others felt there was very little they could do about the delay. Besides, the shipping company had told them that they were going to travel through water infested by pirates. For the most part, the remainder treated the attack like a great adventure and were thankful for the few extra days' vacation in India. The adventure of a pirate attack and a few extra days of vacation to roam around the city of Mumbai would certainly be better than an eight hour shore excursion. This was indeed a trip they would always remember. They would have great stories when they arrived home.

The forensic team from the Indian Naval Science Laboratory began sifting through the debris they had collected. They discovered several pieces of metal, plastic, and pieces of optical quality plastic that were not likely to be found in the dining room of a ship. On closer examination, the pieces of debris were identified as the remnants of a rocket propellant tube, parts of a circuit board, and pieces of a plastic dome which were later identified to be parts of a heat seeking missile.

A chemical analysis of blast residue indicated the presence of HBX, an explosive commonly found in the warheads of missiles. What everyone thought had happened was confirmed. The Sea Traveler had been attacked by pirates using a heat seeking missile. The big question remained: where did pirates from the coast of Somalia get heat seeking missiles? Within thirty-six hours, munitions experts from the U.S. and Great Britain arrived in Mumbai to examine the debris evidence in an attempt to identify who had manufactured the missile. A partial part number consisting of eight clearly visible digits was found on a circuit board recovered from the debris. The numbers helped identify the electronic guidance components used in heat seeking missiles manufactured by the Martin Munitions Company in Ogden, Utah. The propellant and propellant tube appeared to be made in Pakistan.

Chapter 2

Within days of the attack on Sea Traveler, the FBI notified Jim Dunning, CEO of Martin Munitions Company, of the attack and of the apparent connection to Martin Munitions' heat seeking missiles. They also told him to have all records pertaining to the manufacture and sale of heat seeking missiles available for review. The review was to identify how a circuit board that contained the classified logic for the missile's guidance system got into the hands of Somali pirates. Jim Dunning realized that if the security hole was not found and plugged Martin Munitions would lose their government contracts.

The company immediately started its own internal investigation and began gathering the records for the Federal auditors. They were one of two companies that had contracts with the government to manufacture heat seeking missiles and the part number that was found was theirs.

The internal investigation included going through records to identify who had purchased the missiles since they had gone into production. Obviously one of the buyers was the U.S. military. They also had licenses to sell missiles to a number of foreign buyers such as England, Germany, and Israel. The company began researching their records to find the disposition of every missile that had ever been produced, sold, placed in inventory, or destroyed. Additionally, they had to provide records showing the number of circuit boards produced and their disposition including those that had been found defective and had been subsequently destroyed.

Each sale to a foreign country required an EUC (End User Certificate) certifying that the buyer was the final recipient of the missiles, and that the missiles would not be transferred to a third party. Accompanying the EUC was a DV (Delivery Verification) certifying that the buyer had received the number of missiles that Martin Munitions claimed to have sent.

Over the course of the next month the auditors visited each country or organization that had received missiles to verify the existence of the missiles, or reviewed records of their use or disposal. It was frustrating for both Martin Munitions and the FBI when the audit found that each missile that had been manufactured was accounted for. None had been stolen or lost in transit, yet the missile that struck the Sea Traveler used a guidance system manufactured by the Martin Munitions Company.

While the Federal investigation was underway Martin Munitions instituted their own security review. They examined each step of the manufacturing process to see that there was a security procedure in place that could detect the theft of parts, design, or manufacturing technology. Personnel supervisors reviewed personnel histories to see if there was anything that would indicate that an employee was the thief. To further curb the opportunity for theft Martin Munitions instituted a program of lunch box inspections of employees leaving the plant after work. Although they did not expect to find any circuit boards, it drove home the importance of security to all employees. One positive benefit of the inspection program was that Martin Munitions was able to reduce its budget for replacement of hand tools such as pliers, wrenches and screwdrivers. By the end of the month the investigators came back to Martin Munitions and began going over previously reviewed procedures, but as time passed the steam driving the investigation began to wane.

Since the end users could account for all their missiles and parts, the focus of the investigation came back to the Martin Munitions manufacturing plant. No one believed that a terrorist group or a bunch of Somali pirates would have the knowledge, skills, or ability to marry the electronics made by Martin Munitions to a missile manufactured in Pakistan. The source of the parts had to be the manufacturing plant and the modification made by someone who had the necessary skills to work with electronics.

Each step of the fabricating procedure was examined by the federal investigators again in detail to ensure that the electronics could not have been stolen during the manufacturing or assembly process. At the end of another month the investigation had turned up nothing

The FBI interviewed every employee who had handled the missiles, or the circuit boards. As part of the investigation the FBI looked into the financial history of every employee. Those who were even the least suspect were given a more thorough investigation. Everyone at Martin Munitions checked out with financial histories that seemed as normal as one would expect in the general population. Some had significant credit card debt or mortgages; some had money in savings or good investments and others with no investments at all. Everyone was within the norm that you would expect to find in the general population, everything could be explained and nothing raised a red flag. Except for a few DUIs, or domestic violence reports there were no criminal records that made the investigators take particular notice.

Again the focus of the investigation turned elsewhere. Conditions at Martin Munitions slowly began to return to normal. Everyone at the company; employees and management, sighed a breath of relief that the investigators did not find a problem.

Another month passed without incident. Then the USS Nassau (LHA-4), an ASW carrier escorted by two destroyers heading for the Mediterranean, entered the Gulf of Aden. There were a number of radar targets in the area. Some were large enough to be commercial ships and others were presumed to be fishing vessels or local traders.

As a precaution, the task force commander had two recon helicopters out approximately fifty miles in front of the task force to make sure the area was clear. They were at the maximum search range when Hilo Able spotted what looked like boat wakes in the moonlight. As they drew closer they could see that the wakes were caused by four small outboard motor boats, each approximately thirty feet in length. It seemed as if they were headed toward a freighter about four or five miles away.

The pilot decided to go down for a closer look. As he passed over the four boats he could see about ten men on board each vessel. He started to make the turn to come around for another look when a missile threat alarm sounded in the cockpit. When the pilot looked out he saw a light and the smoke trail coming toward him from one of the boats.

"Oh shit!" he exclaimed. "That's an incoming missile!" Then all that followed was static and silence.

A few seconds later the blip representing the helicopter disappeared on the task force's radar screen. By the time the radar operators directed another aircraft to the last position of the downed helicopter it had disappeared; there was no sign of wreckage or the small boats. The following morning searchers only found a few pieces of debris on the surface. The crewmembers were never found.

The only indication of what had happened was the last transmission from the pilot.

The loss of a second helicopter in the same area that Sea Traveler had been under attacked caused the investigation into Martin Munitions and their customers to be resumed with renewed vigor. The investigators wanted to reexamine every record, manufacturing process, shipping method, and re-audit end user records. But they reached the same conclusion; all missiles and circuit boards had been accounted for.

A few weeks later a French freighter was taken by the pirates but the radioman was able to send a message before the pirates cut off all transmission. "They are shooting at us with rifles and a missile has hit the bridge; several killed. . . ." then the transmission was cut off. The transmission did not give a position.

NATO ships in the area where the freighter was thought to have been did not find the freighter or any sign of the pirates.

CHAPTER 3

A short time after the completion of the second federal audit, Jim Dunning, the CEO of Martin Munitions Company, was in San Francisco talking to Alex Pribich, the president of World Bank. After completing their business they left the office and went to a private club on the fiftieth floor of the World Bank building for a drink.

Jim and Alex had been close college buddies. Back at Harvard they'd been interested in the same girl; a beautiful brunette who was studying philosophy by day and waitressing at a local restaurant at night. Neither Jim nor Alex was successful. They were inundated with classwork and couldn't spend as much time as they would have liked courting the woman. Neither of them quite made it past a bungled attempt at asking her out, but they were acutely aware of each other's interest. Even though neither of them won the affections of the brunette, they had remained friends throughout the years and got together when the opportunity arose.

"I am really concerned." Jim began the off-the-record conversation by telling Alex about the theft. "If we can't find out how components manufactured by our company ended up in the hands of Somali pirates, Martin Munitions may be excluded from future Federal contracts."

He took a long sip from his drink. He wasn't in the habit of drinking anything at a business meeting but this had been a tough, tiring day and he needed something cool and relaxing. Restructuring loans with the bank had been difficult and with the company's problems hanging over his head it had been particularly difficult, "If we were to be decertified from bidding on government contracts, we'd have to rely solely on non-governmental business or what we could sell to other countries, we would probably survive but it sure would be tough."

"You have a hell of a problem Jim, You may want to consider hiring your own investigator," Alex suggested."

"A private eye? This is an industrial espionage case not a divorce. I've already got the FBI investigators coming out of my ears. What more could a private I do that a dozen FBI agents can't."

"I don't know Jim, but consider the risk to your company; I would want my own investigator looking into the problem, somebody who was looking after my interest not the governments." Alex signaled the waiter to refill their glasses."

"With the Federal auditors working in there, having a private investigator nosing around might be problem."

"Our bank has used Carl Lukin Investigations to look into security problems in the past. Besides being exceptionally capable; he has always been the sole of discretion. Carl knows how to keep his mouth shut and makes sure his employees do the same."

"Security problems at your bank?" Jim smiled. "Never read anything about that! Maybe I should move my money."

"That's how good Lukin's work is." Alex smiled back. "He found the breach before the Feds got involved. Nothing ever hit the press."

"Well, we're well past that point. The Feds are involved already, and Martin Munitions is about to be fodder for a feeding frenzy by the press."

The waiter arrived with two new drinks. Jim deep in thought took his glass and swirled the liquid around.

"Jim, listen to me, with so much at stake you need someone on your side."

"Ok Alex I'm convinced, give this P.I. friend of yours a call but if he comes across like some TV detective it's no deal."

"Don't worry, he's an interesting guy Jim. I'm impressed every time I meet with him. Over the past few years we have gotten to be close personal friends as well as business acquaintances. He has a small investigation company, fifteen or so investigators, that primarily deal with white color crime in large corporations both here and in Europe. He won't talk about it much but I get the impression he has gotten into some pretty wild stuff from time to time. He's ex-navy, spent most military time as an intelligence officer. His parents immigrated to this country from France when he was very young. They lived in a neighborhood that consisted of a lot of immigrants from the Middle East and Eastern European speaking countries. As a consequence he was exposed to different languages. He is highly intelligent. He speaks five or six languages fluently. In addition he degrees in business and foreign relations. He's tall and looks imposing, and from I've heard he's someone you don't want to fool with. He apparently studied Gracie martial arts and is quite good.

You'll also get a kick out of his girlfriend, she is gorgeous and equally as smart. She's a computer whiz and also speaks four or five languages. She's the office manager but does double duty as an investigator if the job calls for a it. Together they make quite a pair.

"They sound as if they are pretty capable. Sure give them a call, I need help and the situation might get a lot worse if I don't get it."

"Lukin Investigations is located here in San Francisco. Carl might be in town, you might be able to talk to him while you're here. If you like, I can call him for you right now."

Alex and Ann had just returned from a long run and had stepped into the shower together when Alex called. Carl opened the shower door and reached for his wall phone. He looked at the name of the caller, sighed and said "It's Alex I had better take this." There was a short conversation and then Carl put the phone down. He reached for a bar of soap then pulled Ann into his arms saying, "Let me get your back, then he kissed her, at the same time he slowly began soaping her back."

The next morning Alex introduced Jim Dunning to Carl Lukin and Ann Curlin then took them to his private conference room, "Carl, I've already told Jim a little bit about your organization and the work you've done for the bank, and that I thought that you can help him with a problem he is having. I'll leave you three to discuss Jim's problem. You can use the conference room as long as you like. I'll have some coffee brought in."

"Thanks Alex I'll take it from here."

After they sat down Jim described all of the events that placed the company in the trouble that it was now experiencing.

"That's quite a story Jim. From what you have said it sounds like at least a part of the rocket's guidance system was manufactured by your company but not necessarily the whole thing, is that correct?"

"The heart of the guidance system is the circuit board. It contains all the logic to guide the missile. It also contains the heat detection and proximity detection circuits. The rest of the guidance system directs the actuators for the steering mechanism. There wasn't any evidence that our steering mechanism was involved.

We need to find out who is stealing the guidance system and plug the security hole. And we need to do it fast. I don't know if the theft is occurring at out plant or at one of the customers but I have to clear the company, so we'll start there."

After listening to the story and asking a lot of questions there was a lull in the conversation. By this time both Jim and Carl felt comfortable with each other and a plan had begun to form in Carl's mind.

"Do you think you can help us?"

"I don't know, there are no guarantees in this business. But it would be my guess that the thefts are being committed at your plant. If it were to occur at an end user you would have had complaints of equipment failure by now. That's not to say it couldn't happen but it doesn't seem likely.

"If we are to take on this contract you will have to hire both Ann and myself. I would have to work in the unit that manufactures the electronic components and Ann in the accounting unit, specifically, in the section that is responsible for tracking incoming parts inventory and outgoing product. I'll need to get a job that gives me a lot of freedom to move about the manufacturing floor. Obviously some people will have to know who we are and why we are there, but keep the number of people to a minimum and impress on them the importance of keeping the reason we are there an absolute secret. They should not discuss our involvement with anyone, not even with husbands or wives."

"We can hire you as a shop foreman, that will give you all the freedom you need to move around."

"No, I don't want to be perceived as part of management. People won't feel free to talk to me if they think I represent management. I'll need a job somewhere in the manufacturing process that has a lot of freedom to move about but is not considered management."

"I understand. I'm sure we can find a job that fits that requirement. I'll have to let the supervisors in the electronics area know and see what we can come up with. They will have to know about you and

Ann but they have been with the company a long time and have a lot invested in seeing the company resolve this problem."

"Ann and I will be in Logan, Utah within a week. We'll rent an apartment and give you a call when we're settled in. That will give you a chance to figure out how you and your supervisors are going to fit us into your work force and get the paperwork in order. Whatever you do it's got to look like we're legitimate new hires.

"One other thing, can you get me the employee records of all the people who work in the guidance system manufacturing unit?"

"I'll have copies of the employment records ready for you when you get to Logan."

CHAPTER 4

Carl was hired as a parts inspector in the guidance system manufacturing unit. His job consisted of measuring the various circuit boards and other parts to insure that they were made to design specification. Then placing them in a testing device to make sure they functioned properly. Once the parts had been inspected and certified as having passed inspection they are added to the inventory in the parts room located in the assembly area. The work load was not demanding and was currently easily being handled by one man. With two people handling the job it gave Carl time to talk to people and move around the manufacturing and assembly floor.

The other inspector was an older man named Jake Lunemann. Jake was trained in Germany many years before and had some eccentric habits. He arrived at work each morning dressed in a dark blue suit, white shirt, tie, and dress shoes, and wearing a black fedora hat. The first thing he would do on arriving at his work area was to change into a blue work shirt, khaki pants and crepe soled shoes, the last step was to put on a white shop coat. He would wear his fedora all day, or he would place it on the corner of his work bench. His routine never varied.

When Carl first started to work as an inspector, Jake was upset and a little distrustful of Carl. He did not like having to share his job with someone else. He had apprenticed as a machinist in Germany and considered himself more qualified than anyone else at the plant. When he reached the age of fifty-five he began to experience some health problems and was transferred to a job as a parts inspector. Jake felt that Carl, being hired to work with him as another parts inspector, was a threat to his job. To ease Jake's concerns the foreman told him that the company was concerned that there would be a real problem if he were to become ill or have an accident, and that Carl being hired was not a reflection on him, but that management felt that having a second man trained to do the work would insure that the work continued uninterrupted.

Jake could hear a thick German accent. So when he introduced himself he spoke in perfect German.

"You are from Germany?"

"No, I grew up in a neighborhood that had a lot of German families. Some of my boyhood friends spoke German so I learned a little of the language. When I entered high school and later in college I took a few German classes. I am a little self-conscious about my German, I hope it was correct."

"Yes it's very good, if you had not told me where you grew up I would have thought you were from Berlin." With that Jake turned away and went back to his workbench.

Jake was friendly but not very outgoing. He did his work and did not engage in any of the usual banter or social activities that one would find in a manufacturing setting. He didn't go out for smoke breaks although he would occasionally buy a cup of coffee from a vending machine. He didn't engage in any of the card games that always took place at lunch time. He would always eat the lunch that he brought from home at his work bench and read his newspaper.

The fact that Carl could speak German fluently made the situation easier for Jake to swallow. From that point forward all conversations between Jake and Carl were carried on in German and within a few days Jake warmed up to Carl.

Jake and Carl were responsible for inspecting a number of different parts, including the circuit boards for the guidance system. The procedure required that when a batch of parts came into the inspection area they were examined by either Jake or Carl. Circuit Boards that failed to pass inspection were tossed into a box for destruction at a later time. Periodically, the failed circuit boards were ground up into small pieces, and after being weighed, sent to a salvage company for extraction of precious metals.

Since the precise weight of a circuit board was known, the total weight of the ground up circuit boards had to match the number of boards that failed to pass inspection. The company knew how many components they had purchased, how many circuit boards had passed or failed inspection and how many were sent to salvage. They had a foolproof security system with respect to the manufacturing portion of the guidance system; or so they thought.

When the workload was light Carl managed to circulate around the manufacturing floor and talk to people. Occasionally he would join a card game at lunch to catch the latest gossip or he would sit at his workbench with a book. Since his work area commanded a good view of the manufacturing floor he was able to quietly observe the dynamics between the employees. He observed who the jokers were; which employees were engaged in a romance; those who were diligent and those who were not.

Jake finally became convinced that Carl was not after his job so he became a bit more relaxed around Carl. He told Carl a little about his life and his grandchildren. From their talks it was evident that other than his wife, his grandchildren were the important people in his life.

After about six weeks Carl began to notice a pattern. On the days that Jake worked on circuit boards he wore his hat as always to his work bench, but instead of wearing it during the day he would place it on a corner of the bench. During lunch he would handle the hat placing it back on the bench when lunch was over. After noticing this pattern of behavior Carl began to pay close attention to Jake and his hat.

When others had gone to the cafeteria or were eating their lunch and playing cards in the break area, Jake, as always, ate alone at his work bench and read his newspaper. One day Carl noticed Jake fiddling with his hat at lunch. Jake did nothing that would be noticeable if you were not paying close attention. But for Carl the behavior of people, particularly those who handled the circuit boards, was very interesting.

At the end of the day after everyone had left, Carl returned to the work area and examined the inspection box used for failed circuit boards. The tally was correct but one of the boards looked slightly different, not something that would stand out as wrong if you were not looking for it, but on closer examination it was just not the same as other boards. It had the same weight and the components looked right, but still, it was slightly different. After being ground up it would be unrecognizable as a fake and the weight of the boards would tally out correctly. A smile crossed Carl's face when he realized how a good circuit board had been made to disappear.

From then on Carl focused on Jake. He asked others discreet questions about Jake and his family. He found out that Jake was well liked but kept to himself. He was always polite, and willing to help if something needed to be moved or lifted. He was considered a bit of an eccentric but that was attributed to a strict German upbringing. Jake had been with the company for many years and had had a number of opportunities to promote to shop foreman but had turned down each offer. Nothing was known about Jakes personal life.

On the way home from work he was telling Ann that he thought Jake was smuggling good circuit boards out of the plant in his fedora. "No organization other than Airport Security ever checks a person or their clothing, and airport security had to have special legislation to do that. Organizations are afraid of being sued for invasion of privacy. Jake could only have taken one or two circuit boards a month, any more than that would have raised questions about the manufacturing process and invited a very close inspection of the entire process."

Ann thought about what Carl had said, "Okay, now that we know how they are being stolen what are we going to do about it?"

"We're not going to do anything yet. I want to know where the circuit boards are being sent once Jake has smuggled them out of the plant. Who does he sell them to and how do they get in the hands of Somali pirates?

"One other question bothers me; why does he steal the boards in the first place? He has been with Martin Munitions for more than twenty eight years. He's about ready to retire. Why would he risk his job, his pension, and prison for a few circuit boards? Money is the obvious reason, but after spending the past month talking to Jake I don't think that is the only reason.

"We'll have to look into Jake Lunemann's background. We need to find out where he's sending the circuit boards and who he sells them to. I'll talk to Jim Dunning and let him know what we have found and see how far he wants us to follow this trail or if wants to turn this problem over to the FBI."

When they reached their apartment Carl reviewed Jakes personnel file again. It revealed nothing new. It contained personal information such as that he was married and that he had two sons,

Hans and Fredrick, and their mailing addresses. Other information included who to call in an emergency, in Jakes case, his wife. The rest of the information was generic; home address, telephone number, personal description and information required for the pension fund and insurance purposes.

Carl put the files aside the files, yawned, picked up the phone and called Jim. When Jim picked up the phone he said, "I have information when can we meet?"

CHAPTER 5

"I have some news that you need to hear and I think we need to meet as soon as possible."

"Why don't you come to the office in the morning?"

"I don't think that would be a good idea, you know how gossip travels in a company. If someone were to see me going into your office my cover would be blown. Can you drop by Dunkin Donuts on the way to work, say at 6:30 in the morning?"

"I don't think that would be a good idea either, a lot of the early crew stop off there on their way in. If you're free why don't you and Ann come over to my house in about an hour? We're having a few of the neighbors over for a backyard barbecue. No one from the plant will be here. I'll just introduce you as old friends from California. Dress is very casual, Levi's and loafers, bring a sweater or light jacket, it can get cool in the evenings. We can grab a few minutes to talk later in the evening when everyone has left or had a few too many beers to miss us."

When Carl rang the bell at the Dunning household they were invited in and introduced as friends who were in Utah for a short time doing some genealogical research at the Mormon Genealogy

Library in Salt Lake. When Carl was asked what he did for a living he said he worked for the State of California, Department of Finance. Everyone assumed that Ann was Carl's wife and she did nothing to discourage that notion. Within a short time the subject moved to national politics, hunting and fishing for the men; kids, schools, and shopping for the women.

By 9:30 Carl and Jim were able to slip away to the library for some private conversation. Carl filled Jim in on what he had found. When Jim had heard the whole story he sat quietly for a few minute's thinking. Then he said, "I'm both mad as hell and hurt that one of my own employees is screwing the company like that. If this thing is not quickly resolved it could cost the company every government contract that it has. I want to follow this to the end wherever it leads us."

"Do you want to tell the FBI what we have found?"

"No not yet. They have had four months since the attack on the cruise ship to find out what is going on and haven't found diddlly squat. Let's follow this lead as far as we can go then give them a complete package. If we go to them now they are liable to screw it up.

"Okay Carl this is your area of expertise what do we do next?"

"Your loyal employee Ann Curlin is going to quit her job and do a little investigation on her own. She can follow up on the Lunemann family and hopefully find out why after so many years a once loyal employee has begun stealing from the company. Right now it just doesn't make sense.

"If we are lucky we may be able to follow the stolen circuit boards to the point where they are being added to the missiles."

On the way home Carl filled Ann in on the conversation, saying, "You're going to quit your job and investigate Jake's background. You know the routine, with special attention to his financial situation."

"Aren't we going to tell the FBI about what we found?"

"No. Not yet. Jim feels that the FBI has screwed up over the past year and doesn't want to get them involved until we have a complete package."

"What are you going to be doing?"

"I'm going to try to get closer to Jake." After a little thought he added, "You'll probably need Dan Nakamura to give you a hand on your research. Give him a heads up in the morning."

On the drive home Ann leaned her head back against the car seat and let her eyes close for a few seconds. Looking at Carl she said, "Let's forget about Martin Munitions, Jake Lunemann, and stolen circuit boards for the rest of tonight. Let's just go home, crawl into bed, make love until I am exhausted, and then snuggle until I fall asleep."

"Keep that thought beautiful." Carl pressed on the accelerator.

"Slow down Carl, you'll get a speeding ticket."

CHAPTER 6

Dan Nakamura had a Ph.D. in computer sciences and worked in research aimed at developing more secure and robust communication networks. Dan was tall for a man of Japanese descent; he had short black hair and dark eyes that always seemed to be smiling. He was not shy, he simply did not have the time to enter into meaningful relationships. He had close friends and dated when he had the opportunity which was not often and occasionally went to a party, often ending the evening with the prettiest girl there. He had an engaging personality that everyone he met immediately liked, but his focus remained on his work in computer technology.

Tired of working in academia he had joined the CIA where his knowledge of computers and operating system security was vastly increased particularly in the area of breaking security systems. He also became an expert in the more unorthodox use of the technology such as hacking into operating systems and encryption.

Ann's first job after graduating from university was the CIA where she met Dan. Both worked in the same computer research unit. Within a short time they became close friends. Later when Ann joined Lukin investigation she had the opportunity to recommend

Dan to Carl for a job to investigate the hacking into a small bank's computer.

A few years after joining the CIA Dan had attended a party at Georgetown University, had a little too much beer, and had been induced to smoke a marijuana joint, something he would never have done had he not had one too many drinks. The next thing he remembered was waking up in bed with a beautiful blond coed and a huge hangover. His tongue had grown fuzz and his stomach was doing flip flops.

By that evening he had recovered sufficiently to realize that he was going to survive and wondered if that was a good idea. By Monday morning he had returned to normal and reported for work. He told Ann about his experience and swore he would never do that again. All was well until the following week when he was required to report to the medical office. When he entered the office and gave the receptionist his name he was told to go down the hall to the room labeled "Drug Testing." Gong in he was given a plastic cup, pointed toward a door marked MEN and told to pee in the cup then bring it back to the attendant.

The next day he was called into the department manager's office and told he had failed the drug test. He was also told if it were to happen again he would be terminated. Somewhat shaken by the experience he told Ann what had happened and swore that he would never smoke marijuana or take any other recreational drug again.

Nine months later, Ann decided to leave the CIA and join Carl Lukin's private investigating firm located in San Francisco.

Several months had gone by since Ann left. Dan was again invited to a party at the university where many were smoking pot. During the course of the evening he had a few beers and was offered a joint but with a clear memory of his first experience with pot he refused.

Although he had not smoked a joint he was inhaling enough second hand smoke that the THC had entered his blood stream. When he was again tested for drugs later in the week the THC was detected. Although it barely registered in his blood it was enough to cause him to fail his drug test. He was summarily fired and escorted out of the building.

Soon after his dismissal he received a call from Carl Lukin who wanted to know if he was interested in taking a short term job. When Dan asked why Carl had called him he was told that Ann Curlin had recommended him. That was good enough for Dan, he said he was interested.

The job consisted of finding how a hacker had been breaking into a small bank. Within two days Dan had found the back door the hacker had used to get into the bank's computer and identified the hacker. By the third day he had written a report and made a number of recommendations for improving the bank's computer security.

Within a short time Dan moved to Oakland, California and was working as a private consultant in computer security. Although the majority of his consulting contracts came from Lukin Investigations, his company, Scriptorium Guard, was beginning to be recognized as an up and coming computer security company. It was rapidly expanding its customer base and gaining recognition in a competitive field.

Dan had also moved from being solely a business partner to also being a close personal friend of both Ann and Carl.

CHAPTER 7

Ann began her research of the Lunemann family by searching through public records, and obtaining credit reports from the major credit organizations: Trans Union, Equifax, and Experian. They all indicated that Jake Lunemann had excellent credit having never missed or been late on a payment. He owned only one credit card which was rarely used, and if used, he paid it off in full at the end of the month. Jake owned the house he lived in and was a cosigner for a home in Salt Lake City where his son, Hans, had a home and business.

Ann canvassed Jake's neighbors saying that she was interested in buying a home in the area and wanted to learn about the neighborhood. During the conversation a few questions about the Lunemann family always seemed to come up. The picture that emerged was that of a quiet couple who pretty much kept to themselves.

There were no problems with any of the neighbors. The neighbors were all pleased that the Lunemann's kept their home and their yard neat. Although the Lunemann's knew all of their neighbors, they did not socialize beyond a casual, "good morning" or "it's a beautiful day" stage. It was almost as if they were from a distant city and just passing through.

Ann followed Jake or his wife on their shopping trips to the mall, or to church and the post office. After a week she had a fairly complete picture of their daily habits. On the day after payday at Martin Munitions she followed Jake to an ATM machine owned by Zion First National Bank where he deposited his paycheck. That information was passed on to Dan Nakamura.

That evening Dan was able to hack into the bank's computer system gaining access to the Lunemann's checking and saving accounts. Other than the checking and saving account, Dan could find nothing else that belonged to the Lunemanns. No safe deposit box, CD's, mortgage or any other banking instrument. The following day Dan sent Ann an email listing twelve months of the Lunemann's banking activities.

A review of bank accounts revealed that there was very little in savings, and that Jake sent a check each month for a significant amount to their son in Salt Lake City.

At the end of the second week Carl and Ann had reached the conclusion that Jake Lunemann lived a very modest lifestyle and any extra funds they had were being sent to their son. The focus of the investigation then switched to Hans and Callah Lunemann.

When Hans was nineteen he joined the Marine Corps and was sent to Camp Pendleton for basic training. Hans was a big man over six feet tall and heavily muscled. He was an impressive figure in his Marine greens. He liked the discipline of the Marines and was rated expert with rifle and pistol. Even as a boy Hans was always concerned about his personal appearance and maintaining his possessions, this trait carried over to the marines. His bunk and locker were ready for inspection at all times. Hans was considered a squared away marine by the training cadre. When his basic training was complete he was assigned to embassy duty and sent to a special school for training. After graduating his first assignment was the embassy in Algeria.

Hans loved his assignment. He considered the city both beautiful and exotic, a far cry from the environment he had grown up in. He made it a point to take advantage of the local surroundings as much as possible when not on duty. He attended a local church, ate as often as he could afford in restaurants which were not frequented by tourists, and shopped in stores favored by the locals. Rather than spend his off time at the embassy or his room he attended a school and learned to speak Arabic. He found that he had a knack for the language and although not fluent in Arabic, he was soon able to get along fairly well using the language. It was at the language school where he met Callah.

He soon found himself frequently thinking of her and took every opportunity to speak with her. It was not long before he was seeing her away from the school. Whenever he could work it into his schedule they went to the theaters or took long walks. Nearing the end of his tour of duty he decided he was in love with her and proposed marriage, which she accepted.

They decided that when he was discharged they would live in California. Callah could speak a little English but was not fluent. From that point forward Hans became the teacher and she the student. He coached her in English in preparation for the end of his enlistment and their big move to the States. Two months before leaving Algeria they were married. A year later Callah gave birth to a son. Within a short time their son, John, began having difficulty breathing. Hans and Callah were optimistic about their son's health they but soon learned that their son's illness would make life much more difficult.

Ann began spending time in Salt Lake City looking into Hans Lunemann's family lifestyle. Hans and Callah owned a small home that was mortgaged to the Zion Bank of Utah. They also owned a small electronics and appliance store, and an appliance repair business which provided a modest income. The store and the repair business was their only source of income other than the money they received from Jake.

A search of public records did not indicate anything unusual. A review of their credit rating indicated that Hans had been late several times in payments to the Cystic Fibrosis Research Center but had managed to make late payments before they became delinquent and were turned over to a collection agency. The financial picture that emerged was of a family living on the edge. Their total life was dedicated to helping their son overcome his health problems.

Ann visited the Cystic Fibrosis Research Center and using her social engineering skills managed to talk her way into the computer center where she found a terminal that gave her access to medical records. She found only one record with the name of Lunemann. When she pulled up the record she found out it was for John Lunemann, son of John and Callah Lunemann.

When John was born the family was living in southern California. When their son was ten months old he was diagnosed with cystic fibrosis. Cystic fibrosis is an incurable genetic disorder that causes many patients to die young. Very few live to see middle age. The Lunemann's were referred to the Cystic Fibrosis Research Center located in Salt Lake City, where their son now received treatment.

On learning of the work at the research center Hans and Callah decided to move to Salt Lake City. They would rather have lived in California but with so many medical advances being made every day they were hopeful that a cure would be found soon. They wanted to prolong their son's life as long as possible so that he could take advantage of the cure when it became available.

With his son's family living in Salt Lake City Jake and his wife visited their son, Callah and their grandson often and always managed to leave some money to help with medical expenses.

Dan retrieved Hans' banking records and their son's accounting records from the Medical Center. What the banking records indicated was that all funds, including the money that Jake sent were used to pay the Medical Center for John's medication and medical treatments. A review of the account with the Medical Center indicated that the medical bills coupled with normal living expenses were higher than Hans' total income including the money that his father sent. Once or twice a year the Lunemann's could simply not keep up with the medical costs. At those times a substantial amount of money was wired to the Medical center to cover the outstanding debt and leave a positive balance. Six or seven months later the account would again be overdrawn and the Medical Center would receive another wire transfer of funds. The funds were wired from Algiers.

"I don't know Ann, the money being sent from Algeria could be a the payoff for the circuit boards or it could just as well be from a rich uncle who wants to help out with the Medical Center expenses."

"I understand the need that Jake felt to help his grandson with his medical expenses but selling missile technology is not the answer. I also know that families will do the craziest things when the welfare of their children is involved but those heat seekers have already cost eight lives that we know about. As for a rich uncle, I just don't buy it. The money isn't being sent monthly or even bi-monthly. It appears only when it is desperately needed. I just don't think a rich uncle would put a family member through a financial wringer like that, it's much to callous. On the other hand a crook might just do that to string them along, a reminder that if the Lunemann's did not tow the mark the funds would stop."

Carl and Ann met with Jim Dunning at his home in Logan, Utah the following evening and told him what they had found. After discussing the findings, Jim decided that Carl would go to Algiers to find the next piece in the puzzle. After considering what Carl had said, Jim thought it was now time to tell the FBI what they had uncovered. Once the FBI had verified the information and the security hole closed, the cloud over Martin Munitions would be lifted.

Jim said, "I'll call the FBI in for a briefing in the morning. I'll let you know where and when we'll meet."

When Jim called Carl the following morning it was little after 8:00.

A sleepy voice answered on the third ring, "Yeah, what is it?"

"Sorry to wake you up Carl but I just talked to the FBI and they will be in my office tomorrow afternoon. I hate to take your Sunday afternoon for a meeting but this is really important, the FBI wants to be filled in.

Carl pulled himself up on one elbow, "That's okay Jim; give me a few seconds to clear the cobwebs. Okay, a Sunday meeting is not a problem. When and where?"

"The meeting will be in my conference room. The plant will be closed except for a skeleton crew so there is little chance that your cover will be blown. I'll tell the guards you're coming and to let you and Ann in."

"Okay, got it, two in the afternoon, tomorrow, your office. Not a problem, see you then."

Carl slumped back onto the bed rolled over and put his arm across Ann's shoulder.

"I'm awake, tell me what that was all about? I gather we are going to a meeting tomorrow with the FBI."

"Yeah thats it, I guess we'd better get up. I have to write a report for Jim and jot down few notes for the meeting."

He pulled Ann into a hug and smothered his face into her hair and began nibbling on her ear.

She rolled on to his chest and in a low voice said, "I think we have a few minutes yet." Then she kissed him.

The next day Carl and Ann entered the conference room where five people were already seated. Carl and Ann were introduced to FBI Special Agents Jean Peters and Mike Reynolds, and to Jon LaCru, head of security for Martin Munitions.

Jean Peters was a slim five-ten black woman, who was thirty seven years of age but looked to be in her late twenties. She had a light brown complexion and shoulder length hair that had a slight wave to it. An extremely attractive woman with high cheek bones and hazel eyes; she would draw attention in any crowd.

Trained as a lawyer, she entered the FBI academy directly from law school at a time when the FBI was trying to lose the image of a bastion of all white males. At the academy she achieved the highest scores in her class and could out score everyone, including the instructor, on the firing range. What the old guard had not counted on was that Jean was an extremely capable and ambitious young woman. It did not take her long to earn the respect of her supervisors. She was a rising star and had advanced to the rank of Special Agent in charge of a high profile case, the Martin Munitions investigation, an accomplishment that was not often seen at the Bureau.

With Jean was her second in command Agent Reynolds. He was close to forty years of age, had not lost all his hair but it was clearly thinning and he was carrying a few extra pounds. He was trying to keep his weight under control by a lot of exercise; watching his diet was not one of his strong points. It was clear from his actions that he had a lot of respect for Jean and was not in the least concerned about working for a woman.

Jon LaCru was the soft spoken supervisor of the security staff at Martin Munitions. He had been with the company more than twenty three years. He directed the activities of ninety-six security personnel most of whom were guards at the various gates.

Jim started the meeting by saying, "Martin Munitions hired Carl Lukin and Ann Curlin to see if the circuit boards were being stolen from Martin Munitions or from a customer after the missiles had been shipped. Both Carl and Ann have been working undercover at the plant for the past two months and have uncovered the source of the theft." He looked at Carl, "Carl why don't you tell us what you've found."

Carl then explained in detail how the theft was accomplished. Ann picked up the story from there, "I have researched Jake here in Ogden and his son in Salt lake City. There is nothing unusual about Jake, but his son, Hans, is another matter. I found out that Hans has a son with a very serious medical condition and the family is in deep financial straits paying for his medical treatment. Hans and his wife own an appliance store and appliance repair business which brings in a modest income, but not nearly enough to pay the medical bills and living expenses. Jake sends him money every month to help out, but in spite of that, the medical bills are more than they can handle."

Jean Peters asked, "And how did you come by this information Ann?"

"Just a lot of old fashion leg work and social engineering when talking to people." She did not elaborate.

"I know how much Jake is making here and from what I could find out about Hans' finances it became pretty obvious expenses are exceeding their income. When they become behind in their payments a significant amount of money is wired from Algiers directly to the Medical Center. For a number of reasons we don't think it's from a relative."

Jim jumped in saying, "That is why I asked Carl to stay on this case till we have definitive proof that the money is payment for stolen parts." As Jim thought about the theft his voice took on a harsher tone. "The Lunemann's have brought into question the integrity of this company and by God I won't stand for it."

"Mr. Dunning, Carl and Ann are not law enforcement. Outside of this Country they would simply be tourists. They can testify to what they find in any prosecution, but they have no power to arrest anyone inside or outside of this Country."

Jim slapped the table hard causing both Reynolds and Ann to jump and all eyes to turn toward Jim.

"Well if I am not mistaken Jean, the FBI doesn't have any jurisdiction outside of this Country either. And for the past year the FBI has investigated this case sixteen ways from Sunday and has yet to find anything. If it had not been for Carl and Ann the FBI would still be running around with their thumb stuck up their ass and the integrity of this company would still be in question. There is too much at stake. We have to follow through on this for our own protection. I understand your concerns and will assure you that Carl and Ann will keep you informed every step of the way.

"I can't stop you Jim, but I have to keep another government agency informed and they do have an interest in what happens beyond the borders of this Country."

"I understand. Now what is our next step? Carl do you have any ideas?"

"The circuit boards have to get to Algeria some way. I believe that they are simply disguised as part of a toy animal or some other common device, placed in a box and mailed to a family member or friend. Most toys contain mechanical parts and mechanisms to give them a voice. A small circuit board would be assumed to be part of the toy. I don't believe there are going to be too many packages being sent to Algiers from Utah. I would suggest that the FBI and the Postal Service examine all packages being sent to Algeria from Logan or Salt Lake City. That search would have to include FedEx as well as UPS.

"From what I know of Somalia, it would be almost impossible to get an agent or anyone else into the country to follow the missiles to their final destination. The country has a weak central government. The area around the horn of Africa, where most of the pirates seem to be based, is run by warlords who also control the pirates. The warlords get the largest slice of any ransom that's paid. The pirates are poor villagers, typically teenagers or young adults, who only get a small slice of the money. To make matters even more difficult Somalia is a clannish society where strangers would stand out. The chances of putting an FBI operative in that kind of a tight knit clan society following the missiles to their final destination would be next to impossible. The only viable course of action open to us is to convince the pirates that using missiles is not in their best interest.

There is one other reason for me to go to Algiers. I find it difficult to believe that Somalia has the skills to develop their own missile or marry a sophisticated guidance system to an existing missile. I believe that modifications have to be done in Algiers or some European country and the completed product shipped to Somalia."

"That makes sense to me. I suppose the Somalis could simply hire someone to come in and do the work but there's still Hans and Callah's connection to Algeria." Said Jean "What would you do to discourage the pirates Carl?"

"There is another thing that we can do to discourage their use. Each of these missiles has a proximity detection circuit. When a heat seeking missile locks on to a target it follows the heat source, making small corrections in direction as it moves toward the target. Most of the time the missile will hit the target dead-on but sometimes the pilot takes an evasive action that the missile can't follow quickly enough and it will miss the target by a few feet. As it passes the heat source, sensors immediately go black because heat can no longer be detected. At that time a signal is sent by the proximity circuit that causes the missile warhead to detonate. Normally, the missile is close enough to blow off a wing or disable the engine. If we reprogram the circuit to send a signal to detonate the warhead when the missile is launched, those nearby will be killed or severely injured. After a few premature explosions like that, pirates will give up using missiles."

"I can't give the okay for that kind of modification but I'll talk to FBI Director Riley about it. We should have our answer in a few days. If we find any good stolen circuit boards in the meantime we can hold on to them and blame the delay in delivery on the post office. They are always getting the blame for late deliveries anyway. No one will get suspicious if a package is a few days late."

Carl continued, "Lastly, I will be going to Algiers. I hope that the FBI will keep me informed so that I am not flying completely blind while I am over there."

"It seems that the FBI doesn't have a choice but to keep you informed in this matter. Jim is right, we have no authority to operate outside of the U.S. If we want to solve this case we could use your help. The Director might just go for it. I'll also talk to Director Riley about your suggestion and request."

Jim looked at Jon saying, "We will also have a set of surveillance cameras installed above Jake's work station to catch him committing theft. Our security people can have the cameras installed over Jake's work bench this evening. And I'll have engineering get busy designing the bogus circuit boards first thing Monday morning."

CHAPTER 8

It was 10:30 A.M. when Jean Peters pulled up at the gate leading to the CIA Headquarters. After going through the security checks she was directed to the basement parking area set aside for special guests. As she parked her car she noticed a guard standing by the elevator.

When she entered the elevator the guard addressed her by name and asked, "Are you carrying a sidearm?"

"Yes, I'm carrying a Glock 9 MM."

"May I have it please? It will be returned to you when you leave the building."

She removed the clip and pulled the slide back ejecting the bullet from the chamber then handed it to him butt first.

When he had it in his possession he spoke into a lapel microphone saying, "We're clear and on the way up." He inserted a key into the elevator button panel and pushed the button for the seventh floor.

A secretary met the elevator and led Jean to Director Rice's office and opened the door stepping aside to let her enter. Director Rice stepped around his desk and said, "Jean, good to see you again."

Director Rice was a man in his late fifties. An imposing figure who stood six feet tall. He had broad shoulders and weighed close to two hundred pounds. He had steely blue eyes and short salt and pepper hair cut close on the side and square on top. He headed the congressional intelligence oversight committee where he earned the respect of the committee members as well as members of the intelligence community that appeared before the committee. He let it be known that he would not tolerate any bullshit from anyone who appeared before his committee and when it came to National Security, party affiliations stayed out of the committee room. When the job of Director of the CIA opened because of the retirement of the then current Director, Congressman Rice was nominated without opposition.

He led Jean to a small seating area that had a coffee table surrounded by four wingback chairs saying, "Can I offer you some coffee?"

"No thank you Sir, I've had my daily limit of coffee already this morning."

"I have asked Aaron Kovak, my head of Special Operations, to sit in on our discussion since the topic looks as if it may fall into his area of responsibility."

Two minutes later Aaron arrived. After introductions he poured himself a cup of coffee and sat down.

Aaron was a slight man with non-descript features. He had black eyes that seemed to look into you rather than at you. He had a slight accent but Jean was not sure where it came from. Aaron had been a field agent for fifteen years before being asked to run the Special Operations Section. He was responsible for field agents in virtually every country on the globe whose job it was to gather bit of information. Additionally, he had a team of analyst who were excellent at piecing information together in such a way that it made sense.

Most of his people were assigned to hot spot countries. A few were assigned to embassies in countries that were considered as friendly backwater countries that from time to time offered useful bits of intelligence.

"Okay Jean, why don't you tell us what prompted this meeting."

"We are investigating the industrial espionage case involving the theft of technology related to the missile attack on a cruise ship and the downing of a military helicopter by Somali pirates." Jean told the Director and Kovak the story from the beginning. She did not gloss over the FBIs failure to find the source of the theft. She explained Jim Dunning's frustration at the lack of progress that had been made by the FBI, and that he had hired his own investigator. She went on to explain Carl's role in the investigation, and how he had been asked to continue working the case and find out who was making the modifications.

She pointed out that Hans Lunemann's wife Callah has a brother living in Algiers who happens to be an electrical engineer. "We suspect he's involved in this mess but we don't have any evidence to that effect.

"We have a watch on all packages being sent from Utah to Algiers. Hopefully we will be able identify the person receiving the parts and who is making the modifications. At this point in time we believe the parts are shipped to Callah's brother but since we have not intercepted any parts being sent to Algeria we are not sure."

"You're not suggesting that a small machine shop in a second rate country is capable of building surface to air missiles are you?" asked Director Rice incredulously.

"No, I am not. But what if these people were able to get their hands on older surface-to-air missiles? In the attack on the cruise ship a Pakistani missile was used. But it could have been any kind of missile that used a guidance system. The fact that a missile could be modified to use the new technology is a major concern. Circuit boards that could give older missiles heat seeking capability is just plain scary. What if the basic missile already had a guidance capability that could be simply updated with the newer technology? I don't know the answer to that one but the prospect is rather frightening, particularly when you think the owner of a machine shop in a small country like Algeria might be capable of doing just that."

"You're right Jean that is a damned scary thought."

"Since FBI jurisdiction is investigations in this Country unless special authorization is given to go overseas, the CIA may have to become involved. There is one more thing; the munitions company is sending their investigator to follow this thing to the end. So at some point he will be heading to Algiers."

"Who is this guy and what do we know about him."

"He seems pretty capable but at this time we don't know much. We're investigating his background to find out more, when I get the background report I'll pass it on to you.

"In the meantime we're working with the postal service to look at all mail that's being sent to Algeria from Salt Lake City or Logan, Utah. The parts are small enough to be easily concealed in a small package, or hidden in doll or other toy, and not be detected going through the mail.

"If we find a circuit board we will make a substitution with a board that has a modified proximity circuit. The modified proximity circuit will cause a premature explosion if the missile is fired. Our problem is that we don't know when the next shipment will be made. When that happens we'll be waiting to make the exchange and Carl Lukin will make his trip to Algeria to be there when the package arrives. In the meantime we'll see what kind of information we can develop concerning Mr. Lukin as well as the Lunemann family in Utah and in Algiers."

The Director looked at Aaron, "What kind of assets do we have in Algeria?"

"We only have one asset in Algeria and he's attached to the embassy gathering information in the diplomatic circle. We can keep him posted and he can keep an eye on Mr. Lukin when he arrives. But beyond that, Mr. Lukin will be pretty much on his own."

The Director looked at Jean, "Please keep us informed. It looks like the roots for this particular problem could travel far."

"Yes sir, I'll pass along any information as we receive it, please do the same."

"We will do what we can but you know the CIA is restricted by law as to the information that we can share."

CHAPTER 9

Carl and the FBI were beginning to question their theories concerning the method of shipment. Although using the postal service was the easiest and most logical method, they could choose to use UPS or FedEx. Meanwhile the FBI and Postal Inspectors were also considering whether or not to cancel or continue the surveillance of mail to Algeria. While these discussions were underway they received word saying that the Lunemann's had just mailed a package to Algiers.

The package was addressed to Callah's brother, Taos Kassini. The x-ray of the package showed a stuffed animal with a built-in mechanical device.

The FBI quickly photographed the package from every angle, and photographed every step of the opening process. When it was open they found a large pink stuffed rabbit. After cutting the stitching in the abdomen they were able to extract a bundle of six circuit boards. They replaced the bundle with six circuit boards that had modified proximity circuits. The incision was closed and "Peter Rabbit" as it was named by the federal agents was pronounced well enough to travel. The package was resealed and held for four days to allow time for Carl to arrive in Algiers.

CHAPTER 10

When Carl arrived in Algiers he rented a car then set out to locate the Kassini home. Twenty kilometers from the city he found the address in a group of homes that overlooked the Mediterranean coast. He spent an hour getting familiar with the surrounding area before he returned to the city to find the Kassini Machine shop.

The machine shop turned out to be a large brick building with a storage yard in back. The storage yard was surrounded by a ten foot high chain link fence. It was also guarded by a large and very mean looking black Doberman Pinscher. The building and storage yard covered most of a city block. There were two large rollup doors, one that allowed access from the street for pickup and deliveries, and the other from the building to the storage yard. There was a side door in front of the building that led to an office area. From the apartment building next door Carl could see a second door that allowed access to the roof of the building. On the roof there was a small covered patio where employees could eat their lunch or take a smoke break.

There were a number of questions that had to be answered. Had the missiles arrived yet? If not, would they arrive later or might be sent to a different location.

To further complicate matters the circuit boards were small enough that they could easily be concealed in a pocket or briefcase and passed on to another person if the work was to be done elsewhere. If that were to happen he might never find out who was modifying the missiles. Carl wished he had help in keeping an eye on both Taos Kassini as well as his machine shop.

To determine if the missiles had arrived yet, Carl had to get in the machine shop for a quick look around. The roof appeared to be the easiest point of entry to the building. Once on the roof he would not be visible to anyone on the street. Using the cover of darkness he could reach the roof from the alley using a grappling hook and rope.

It was after midnight when Carl climbed to the roof. After pulling up his tools and the climbing rope Carl examined the door that led into the building. The hinge pins were welded on the bottom to prevent their removal without first grinding off the weld. It was a substantial door except that they had used a simple spring lock instead of a dead bolt. Carl slid a thin strip of spring steel between the door and the door jamb. He moved it down to the bolt and then using a second tool was able to slide the bolt back until the door could be opened. He used duct tape to prevent the bolt from moving forward again and locking.

He stepped in and examined the door frame for any indication of a burglar alarm. He found a set of broken wires that had been twisted together completing the circuit, effectively disabling the alarm for that door. The alarm had probably been deliberately disabled by the workmen to make reaching the break area on the roof easier. Carl then moved down the stairs to the main floor.

There was a single light that was used at night to permit the night watchman to move around the equipment without getting injured. The light was bright enough to cast shadows but not enough to comfortably read by. There did not appear to be anyone in the building.

Along one wall there were four rooms. The last one in the far corner of the building was a bathroom. Of the remaining rooms one was obviously a tool room, one appeared to be an office, and the third was a workshop or assembly area. Carl looked around the main floor, office, and assembly area but did not find anything of interest. There weren't any boxes big enough to ship or hide missile assemblies or launchers.

Carl was just about to leave when he heard a key in the personnel entry door at the front of the building. Ducking behind a milling machine he watched as the night watchman walked in.

The watchman had apparently heard something because he turned on his flashlight flashing around the room and started to walk through the shop. After a couple of minutes he had reached the far wall looking behind machines and boxes as he went. When he reached the wall he began calling "Mimi." Carl watched as the watchman turned and began moving in his direction.

A cat that had been curled up asleep on a nearby box got up, stretched, and purring walked over to Carl. The guard was still moving in his direction. Carl flicked his finger at the cat's nose and it ran toward the watchman. Carl could feel his heart begin to thump loudly in his chest as the adrenalin flow increased in his body. Holding his breath he bent his head down to his chest to reduce the amount of the white skin of his face reflecting light. He hoped that the guard could not hear him breath or his heart beating; he crouched behind the milling machine remaining absolutely motionless.

The watchman stopped about twenty feet away, bent down and picked up the cat saying, "There you are Mimi, I brought you something to eat." Petting the cat for a moment he walked back to the front of the building and put it down in front of a plate to which he added some food. He stood there for a minute watching the cat then turned and walked toward the office.

As he walked into the office Carl let out his breath out slowly. Once in the office the guard sat in a comfortable chair, stretched, yawned, leaned back and was soon sound asleep. Carl listened to the snoring for fifteen minutes then left the building the way he came in.

CHAPTER 11

The package was addressed to Taos Kassini's home located on the Mediterranean coast. The home was located in an upscale neighborhood that overlooking the Sea. The homes in the area were obviously those of the rich or near rich, the Kassini house was one of the latter.

Most homes were of white stucco construction with red tile roofs and landscaped with lush gardens. Most were covered with flowering plants or bougainvillea vines. The Kassini home was no different.

Carl had a chance to become familiar with the area surrounding the home long before the package arrived. He was seated in a car that was parked on a hill just up the road from the house. From this vantage point he could see the line of mailboxes near the Kassini home. He had driven by the mailboxes earlier and identified the one belonging to the Kassini family.

To provide a cover for his presence in the area, Carl had purchased an easel, folding chair and a box of art supplies. He would drive to the small hill that overlooked the Kassini home and set up his easel and begin to sketch the scene in front of him. While he sketched he could watch the postman as he drove down the street making deliveries. Within a few days Carl was familiar with the postman's schedule.

The post office in the U.S. could provide an approximate date for delivery of the package to the Algerian postal service but could not provide any time frame for delivery of the package to the house. The only thing Carl could do was remain as inconspicuous as possible, wait, and watch, in effect he had decided to hide in plain sight.

Each day Carl would set up his easel and canvas, and sketch the street and homes. When the postman drove up he would pull out his binoculars and watch to see what had been delivered.

It was not long before a number of children began gathering around Carl to watch him sketch. Children would ask questions as children do, such as, "Why are you drawing pictures of those houses?"

"Because they are nice looking houses and I want to draw a picture of them."

"What are you going to do with the picture?"

"I am going to color it with paint when it's done."

"Then what are you going to do?"

"I am going to sell it."

So it went for a few hours. The children would ask questions and Carl patiently answered each one.

A short time after the postman had gone by Carl would pack up his art equipment in preparation to leave. When the children asked why he was leaving he would say, "The light is no longer right for painting."

"But you are not painting you are drawing."

"Yes, but in my mind I see the drawing as I will paint it and the light is not right for painting."

The following day the process was repeated with the children arriving a short time after Carl had set up his easel. They asked many of the same questions and a few new ones but it did not take as long for them to lose interest and leave.

By the end of a week Carl had a very detailed sketch and was beginning to add paint to the canvas. For a few days children stopped to watch Carl paint. His progress was so slow that they soon became bored and went away. Within the neighborhood Carl soon developed a reputation for being a crazy Frenchman who, at the rate he painted, would soon starve to death.

Carl was focused on the Kassini home and did not notice that each day he had been followed and watched from some distance away. When he finished his painting for the day and drove back to the hotel the watcher would discreetly follow along.

In the early evenings Carl would walk around the city to become familiar with its streets and shops and later dine at a good restaurant. Late in the evening he would find a seedy workingman's bar near the Kassini Machine Shop where he posed as an obnoxious German businessman who was not opposed to buying a few rounds of drinks although he could not hold his own liquor very well. By the end of the night he would be dropping hints about his connection to the weapons trade and his connections in Sudan, Somalia, Congo, Sierra Leon and a few other African nations. Though his voice would tend to slur he occasionally made casual comments about the need for help in upgrading or repairing equipment.

As the nightly outings continued Carl could not shake the feeling that he was being followed, although he couldn't identify the person following him. Carl was always conscious of his surroundings and the people around him but he didn't notice anything unusual. As the days passed Carl's feeling of unease heightened.

On the tenth day of watching the Kassini house the postman tried to fit a package into the mailbox but couldn't so he walked it to the front door. That evening Carl sent a text message to Ann saying,

"Peter Rabbit has arrived. I love you and miss you." Ann passed the message concerning Peter Rabbit on to Jean Peters who in turn called Aaron Kovak but Aaron was already aware of the delivery.

Carl continued watching the Kassini home hoping to see the package being moved to its next destination. He also continued to frequent the more unsavory bars every evening trying to get a lead on the name of someone who might be willing to modify weapons.

Late one evening he left a bar with two men who said that they could introduce him to a businessman who did that kind of work. As they were walking down the street he sensed that there was someone behind him and was starting to move to one side when he was hit a glancing blow to the head and left shoulder. He was knocked to the ground in a daze and quickly pulled into an alley. As the men started going through his pockets a shot rang out, the bullet chipping brick from the wall just above their heads. His attackers jumped to their feet and ran down the dark alley. A second shot encouraged them to keep running.

Carl was helped to his feet by a slightly overweight middle aged man. He leaned against the wall to steady himself. He tried to see the man who came to his assistance but the alley was too dark to get a good look. He finally said, "I don't know who you are but you saved my ass."

"Those ruffians would have taken everything you had if I hadn't come along. Come on I'll help back to your hotel."

"Who are you and how do you know where I am staying?"

"My name is Macintyre, Ian Macintyre. We had better get moving, I doubt that they will come back but better to be safe than sorry."

Carl pushed away from the wall and rubbed the back of his head. As they passed a lighted window in a small restaurant he took a long hard look at his benefactor. The man was about fifty, five ten in height, thinning gray hair, and about thirty pounds overweight. He was dressed casually, but had obviously paid some attention to picking clothes that matched; definitely a man who cared about his appearance.

"I've seen you several times in the last few days. It appears that you've been following me. I don't know why you're tailing me but thanks for your help. Those bastards play rough."

"Not now old boy, plenty of time for questions when we get back to your room."

CHAPTER 12

Carl leaned over the bathroom sink and washed his face. He had a small laceration on the back of his head. Although his head ached it had stopped bleeding. He took two aspirin to ease the pain and reentered his bedroom.

The room was like thousands of other hotel rooms around the world. A large bed, an easy chair, a television set, a dresser, and a small round table with two chairs and two scenic pictures on the walls. There was a desk lamp on the table and a small alarm clock radio next to the bed.

Ian Macintyre was sitting in one of the chairs patiently waiting for Carl to wash up. When Carl entered the room he asked, "Why have you been following me?"

"I have been asked to by your friends."

"I haven't told any of my friends where I was going or what I was going to do. So tell me again, why have you been following me?"

"You have more friends than you know about. People in the organization I work for have asked that I keep an eye on you."

"Okay let's start there, who do you work for?"

"People who don't want to see you get hurt."

Carl sat quietly for a few seconds thinking.

"I've got friends that I don't know about, and people who don't want me hurt, but you can't tell me who they are. And the man who saved my butt won't tell me who sent him to watch over me.

"I apparently can't persuade you to tell me who told you to follow me and since you saved my ass I can't very well beat it out of you, so let me ask you, are you going to continue to watch over me?"

"I don't know, are you planning to get into more trouble?"

"Let's make this easy on both of us. Why don't you meet me in the hotel restaurant at nine tomorrow morning and I'll buy breakfast. In the meantime you can talk to your boss or whoever you work for and find out what you are allowed to tell me. In the meantime I'll make a few calls and find out who the hell you are and who you work for."

Both men stared at each other for a moment, finally Ian said, "Okay, It seems we have reached an impasse. I work for the American Embassy as a Commerce Attaché; I just happened to be walking along the street when I saw those three hoodlums trying to roll you and decided to even the odds a bit."

"You're not going to tell me the truth are you? So let me guess. You work for the American Embassy; that's probably true. You carry a gun which a diplomat is a not allowed to do and you have been tailing me ever since I got off the plane. So I'd have to guess you're CIA. Now the question is, why is the CIA tailing me? My guess is that the FBI has talked to your boss and your boss is interested in solving the same problem that I am. How am I doing so far?"

"That knock on the head obviously didn't do much damage. Those missiles have been used against British and American naval aircraft killing a number of good airmen. They hit a cruise ship and several freighters killing more people. We want the dealer who is selling the missiles to the Somali pirates, and like you, we are interested in the man who is making or modifying the missiles. What do you intend to do next?"

Carl thought about what McIntyre had said and decided that they might just as well join forces. It didn't look as if he was going to be able to get rid of Ian McIntyre.

"I assume that your boss has filled you in on what is going on?"

"Somewhat. Guidance electronics for heat seeking missiles are being stolen from an American company and used to modify or build heat seeking missiles, probably here in Algeria. You are following the stolen parts to find out who the buyer is and who is selling the finished product. Does that about cover it?"

"Yeah that about covers it. A set of circuit boards for the guidance system arrived by mail at the Kassini home today so I thought I would make a visit to the Kassini Machine Shop tonight and see if the missiles are there. Those missiles have to come into the plant someway and they have to be shipped out to their final destination. If the work is being done by the Kassini Machine shop there must be records of their arrival and shipping invoices to the Somalis or some other destination when the modifications have been completed. If I'm lucky I might be able to find out where they are coming from and who is sending them.

"On the other hand, Taos Kassini may simply give the boards to someone else, in which case I'll try to follow them. But that would be difficult since they are small and can easily be hidden in a coat pocket and then simply passed on to someone without being noticed. But I am betting the work is being done by Taos Kassini. He has the facilities and he is an electrical engineer so he has the basic skills necessary for the job.

"I know the circuit boards are here so I am going to keep an eye on the machine shop and try to find out where they came from and how they're being sent to Somalia."

"Well, don't get caught, an Algerian jail is not a fun place to be. When do you intend to do this bit of breaking and entering?"

"I'll get a good night's sleep, buy the things I need tomorrow and go in tomorrow night. The new parts arrived yesterday morning. I want to find out if the missiles have arrived. If they have maybe I can get a look at the shipping crates they came in. Maybe get a handle on where they came from and how they're being shipped. If they have not arrived yet I'll watch for them."

"What kind of equipment do you need?"

"If you have an extra pair of night vision goggles lying around I sure could use them, I can buy a camera and the rest of the things I'll need at a hardware or sporting goods store."

"I'll be back at seven tomorrow evening with the night vision equipment."

"Good, if you're interested I'll buy dinner instead of breakfast and thank you properly for saving my hide."

Chapter 13

Putting down his coffee cup, Carl said, "I got in through the roof without any problem and got a look around most of the building except the office before the night watchman came in. He had apparently gone out for something to eat. He almost caught me but he didn't see me. Luckily, after feeding the cat he went into the office and went to sleep giving me a chance to slip out. But I don't think what we were looking for was there. I didn't see any shipping crates big enough to ship missiles or launchers; they most likely haven't arrived yet. Having a bunch of rockets just sitting around waiting for circuit boards to show up would be dangerous and certainly raise a lot of questions from those employees who are not involved with making the modifications."

Ian considered what Carl had said then asked, "What are your plans now?"

"I have two options. The first is simply to get on a plane and head home. But I just can't do that, I don't like leaving a job half done. The second option is to watch the Kassini factory for the next couple of weeks and see if the missiles come in or not.

"I guess I'll stick around for a while and see what happens. I could use your help, but if you would rather not get involved I can hire a couple of thugs."

"That depends on what you have in mind? I'm a little old to go climbing over rooftops and you may have notice I am not the trim muscular man that I once was, besides I have been sitting behind a desk for too many years. Second story work was fun when I was younger but it's not something I like to do now. You know how it is as you get older and you get a little bursitis or arthritis."

"I know what you mean. I'm not your age but I am beginning feel a few aches when I get up in the morning.

"The night watchman apparently goes to get something to eat about eleven at night. When he comes back he goes into the office for a nap. I need someone to keep him busy at dinner for as long possible so that I can get a look around. I can't watch both the front and back of the building at the same time so a warning when he is coming back to the building would really help. I almost got caught last time I went in, but Mimi saved my ass."

"Who the hell is Mimi?"

"Mimi is the shop cat that the watchman feeds every night."

"Okay, I can do that for you. I'll check around today and see if there are any all-night café's in the area and I'll pick up a couple of radios so that we can keep in touch."

"That sounds good. I appreciate the help."

Carl rented a room above a bakery just down the block from the Kassini Machine Shop. From there he could watch the front door of the building. During the day a delivery van driven by a young man made trips delivering finished work or picking up supplies and parts that required machining. About five in the afternoon Ian would come and relieve him so that he could get a bite to eat and a few hours' sleep before entering the machine shop at night.

Each night Carl waited until the watchman left for his meal break, he would then climb to the roof and entering the building. Now that he had someone keeping an eye on the watchman he had an opportunity to go through the files in the office. He didn't find any shipping or receiving invoices for Somalia, nor did he find any unusual shipping records to other countries. It seems that the most business was based on supplying services to other local businesses in Algiers or surrounding towns. The missile upgrades were obviously done were done without any records being kept. Only occasionally would the machine shop receive work from outside of Algiers.

It was Friday of the second week that there was a change in the normal machine shop operating routine. Instead of the van being locked up in the machine shop over the weekend Taos Kassini and another man drove out with it in the early afternoon and did not return until well after normal business hours.

When Carl made his early morning inspection he found the van in its normal parking place. There was nothing unusual on the floor of the machine shop, except that the assembly room which was normally unlocked was now locked. Carl managed to pick the lock and open the door.

Inside there were six wooden crates, each about twelve inches high and wide and six feet long. The crates had not been opened but there was little doubt that they contained the missiles that Carl was looking for.

Each of the boxes had a shipping label addressed to Kassini Machine Shop, and a shipping invoice saying that the box contained hydraulic cylinders that required repair and were sent by the Coussach Tractor Company in Kiev, Ukraine. He photographed each box and the attached shipping invoices. He lifted one of the boxes to get an idea of the weight. He estimated that each box weighed about 90 pounds. The missiles themselves would not weigh that much but the wood shipping crate, and metal shipping container inside added to the weight.

Carl was back on the roof when he got the call from Ian saying that the watchman was on his way back. He responded with, "They're here. Come to my hotel, I've got photos."

When Carl entered his hotel room Ian was waiting for him. Removing his camera from his backpack Carl turned it on and he and Ian looked at the photos on the camera's digital display.

Ian spoke first saying, "I'll wager my girlfriend's virtue that those boxes contain what we are looking for."

"You can keep your wager, any girl that would go out with you lost her virtue a long ago."

They both chuckled, Carl said, "Now what? Do you think the people you work for can do anything with these?"

"Yes, I believe they will certainly be most interested."

"They came in late on Friday after the shop closed for the weekend. Taos and his friend picked them up from the shipping company Friday afternoon and made sure everyone was gone for the weekend before moving them to the assembly room. I'll bet Kassini told the weekend guard that he could take the weekend off. That he would be in the machine shop on a special project and there was no need for both of them to be working.

"I'll go in Saturday night after Kassini and his friends have gone for the day and try to get some photographs of the missiles. If we are lucky we'll get some indication of where they're being sent once they're modified. By the way, do you have any bugs that we can put in the assembly room?"

"Yes, I believe I can manage that. I'll bring them over this afternoon."

Saturday morning Taos Kassini parked his S600 Mercedes in front of the machine shop. His friend was already there waiting for him. Although both doors to the machine shop were closed, lights could be seen through the office windows. About two in the afternoon the two men left the building going to a small restaurant a short distance away. They returned about ninety minutes later and continued work in the machine shop until seven that evening. As usual, at eight that night the watchman returned for his normal work shift.

Taos appeared to be near Carl's age, thirty five to forty years of age, dark hair, brown eyes, and suntanned skin. He had a pleasant smile and a mole on his right cheek. He was 5'8"and slim. He looked and moved like he was athletic, possibly tennis or swimming since he lives near the coast. Altogether a rather handsome businessman.

When the watchman went for his supper, Carl reentered the machine shop going straight to the assembly room. There were two stacks of crates. One stack had obviously been opened and resealed; tool marks were clearly visible. The other crates had been untouched. Carl found a crowbar and pried the lid off of one of the previously opened boxes. Inside was a metal container which he lifted out setting it down on the workbench. When he unlatched and opened the lid he could see a shoulder held rocket launcher. He lifted the launcher from the metal container so that the numbers and writing on the side of the launcher were clearly visible.

He photographed the launcher from several angles. He didn't need to remove the missile from the launcher. He carefully placed the launcher back in the metal case then put the case back in the shipping crate nailing the lid back on.

There was no need to photograph the crate again. No new labels or addresses had been added. He put the tools back where he had found them and was getting ready to leave when his radio crackled with Ian's voice, "Get out of there he is on his way back." Carl did one last check of the assembly room and turned off the lights. He started to leave then remembered the bugs. Removing the plastic strip covering the adhesive from the back of the microphones he quickly stuck them under cabinets that hung over the work bench. He stepped out of the assembly room and locked the door behind him just as he heard the key in the front door. He ducked behind a lathe and froze, hardly daring to breath.

The guard walked over to Mimi's feeding dish and dropped some food in it. He called Mimi who sauntered over, stretched, rubbed her head against the guards leg and began to eat; the guard petted the cat a few times then yawned and headed to the office. Within a few minutes Carl could hear the guard snoring loudly.

Chapter 14

The next day Carl and Ian watched as Taos parked his Mercedes at the curb and entered the machine shop with his friend. A few minutes later the bugs picked up the sounds of the assembly room door opening and the voice of Taos Kassini on the monitor saying, "Hand me the crowbar." then came the sound of boards being pried up and the screech of nails being extracted from wood. There was the clatter of tools and wood as the crate lid was leaned against the wall.

"Pick up the other end of this thing Lazio, and be careful, I don't trust these things. Good, now lift it out."

There was the sound of the missile case being placed on the work bench and the latches being released, then the metallic sound of the missile launcher being set down on the workbench.

"Lazio, hold the launch tube while I take out the missile."

Then came the sounds of tools being picked up and put down, and Taos' voice saying, "Lazio, plug in the soldering iron and get me the new batteries."

After an hour Lazio asked, "What is wrong with this thing that we have to change the electrical parts?"

"This is the first model ever produced by the Pakistanis. If it hit its target it was to everyone's great surprise, but it missed its target many more times than it hit. We add the new circuit board and fresh batteries and all of a sudden it doesn't miss anymore."

"Who is this owner that we do this work for and what does he do with the rockets?"

"You don't want to know who he is, it is safer that way. I don't know where he uses them or sells them and I don't want to know either, it's none of my concern or yours. It is safer for both of us if we don't ask too many questions."

By the end of the day the remaining missiles had been modified. While Taos worked on the missiles Lazio painted over the Kassini Machine Shop name that had been on the shipping crate and added a fictitious name of a non-existent company. The last step was to load the boxes into the back of the van.

That night Carl made one final entry of the Kassini Machine Shop. He went straight to the assembly room and removed the two bugs he had placed there the night before. Then to the van where he photographed the missile crates making sure that the new paint on the shipping crates was visible. There was no shipping address or any other indication of where the boxes were to be sent.

By the time the guard finished his supper and returned, Carl had finished taking photographs and was gone.

There was nothing more that Carl could do except follow the van the next morning. Ian and Carl watched the machine shop all night to make sure that the van was not moved without being followed.

Arriving at six the next morning, Taos Kassini drove the van to a small airport that handled corporate jets and a couple of small freight carriers.

He stopped at the gate and talked to the guard telling him that he had engine parts for the maintenance crew at the Sarcozy Freight

Company. After the guard waved him in he drove to a large hanger. The doors were open and he was able to drive in and park next to an old Hawker Siddeley HS748 where two men were standing. The HS748 was a cargo plane designed as a STOL aircraft (short takeoff and landing) ideal for operating in Africa or the Middle East.

Following a short distance behind Taos, Carl drove up to the airport gate. When the guard approached, he said, "I was told to come here and meet a Mr. Angeles, Vice President of a freight company, but you know how it is, I had a few drinks the night before and can't remember the name of the company. Can you help me?"

"There are only two freight companies here, Sarcozy Freight, and Ghana Air, but I don't know the names of any of the people that work there."

"I'll just go to the freight office and ask for Mr. Angeles."

"I'm sorry, without a pass or your name on my list I can't let you in."

"Take another look at your list I'm sure my name must be in there. Here is my business card, it may help." Carl reached for his wallet and withdrew a $100 dollar bill passing it to the guard.

Looking in both directions the guard took the money and said, "Sarcozy is in the big hanger, Ghana Air is in the building next to it."

Carl pulled out another $50 dollars, saying, "Where did the van that just came in go?"

Taking and pocketing the money he said in a conspiratorial voice, "Sarcozy Air."

"Thank you." Carl drove slowly toward the big hanger. The doors were open and as he drove by he could see creates being loaded onto the plane.

Twenty minutes later the van drove out of the hanger and headed toward the gate.

Carl called Ian and told him what had happened. He said that he was going to wait and see if he could get a look at the tail number on the aircraft.

"I'll try and pick up our friend in the van. I'll call you later."

Carl's phone rang an hour and a half later. When he answered it Ian said, "I picked him up just as he was entering the city. He stopped at a restaurant and then headed straight back to the machine shop."

"Thanks Ian, I'll keep an eye open out here."

Three hours later a car with two men drove up and parked next to the hanger. The men got out of the car, one carried a briefcase, both had a small suitcase. They entered the hanger and boarded the aircraft. Ten minutes later a small tractor towed the plane out of the hanger and faced it toward the runway. Clearly visible on the tail was the number SA5757. The photographs that Carl took would help in identifying the men and the airplane.

Carl called Ian and gave him the information.

"I'll pass the information on and meet you at your hotel. We can have a late breakfast."

Later at breakfast Ian said, "I spoke to some friends at the air ministry and they said that a flight plan had been filed for SA5757 to fly to Libya, Sudan, Ethiopia, Somalia, Cairo, Egypt, then return to Algiers. So now you know how the missiles get to Somalia. The big question is who sold them to the Somalis. Are you going to follow up on this problem or are you going to quit and go home?"

"I don't know Ian. I'll probably go home in the morning and talk to the people who hired me and see what they want me to do."

"Ian, I want to thank you again for saving my ass and all your help."

"Think nothing of it. I haven't had this much fun in years. Quite frankly I was getting tired of being stuck behind a desk, or being forced to attend embassy parties, dancing with beautiful women, eating good food, and drinking too much. Perhaps we'll have the opportunity to work together again."

CHAPTER 15

Carl and Ann sat across the conference table from Jim Dunning, Agents Jean Peters and Ron Anderson giving a briefing on his Algerian trip.

"We know that the Kassini Machine Shop is where the missiles are being modified and that Taos Kassini is doing the work. We have pictures of the missiles, and a recording of Taos discussing the missiles with an assistant. Ian Macintyre has sent photographs of the missiles and shipping cases to the CIA. Maybe they can identify where they came from.

"We know that the missiles are being shipped to Somalia on Sarcozy airline, a small time freight carrier. The airline makes stops in several countries that are having problems with insurgencies. I think it's reasonable to assume that they may be carrying other illegal contraband.

"We have pictures of the missiles and can identify who makes them but we don't know who in Pakistan is selling them or who the buyer is, and we don't know who is buying the missiles once they are modified.

"All we know is that they end up in the hands of the pirates and probably other groups.

"You could arrest the Lunemann's which would end the theft problem and clear Martin Munitions, but I doubt that it will stop the flow of arms to the pirates. But once you do, everyone in the pipeline will know about it and head for cover. The worst part is that it will only be a matter of time before the arms dealers, whoever they are, will find another source for missiles.

"If we want to identify who is buying and selling the missiles we need more information."

Jim said, "It gall's me to think that someone who stole our circuit boards then sold them to pirates might get away with it. I would like to get this guy whoever it is. What do you think Jean?"

"Carl's right, we have enough information to indict the Lunemann's and close down the theft operation. But now the CIA is involved and my guess is that they would like to find who is selling missiles to the arms dealer. Even though the pipeline for the circuit boards will be closed it's likely that the arms dealer will have contacts in other countries that make heat seeking missiles. The question is how can we proceed without alerting the Lunemann's, Kassini's, or the arms dealer before we are ready?"

"I can go back to Algiers and have a private conversation with the airline pilots and Taos Kassini. I doubt if the airline pilots know anybody else in the pipeline but it's worth a shot. I suspect they're just paid to fly the plane.

"Taos is a different question, there is no guarantee that he won't call his sister, but maybe I can persuade him that the consequences would be very costly to him. In any case, we might get more information than we have now. With a little luck they might give us a clue to the arms dealer. Once we have that, the rest will be pretty much up to law enforcement."

Jim said, "I'm still pretty much burned about the way my company has been used, I would like Carl to go back one more time. Personally, I would like to see this mess cleaned up and those responsible in prison. But above all I want to see my company's good name restored. Are you up for another trip to Algiers Carl?"

"Not a problem. Give me a couple days to get a little rest and I'll head back for a private talk with a couple of airline pilots and Taos Kassini."

CHAPTER 16

Carl had stopped at the Briska Airport operations office and found the name of the pilot who flew for Sarcozy the previous week. The Airport operation office gave him the name of the pilot, as Carlos Mendoza. Undoubtedly Mr. Mendoza would be very reluctant to discuss his work with a stranger, particularly since that line of work could land him in prison for a very long time.

Particularly since there was no obvious proof that he knew he was carrying illegal cargo; he may have been totally unaware of the missiles and just flew the plane. Although, in this part of the world it is doubtful that law enforcement would care whether he knew that he was carrying illegal cargo or not.

In any case, there would be no point in trying to have a rational discussion with Mr. Mendoza. Carl would have to open the discussion with a very forceful and persuasive argument; an argument that Mendoza couldn't ignore or say no to.

After driving to Mendoza's apartment, Carl pulled on a pair of light leather driving gloves and knocked on the apartment door. He got ready to make his opening argument. He knocked on the door again and waited, then knocked louder.

From inside he heard "Yeah, yeah, just a minute."

The door was opened by a man who looked to be about forty-five years old and was beginning to show signs of balding. He was not fat but he had a layer of flab around his middle. He looked at Carl through sleepy eyes and in a very irritated voice asked, "What do you want?" His breath reeked of cheap wine. And his eyelids were droopy with sleep. He had a heavy Spanish accent.

"Carlos Mendoza?"

"Who wants to know?"

"I do"

Carl rarely ever used violence; it simply was not in his nature. Since his investigation business usually dealt with white collar crime he seldom had need for it. Although he disliked physical violence he recognized that sometimes it was necessary. On those few occasions when he had to use force his martial arts training simply took over. This was one of those times.

Carl's fist slammed hard into Mendoza's face, knocking him back into the room. Carl stepped over the man sprawled on the floor and closed the door behind him.

Mendoza's nose was pushed to one side of his face; obviously broken. Blood gushed down over his upper lip and dripped onto his chin and down the front of his shirt. In a whining voice he said, "You broke my nose! Who the hell are you? Why the fuck did you hit me?"

"I have a few questions for you and I want to make sure you understand how important the answers are to your well-being. If you lie to me I can assure you that your nose won't be the only thing that is broken. Do you understand?"

Carlos stared to get up but the tip of Carl's shoe smashed into his ribs, "Don't try to get up. Answer a few questions and I will be out of here and all this will be just a bad memory."

Mendoza rolled over in agony, and gasped for breath. His arms were across his chest holding a cracked rib.

Finally in a raspy voice he asked, "What the fuck do you want to know?"

"Seven days ago you flew to Somalia carrying six crates. Who sent the crates and who did you deliver them to?"

"I don't know anything about…." The toe of Carl's shoe slammed into his thigh muscle.

Tears streamed down a face that was covered in blood and contorted in pain. In short panting gasps of breath he moaned, "I don't know who sent the boxes. You have to talk to Thatcher."

"Who is Thatcher?"

"He's flight operations manager and dispatcher. All I do is fly the damned plane."

"Who picked up the boxes in Mogadishu?"

"The boxes weren't on the plane when we got to Mogadishu."

"What do you mean they weren't on the plane? Where were they?"

"Thatcher told us to make a stop at a small landing strip near Dhurba and to not put it in our flight plan or log it. He gave my copilot and me an extra five hundred Euros each."

"Where was this landing strip?"

"I told you, near Dhurba, he gave me the GPS coordinates. He said it was a landing strip built during the last war by the British."

"Okay, what were the coordinates?"

"I don't know, Thatcher wrote them on a piece of paper and I threw it away before we took off again."

"Why did you do that?"

"I didn't want it on me in case we were stopped by the police."

"Then what did you do?"

"Nothing. We took off and headed to Mogadishu."

"Who did you give the boxes to?"

"I don't know. Three men were waiting for us. When the cargo door opened they just climbed in the plane and unloaded the crates onto a pickup truck and left. They didn't say anything, just took the fucking crates and drove off."

"What was the name on the shipping invoice?"

"What shipping Invoice? There was no shipping invoice, no paperwork of any kind. All I was told was that I would be met and that they would offload the crates. I don't know who they were or where the crates were supposed to go, who sent them, or what was in them."

"Were do I find Thatcher?"

Mendoza managed to roll to a sitting position then crossed his arms over his chest holding his ribs. "He works at the hanger all day, you can find him there."

"What does he look like?"

Mendoza tried to cough but because of the pain in his ribs rolled onto his back. Looking like he might pass out. After a few seconds he said, "You broke my fucking ribs!"

"I'll break a few more if you don't tell me what Thatcher looks like and where I can find him"

"You can find him at the hanger. He drives a shiny new blue Mercedes, he's about fifty, fat, and he has blond hair."

"If you lied to me or tell anybody about our conversation, Thatcher or anyone else, or let Thatcher know that I am coming to talk to him we will continue this conversation in far more detail. When I am finished with our conversation you will spend a lot of years in an Algerian prison for smuggling weapons. Do you understand?"

His eyes showing fear, Mendoza looked at Carl and nodded.

"Have a pleasant day Mr. Mendoza. If I were you I would have that nose looked at."

That afternoon Carl visited the airport. He spotted the blue Mercedes parked inside the hanger near what appeared to be an office. Carl drove onto a side road outside the airport gate where he could watch cars leaving at the end of the day. Shortly after 4:00 in the afternoon a blue Mercedes, driven by a blond man came out and headed toward Algiers. The blue car took a road that followed the coast and soon stopped at a small cottage that sat on a hill that overlooked the coastline. As Carl drove by, the thought occurred to him that smuggling must be a lucrative business if Thatcher could afford a rather pricey home and an expensive Mercedes. Turning around, Carl drove past the house again then found a wide shoulder on the road where he could park and watch the house for a while to see if there was any one else living there.

About an hour later, Thatcher, dressed in sports clothes, came out and got in his car. He drove to a restaurant and bar not far from his home. He had dinner and a few drinks at the bar where he stayed until ten that night then returned home where Carl was waiting. He parked got out and locked his car. Turning around he saw a big man standing next to him. In the next instant he felt a fist sink deep into his stomach. He doubled over and dropped to his knees. A hand grabbed his hair jerking his head up as a fist slammed into his jaw splitting his lip, he fell to his side and started to retch.

"Do I have your attention?"

Between gasps Thatcher's voice whined, "Take my money and leave me the hell alone!"

"I don't want your money, I want information, and if I don't get it or if you're holding out on me I will continue to beat the truth out of you. When you recover, if you do, you will spend the rest of your life in prison for smuggling weapons and murder. Do you understand?"

"Are you crazy? I don't know anything about smuggling weapons or any murder."

A second blow to the face closed one eye. Thatcher dropped back to the ground in pain.

"Who paid you to smuggle six crates of missiles to Somalia last week?"

Thatcher did not answer right away instead he started to get to his feet. Carl grabbed his hair pulling his head up and slammed a fist into the right side of his face. Thatcher's other eye began to swell shut. And he fell back to the ground.

In a weak voice, Thatcher gasped, "He said his name was Jules"

"Okay, that's a start. What was his last name?"

"He wouldn't tell me his last name

"How much does he pay you for a delivery?"

"He pays me four thousand Euros each time.

"How does he contact you?"

"He just calls me when he has a shipment."

"When was the last time he called you?

"He came by about two weeks ago. Said he had a shipment for Somalia"

"What did you tell him?"

"I told him to deliver his boxes directly to the hanger on the day of the flight. He said the plane would be met when it landed. That was all."

"Where in Somalia did he tell you to deliver the boxes?"

"He gave me the GPS location for a landing strip near Dhurba. Said it was a landing strip the British had built during the war. He said there would be somebody there to unload the boxes."

"He gave me half the money and said that I would get the rest when he received word that the boxes had been delivered. That's all I know."

"How do you contact Jules?"

"I don't contact him he said he would call me the next time he had cargo to be delivered. I don't know his last name."

He put the other hand up as if to ward of more blows. "I don't know anything else. I swear."

"If I find out you're holding out on me I'll be back and we'll talk some more, do you understand?"

"Yes, yes I understand."

Carl told Thatcher the same thing he had told the pilot about keeping his mouth shut and spending time in jail then he turned and walked away.

When Carl returned to the hotel he found Ian Macintyre waiting for him. "I heard you were on your way back to Algiers, When did you get in?"

"I got in this morning. I was going to give you a call but I got a little busy. I'll buy you a beer and we can talk."

"I suppose your room would be quieter. You do have a mini-bar don't you?"

When they reached the room Carl opened the mini bar and pulled out two beers. Opening the bottles he handed one to Ian saying, "I persuaded the pilot to talk to me. He delivered the missiles to a landing strip near Dhurba but he doesn't know anything else. He says he just flew the plane. He didn't even unload the cargo. He said the dispatcher, a guy named Thatcher, made all the contacts. I persuaded Thatcher to talk to me and he said that he was approached by a guy named "Jules," but he didn't know the man's last name. He said that Jules just dropped a wad of cash on him and said that if he needed anything else delivered he would call. Jules did not give Thatcher a way to reach him saying only that he would call Thatcher when he needed something else shipped."

"I'll have my friends run the name Jules through the computers and see what they come up with. What is your next step?"

"In the morning I'm going to call Taos Kassini and set up a meeting with him."

CHAPTER 17

When Taos entered the restaurant he spoke to the hostess and was shown to Carl's table. Carl stood and shook hands with him then offered him a seat. When they were seated they orders drinks.

"Thank you Mr. Lukin for your kind invitation to lunch. I hope that the Kassini Machine Shop can do some business with you."

When the drinks arrived Carl pushed an envelope across the table saying, "Perhaps so Mr. Kassini, but first you had better look at these photographs before we talk."

Taos, with a puzzled look on his face, opened the envelope and pulled out the photographs of missiles on his workbench. His face blanched, not breathing for a few seconds, he finally said, "Where did you get these?"

"Those were taken eleven days ago in your machine shop before the missiles were placed back in the shipping crates and taken to the Briska airport by you. As you well know they were loaded on a plane in the Sarcozy hanger. What you may not know is they were flown to Somalia and given to the pirates that have been raiding ships in the Gulf of Aden. The missiles that you modified were used to kill many people. That makes you an accomplice to murder."

"Who are you, the police? What do you want from me? Money?"

"No, I don't want money, I only want one thing; the name of the man who hired you to make the modifications."

"I don't know his name he simply walked into my office and offered me a lot of money and threatened to kill my wife and children unless I agreed to make modifications to his missiles."

"Come now Mr. Kassini, I can assure you that I am not stupid. Please do not lie. A man does not just come into your office and threaten you and your family, offer to give you a lot of cash to modify missiles, and you just smile happily and say yes."

In near panic Taos said, "The man had pictures of my wife and children, he knew their names, he knew my wife's name, and where we lived. He knew where the children went to school, he knew everything. He said he would kill them if I did not cooperate or if I went to the police. I knew it was not an idle treat. What could I do?"

"Alright, calm down, what was his name?"

"I don't know!"

"Perhaps you had better hear this tape recording." Carl pushed a tape recorder across the table.

Taos, his hands trembling, placed the ear bud in his ear and pushed the play button. He listened then said, "As you can see I told my helper that I did not know the name of the man."

"You told your helper that he did not want to know the name, implying that you did. Don't lie to me Taos. If you lie to me again all the information that I have will go to the authorities."

"I don't know his name. He said that if I did not help him I would never see my family alive again, that is all I know."

"Why did he pick you to do the work?"

"I have a degree in electrical engineering and he knew that I could make the modification once I had the circuit board. The circuit board already had a flash memory chip with all the logic for the guidance system. I didn't have to know how the logic worked. All that was needed was the connection to the existing servo units used for steering."

"Where did you get the circuit boards?"

"He sent them to me."

"I told you not to lie to me. Your sister Callah sent you the circuit boards and she's going to go to jail with you. Now what is the name of the man who is paying you for the work? If you want to see the rest of your family in jail as well just keep lying."

His hands were shaking and beads of sweat began forming on Taos's forehead, he finally said, "Jules."

"Jules? What's his last name?"

"I don't know for sure, he received a mobile phone call when he was in my office. When he stepped to the side of the room to answer the phone, I think he said Dunbar, but I could be wrong, he spoke softly."

"Where is Mr. Dunbar from?"

"I don't know, but he had an English Accent."

"You're sure it was English and not American?"

"Yes, yes, English."

"How do you know where to send the missiles when you are done?"

"I didn't know. All I was told was to call a man named Thatcher at Sarcozy Air Freight and tell him that Mr. Jules had some boxes to ship, and he would take care of it."

"I have some very important instructions for you, so listen very carefully or I will pay you another visit and I can assure you it will not be as pleasant as this has been. First, do not tell anyone about our discussion, do you understand? Not your wife, not your sister Callah, not Jules, not Thatcher, no one, do you understand?"

"Taos nodded."

"Second, you are going to call me if you hear from Jules. If you cooperate your help will be taken into consideration at your trial. The number I'll give you is to a switchboard at the American embassy, ask for Carl Lukin. The gentleman who answers will call me with your message. If you want to talk to me I will call you back. Is that all clear?"

"Yes, I understand."

"OK Taos. That is all for now but I will be watching you. Now would you care to order something to eat? It's on me."

"Are you crazy? Not now. I'm ready to throw up."

Returning to his work, Taos locked himself in his office to calm his nerves. The next few hours were spent thinking about his problem, he had to come up with a plan or he would lose everything and end up in jail, or he and his family would be killed. Finally, in the late afternoon he went home.

That evening after the kids had gone to bed he sat with his wife and did what he dreaded most; he began to explain the predicament that they were in. He told her about the threats Jules had made on her and the children, and his feeling of helplessness and fear. How he had finally succumbed to Jules demand. He told her how for 18 months he had been modifying missiles. And finally about Carl's visit and threats.

His wife broke into tears He took her into his arms and cried with her. After a while she looked up and asked, "What are we going to do? If we stay we'll all be killed; if we try hide the police will eventually find us and we'll all be put in jail."

"You will not be jailed, you have done nothing wrong. We only have to be afraid of Jules, and with the Americans after him I don't think he will be a problem for long.

"First we'll go to Madrid, from there you can stay with your aunt in France and I'll go to Brazil. If there is a problem I can come back quickly. But for now it is important that we go someplace where Jules can't find us.

"Then After a while maybe we can move back to Algiers. Frank is running the machine shop and it's still making a profit, we will have an income."

The next morning he went to the machine shop to tell them he would be on an extended vacation and that Frank the shop supervisor would be responsible for the business. Next he visited the bank and drew out all of his personal funds. He made arrangements to have funds wired whenever he required them. Then he had his car serviced for the trip to Morocco. When he had completed all his preparations it was late in the day and he drove home. That evening he called and warned Callah about the impending arrest on charges of theft and possibly accomplices to murder. He told her that he loved her and that he was taking his family and going into hiding in some other country, he didn't know where yet but at some point he would try and contact her.

Early the following morning Taos loaded his family into their car and drove to Ceuta, Morocco, where they caught a ferry to Gibraltar. To make his movements a little more difficult to trace Taos simply left his car on the street in Ceuta with the keys in the ignition. By the next day the car had been stolen, painted a different color, and had a new set of license plates.

When Taos and his family reached Madrid he placed his wife and children on a plane to Paris, from there she would have to take a train to Calais. He booked a flight to Rio De Janeiro, Brazil.

CHAPTER 18

Carl watched the Kassini Machine Shop for the next two days. The afternoon following the meeting, Taos left the machine shop early and only returned for a short time the next day. On the third day he did not come in at all. Carl called the machine shop and asked to speak to Mr. Kassini.

"I am sorry Mr. Kassini is not in today can the shop supervisor help you?"

"No I'm afraid not. When is Mr. Kassini expected to return?"

"Mr. Kassini is on an extended vacation and is not expected back for some time. He left Mr. Frank, the shop supervisor in charge until he returns, perhaps he can help you."

"No thank you I'll call at some other time."

Carl called the Kassini home but got no answer. He drove by the house a short time later but the house was dark and the car was gone.

Carl then called Ann telling her about his discussion with Taos and that Taos appeared to have left Algiers in a hurry. Ann in turn called Jean Peters with the news.

"There is not much more that I can do in Algiers. I'll try and catch a plane this afternoon, or tomorrow at the latest."

Carl called Ian and set up a lunch meeting to tell him that he was leaving and fill him in on the latest information.

"Sorry to see you go. I haven't had so much fun since the last time you were here. I heard from my friends recently and they have some information that you might be interested in. They informed me that they have identified Jules as Jules Dunbar, an ex British SAS officer now living in Antelope, California, a small community near Sacramento, sorry not street address.

"He appears to be self-employed working as a security consultant to firms in Europe, Africa, and the U.S. Apparently he will work for any organization that is willing to pay for his special talents.

"Among his acquaintances is Paul Hamit an American arms dealer who has offices in San Francisco. Jules has done a considerable amount of travel throughout Europe, the Middle East and Africa, although he is not an arms dealer he appears to have a close connection as a salesmen or facilitator to Mr. Paul Hamit.

"Paul Hamit is a licensed arms dealer, but he is careful to only sell weapons to belligerent parties the United States supports. Hamit knows that if he sold to a group not supported by the United States it would lead to an immediate revocation of his license.

"By the way, the FBI has asked Interpol to be on the lookout for Taos and his family. We also have our people watching for him. It should not be too long before he shows up on somebody's radar.

Other than the normal pirate activity in the Indian Ocean and Gulf of Aden things have been quiet.

Chapter 19

When Callah finished talking to Taos she immediately told Hans. Because of the time difference between Algiers and Utah it was just before eleven fifteen in the evening when Hans called his father telling him that the authorities knew of the theft and that they would all probably be arrested soon. When his wife asked Jake who had called so late he simply said that he had been asked to go to work early the next morning.

Jake simply could not tell his wife that he had been involved in stealing from the company he had worked for so long. To tell her that he would soon be arrested and that she would be married to a criminal was beyond his capabilities; he simply could not do that.

Jake was a proud man who had always led a moral and honest life until becoming involved in Hans's scheme to raise money for John's medical bills. That part if his life was something that was kept between his son and himself. He knew that his wife would support him but that her pride in him would be diminished, that was something that he could not stand. He also knew that his arrest and conviction would mean the end of his job, his pension, and the beginning of a long prison sentence. All because he wanted to keep his grandson alive.

His wife of forty-five years would be left without an income except for a small amount from social security which was not enough to live on.

He thought about John and his medical problems. With his mother, father and grandfather in prison John would be at the mercy of whatever the county social services were willing to provide in the way of medical care for him. The thought of any member of his family being dependent on public assistance for anything was abhorrent to Jake. For Jake, pride was an unforgiving taskmaster.

Jake had been prudent enough to buy a substantial life insurance policy but that would only be available on his death. He would probably live a long life in prison. The prison system works very hard to keep you healthy while you are in their care. You are well fed and receive better medical and dental services then many of the people who are not incarcerated. It is the goal of the prison system to keep you healthy so that you can serve your entire sentence.

If he were to be put in jail there would be no way to pay for his life insurance premiums. He would lose a significant part of his life insurance that he counted on to take care of his wife when he passed on. He thought about how he could save it all; the insurance as well as his pension. He lay awake thinking about his problem. When he finally reached a decision his mind became peaceful and he was able to get a few hours of sleep before putting his plan into effect.

On hearing that Taos Kassini had called Callah, the FBI made the decision to pick up Jake, Hans, and Callah in simultaneous raids at their homes early the following morning. They would be held on charges of industrial espionage, piracy, accomplices to murder, and a few other charges to be added later.

Jake woke up several hours earlier than usual. He got dressed and made his coffee. His wife came into the kitchen and asked him why he had not awakened her so she could prepare his breakfast. Then she started to pack his lunch as usual.

After eating he put on his coat, kissed his wife, hugging her a little longer than usual, then told her that he loved her, which he never did. He went to his car got in and made sure his seat belt was on then backed out of the driveway. A few minutes later he was driving toward the Martin Munitions Company.

After leaving the city and surrounding farms he entered the open desert. He pressed the accelerator to the floor. Soon his old car was moving as fast as it would go; a little more than a 105 miles an hour. He thought about his wife, his pension, his life insurance, and the fact that he had lived a good life. Then he stepped on the breaks hard and turned the steering wheel sharply to the right. His car immediately went into a skid, rolled over several times then flew off of the highway into a deep ravine where it continued to roll several more time before coming to a stop against a large boulder and bursting into flames.

Callah and Hans lay awake talking most of the night; they didn't know what to do. They could not just run; where would they run to? It is true they did participate in the theft of the circuit boards and they did mail them to Taos. But the idea that they might be accomplices to murder was too farfetched for them to comprehend. The only thing that they could do was wait for the FBI to arrest them. Finally, just before dawn, exhausted they dropped off to sleep.

A short time later the phone rang. When Hans picked up the received he heard his mother's hysterical voice, "There has been a terrible car accident and your father is dead. He was killed on his way to work this morning. Now the FBI is at the door saying they are here to arrest him and that they have a warrant to search the house."

Hans tried to calm his mother but there was not much he could do. He told her that he would drive up immediately and deal with the authorities. It was a promise that he would not be able to keep.

Just as he hang up the phone there was a loud knock at the front door. The FBI was there to arrest Hans and Callah. They had a search warrant for the house, car and the appliance repair business.

John was taken to FBI headquarter for questioning but not arrested. He was released late in the afternoon. When he returned home he found the FBI still searching the house. The only thing he could do was get in his car and drive to his grandmother's house. When John arrived he found her extremely upset and in tears. Aside from trying to cope with the death of her husband she had to deal with a number of FBI agents who had been executing a search warrant and were now getting ready to leave with several boxes of papers, bank books, mortgage papers, bank statements, et cetera.

In the following weeks the FBI questioned both John and his grandmother several times adding to their stress level. The added stress aggravated John's cystic fibrosis to the point that he had to be taken to the Cystic Fibrosis Research Center for treatment. He nearly died and was admitted to the hospital where he spent the following week in intensive care.

Further aggravation to the family was caused by the insurance company who claimed that Jake had committed suicide and therefore refused to honor Jakes life insurance. It would take the courts nearly six months to determine that Jake had no history of mental problems or shown any sign of suicidal tendencies prior to the time of his death. Although he had known that the FBI was aware of his theft from Martin Munitions, he had no indication that he would soon be arrested. The courts decided that based on the evidence it was unreasonable to assume Jake had committed suicide. Therefore Jake Lunemann's widow was entitled to the full amount of the insurance policy, plus she was entitled to six percent interest on the funds that she was to receive as a result of the insurance company's delay in making payment.

The courts also decided that since Jake Lunemann was an employee of Martin Munitions at the time of his death and had not been charged or convicted of any crime, there was no valid reason to deny his surviving widow the pension benefits to which she was entitled.

CHAPTER 20

A week after leaving Algiers Carl was sitting at his desk in San Francisco. He and Ann were going over the various cases that the Lukin Investigation Agency was actively working on when Carl received a call from Jean Peters, saying, "Since you two were so heavily involved in the Martin Munitions case I thought you would like to know a few of the details that we have."

"Just a second Jean, I want to put you on the speaker phone so that Ann can hear you."

When Jean heard the click of the speaker phone she said, "Hi Ann, I'm glad you could join us.

"First off, we have just had a report of an explosion on a pirate boat. The boat was sunk and it appears that several were killed or injured. If any more information comes in on that I'll let you know.

"We have been talking to the Bank of Algiers about the wire transfers to John Lunemann's account at the Cystic Fibrosis Center. They're saying that periodically a man would walk into the bank with cash and ask for a wire transfer. The cash was usually in Euros. Although the description is vague it could be our friend Jules Dunbar.

Unfortunately the surveillance tapes have been recorded over many times since Dunbar's last transaction.

"We haven't found any evidence to indicate that Hamit is involved but we'll keep looking. It could be that Dunbar was selling the missiles to the Somalis on his own."

"That's a possibility Jean, but there are a lot of unanswered questions. How did Dunbar or Hamit make contact with Jake Lunemann, Hans, Callah or Taos? They all led quiet lives in Utah or Algiers. Someone had to know that Jake was involved in the manufacture of the circuit boards and passed that information on to Hamit or Dunbar. They would have had to know about John's cystic fibrosis and the family's financial problems in order to induce Jake to risk everything by stealing the boards. How and from whom did Hamit or Dunbar get that information? One other thing Jean, the CIA guy in Algeria mentioned that Jules was thought to be working for a Paul Hamit from San Francisco but that they didn't have more information."

"Okay , I'll look into Paul Hamit.

"I don't know Carl, the people at the Research Center would know about the family's financial problem but not necessarily about the details of Jake's job or that Jake was giving Hans and Callah financial help. How would Jules know to talk to the research center in the first place? The information would have had to come from someone with a close relationship to the family. The only other person who might know is Jake's other son Fredrick who lives in San Francisco. Fredrick is a financial advisor and not connected to the arms business. We have interviewed Fredrick but he has very little contact with his father or brother other than at Christmas holidays and the occasional phone call. There is no indication that he was in any way involved. We can't find any connection between Fredrick, Dunbar, Hamit or the arms trade."

After a pause Jean continued, "Callah and Hans both told us that a man named Jules approached them about stealing the circuit boards in exchange for enough money to pay the research center for John's outstanding medical bills. At first they turned him down. They realized they only had three options, face financial ruin, forego medical treatment for their son, which in their minds was not really an option, or approach Jake for help. They elected to approach Jake. Apparently Jake was reluctant at first but finally agreed to help. The thought of forcing his grandson onto welfare in order to get minimal health care was too much for Jake's pride. After a few weeks of wracking their brains they came up with a method they thought would work. The plan would satisfy all of the security measures that were put in place by the company.

"In the beginning, Callah didn't know that Taos was involved in the scheme until she was given the address where to mail the circuit boards. According to Callah, Taos didn't know it was the Lunemann family supplying the boards until she called him, but by that time it was too late, they were all involved and felt that they didn't have a way out.

"That's all I can tell you Carl, if you come up with anything please give me a call. In the meantime we are going to take a close look at Paul Hamit."

When the telephone connection was severed Carl sat thinking for a few minutes then turned to Ann saying, "Talk to Dan and see if he can find out if any other cash wire transfers were made from the bank of Algiers on the same day as the transfer to the research center. I suspect the FBI request for information was restricted to parties that the investigation had identified as having involvement, which at that time was the research center, Jake and Hans and Callah Lunemann. The FBI just can't go fishing for anyone's financial or private information, they are restricted to those people under investigation. If they want to look at anyone else's private information they have to get a court order and show probable cause. They could not ask the Algerian bank if anyone else was sent a wire transfer on that day."

Two days later Ann walked into Carl's office saying, "Dan just called saying that on each day that money was transferred to the research center a wire transfer for five thousand dollars was sent to an account at the Union Bank in San Francisco. I talked to a friend of mine who works at one of the bank's branches and found out that the account belongs to Lunemann Investment Company. That's too much of a coincidence to be unrelated."

"It looks like we are going to have to take a closer look at Fredrick."

"Have you forgotten we're no longer working for Martin Munitions?"

"Yeah, I know, maybe it's my military background, but I'm having a hard time letting go of this one. The death of those helicopter pilots and the seamen who were just trying to earn a living really bothers me. I really want to see the bad guys behind bars.

"Ann, you are going to the Lunemann's house and do some more research."

"Okay who am I going to research this time?"

"Find out all you can about Fredrick, and the Fredric Lunemann Investment Company. He is the only other person that might have had the information that was used to pressure Jake, Hans, and Callah. He was the only other person who would know about John and his medical problems as well as Jake's job at Martin Munitions."

CHAPTER 21

As Ann approached Fredrick Lunemann's residence she noticed a small girl's bike leaning against the garage wall. She rang the doorbell.

It was answered by Fredrick's wife, a slim, attractive woman with ash blond hair. She was dressed in jeans and a light yellow blouse, "Can I help you?"

"Hi, my name is Ann Curlin, my husband and I are thinking of buying the house that is for sale on the corner and I was wondering if you could spare a few minutes to tell me a little bit about the neighborhood? I noticed the kids bike leaning against the garage wall and thought you would know something about the local schools."

In a tentative voice Mrs. Lunemann said, "I guess so. My name is Lynn Lunemann; I was just going to sit down with a cup of coffee, would you care to join me?"

"That would be great, thanks."

Ann stepped into the house. Mrs. Lunemann closed the door and led the way into the kitchen saying, "It seems that house has been for sale for some time."

"The real estate agent said that the price started out pretty high even for the San Francisco Bay area but that it has dropped quite a bit since it was first put on the market. I guess the bad economy has really hit the housing market. We were lucky to have sold our house back east when we did. My husband got a job at Microstar Systems last month and we have been looking for a place ever since we got here. But San Francisco area housing prices are so high."

"You're fortunate your husband could find a job. My husband is an investment advisor and has been having a tough time for the past year because of the poor economy. If it hadn't been for a few Clients with foreign investment accounts paying off we would have been in financial trouble. You said that you were looking at schools?"

"That's right, I have two daughters; six and eight, and we're really concerned about the quality of schools they will be attending."

"The schools here are excellent. With all the computer development companies in the area the school districts are big on sciences and math, and most schools have accelerated learning programs."

Looking a little on edge Mrs. Lunemann poured more coffee into the cups then said, "Please call me Lynn, Mrs. Lunemann sounds so formal."

She took a sip of her coffee then said, "It's a pretty quiet area, not much to do, most of the men play golf, or tennis, my husband likes to spend time at the local Indian casino and occasionally he has to fly to Las Vegas to meet with clients that fly in from Europe. Of course there are the usual neighborhood bar-b-cues and poker parties. It's really a quiet, friendly neighborhood."

"My husband is always looking for good investment opportunities, what company does your husband work for? Maybe they can do some business together."

"He has his own company it's called Lunemann Investment Company. I'm sure he can help your husband."

The mention of foreign investors triggered a thought: could the investors be in Algeria and Somalia or people doing business in those areas. That would certainly tie with the rest of the Lunemann family. If Fredrick's clients are doing business in other African countries besides Algeria they have to be moving or investing their money somewhere. But why with a little known company like Lunemann Investments? The only common denominator she could come up with was the theft of missile parts and the rest of the Lunemann family.

Later that same day Ann called Dan Nakamura and told him to take a close look at Fredrick's credit reports, property taxes, and bank accounts and the Lunemann Investment Company client list in particular, and anything else that looked interesting.

CHAPTER 22

In the past the general had demonstrated a willingness to sell weapons, mostly old Russian weapons, AK 47's, ammunition, grenades, mines, etc., that had made their way into Pakistan from Afghanistan. Although many of the weapons were old, so long as they were serviceable Jules would buy them and would later sell them in Africa and elsewhere.

One night over dinner and many drinks the General had asked, "Are you interested in acquiring any heat seeking missiles?"

"I am always interested in getting missiles. What kind are they and how many are we talking about?"

Leaning back in his chair the general smiled, "As you know I am in charge of training for the Pakistani army which gives me access to a lot of equipment. It so happens we have a whole warehouse full of first generation shoulder launched heat seeking missiles that are considered old technology and that worked so poorly they are only used for training purposes. Unfortunately, they miss their target most of the time. Selling them is no trick at all, there is practically no record keeping on them."

"I'm very interested. How many are you willing to sell now?

"I can probably let you have thirty now and perhaps more later."

"You have a deal. I may even have a way to upgrade the electronics a bit. Give me a few weeks to see if I can work things out."

After leaving the General, Jules flew to Utah to again meet with Hans and Callah. He again held out the promise of enough funds to insure that John would not be denied clinic treatment because of a lack of funds. He added to the pressure by adding that they had only three days to give him an answer or he would go elsewhere.

That night Hans drove to Ogden to meet with his father. "I am at the end of my rope. Even with the money you have been helping with I can't continue to keep John at the clinic. We're falling further and further behind. We will soon be forced to ask the county for financial assistance for his treatments. I have been told that the county will insist that John receive treatment from a county free clinic where he will only receive minimal care. Callah and I are afraid that if he goes to the county clinic that he will not survive long."

"No! We will not go on welfare to get help for John. The Lunemann family has always paid their way and has never had to beg for money. And we will not do it now. There must be something we can do."

"There is father but it is distasteful to me and I don't want to ask your help but I don't see any alternative. There is a man who is willing to buy the guidance system circuit boards that Martin Munitions makes. If we can find a way to take two or three a month John will receive the money he needs to survive. I know that you work in that area that makes the boards. Is there any way we can take a few each month that they will not be missed?

Jake was horrified at what Hans was proposing but the thought of his grandson being forced to go on welfare was even worse. Hans and Jake discussed the problem into the early morning hours and finally came up with a plan that would yield two or three circuit boards a month with little chance of being caught.

Two days later when Jules called Hans he was told that they would be able to get two or three of the needed parts each month. Jules tried to pressure Hans to get more but Hans would not go further saying, "It is risky taking two or three, any more than that will result in an investigation, and then you will not get any."

Jules realized that he could push no further, "OK three each month. I'll let you know where to send them later."

The last stop Jules made was in Algiers at the Kassini Machine Shop. At first Taos turned down all offers to participate in Jules' plan, but a discussion about his family and pictures of his wife and his children going into their school soon convinced him to reconsider. Taos did not know that Callah or her family were involved until he received the first shipment of circuit boards and saw the return address on the package.

As Jules flew to Islamabad to close the deal with the General he thought about his project. He had all the pieces in place, now all he needed was the Pakistani Missiles, and he knew that would not be a problem; the General was a greedy fool. He would take a night to get a good rest then meet the General in the morning.

General Karim said yes the missiles were still available and then told Jules his asking price. Jules looked shocked. He began to haggle over the price with the General. If he paid too high a price he would be forced to pay a premium price for all items he bought from the general. Jules had been around this block before. He knew how to negotiate for the best price. After an hour and two pots of tea they reached a mutually agreeable price.

CHAPTER 23

The day after after Ann's visit to the Lunemann home Carl walked into the offices of the Lunemann Investment Company and asked to see Mr. Lunemann.

"I'll see if he is available, can I give him your name?"

"Yes, tell him Carl Lukin of Lukin Investigations." He handed the secretary his business card, then stood waiting at her desk while she used the intercom to inform Fredrick of his presence.

She finally hung up the phone saying, "Go right in." She pointed to a door to the left of her desk.

When Carl entered Fredrick looked up and said, "How can I help you?"

"My name is Carl Lukin. I have been hired by the Martin Munitions Company in Logan, Utah to investigate the theft of proprietary property. Unfortunately, your father and brother are involved in the theft." He failed to mention that he no longer worked for the munitions company.

A surprised look appeared on Fredrick's face but he said nothing.

"As part of that investigation we are looking at others who might have some knowledge concerning the theft. Although we have no evidence that you were involved with the theft it is possible you may have information that will shed some light on this case."

"You obviously didn't know my father or you would not suggest that he was involved in anything criminal. My father died a short time ago in a car accident. And I don't appreciate you coming in here now and telling me he was a criminal."

"Quite the contrary, I knew your father very well. Regardless of what you believe, I can assure you he was involved in the theft of highly secret weapons technology."

"I have already been interviewed by the FBI. I don't know anything about that case. Why would I want to help you in building a case against my family? I think you had better leave now."

"Mr. Lunemann, I am not building a case against your family, quite the opposite. That is the FBI's job. I am trying to find those responsible for involving your father and brother in these thefts. I knew your father before his accident and I have met your brother. They are not the kind of people that would involve themselves in industrial espionage willingly. If I can find those responsible for inducing your family to participate in this affair I may be able to help your brother and his wife."

"Why do you want to help my brother?"

"Because I know he was only trying to save his son's life. What father wound not want to do everything possible to save a son or daughters life?

"The electronic parts that your father stole from Martin Munitions eventually ended up in missiles that were later sold to Somali pirates and used to kill American and British airmen, and a number of sailors on a cruise ship. The missiles have been used on a number of other vessels as well. The people that involved your family in their scheme and later sold the missiles with the stolen technology are the scum that we want to catch. They took advantage of Hans' financial problems in trying to save his son's life by pressuring him and your father to participate in the thefts.

"During my investigation, a number of names have come up that might have some bearing on the case, perhaps you know these people. Have you met or heard of Jules Dunbar?"

"No. I've never heard that name before."

"How about a man named Paul Hamit?"

A scowl flashed across Fredrick's face, "Yes I know a Paul Hamit. I provide investment counseling services for him. Is he involved?"

"We don't know that he is. As I said his name came up in the investigation and we are simply following up to see if he has any relevance to this case. How well do you know Mr. Hamit?"

"I provide investment advice to him concerning stock purchases and sales, and research investment opportunities here and in Europe."

"What kind of stock investments does Mr. Hamit have, foreign or domestic?"

"I'm sorry I can't discuss that with you. You will have to talk to Mr. Hamit."

After a short pause Carl said, "Pardon me for saying so but you are not a big name investment management company. How did you come to meet Mr. Hamit?"

"I met him on a plane to Las Vegas a few years ago. We were staying at the same hotel and decided to have dinner together. During dinner we found out we had many of the same interests and decided to play golf the next day. We happened to meet on several other trips and became friends. He started to throw some business my way and I gave him some advice that worked very well for him. Our business relationship grew from there."

"Has Mr. Hamit met any of your other family? Your mother, father, brothers or sisters?"

"No. He has only met my wife on social occasions."

"Have you discussed your family with Mr. Hamit?"

"No, other than the normal tidbits that come up in general conversations, such as, what does your father do for a living? Do you see your brother often? You know, the kind of small talk that usually comes up over dinner or drinks. Only casual conversation, we didn't discuss anything of any consequence."

"Thank you Mr. Lunemann, if anything else comes up I'll give you a call."

Following his meeting with Fredrick Carl called Jean Peters and relayed the gist of his conversation with Fredrick Lunemann, finally summing up with, "Fredrick has a personal as well as a business relationship with Paul Hamit. He may not have intentionally told Hamit anything useful that directly led to the theft, but over time he may have dropped enough bits of information that Hamit could put together a good picture of the family's financial problems. As an arms dealer Hamit would already have a good deal of knowledge about Martin Munitions. It's quite possible he could see a business opportunity by using the Lunemann family.

"Fredrick says that he doesn't know Jules Dunbar but Hamit might have passed on the information that came to him regarding the family.

"By the way Jean, you may want to go back and take another look at the Bank of Algiers' wire transfers to the Cystic Fibrosis Research Center, and any other wire transfers that were made on the same day that were paid for in cash."

There was a few seconds of silence, "Why would we want to do that?"

"Because wire transfers were made to Fredrick's investment company on the same days that money was sent to the research facility and I just don't believe in coincidences."

Jean said, "It sounds like the FBI needs to have another look at wire transfers and another conversation with Fredrick Lunemann."

"If you do go back to see Fredrick, I would go in with warrants to look at Hamit's business records and I'd place a tap on his telephone to see who he calls after you walk in the door waving warrants."

While Carl and Jean were talking about Fredrick, Fredrick was on his own phone calling Paul Hamit. When Paul came on the line he said, "Yes Fredrick what can I do for you?"

"Sorry to bother you Paul, and I know this is a stupid question, but are you involved in anything illegal?"

"That's a hell of a question Fredrick why do you ask?"

"I've had this private investigator named Carl Lukin, from Lukin Investigation Company in my office for the past hour asking questions about you and some guy called Jules Dunbar."

"What did you tell him?"

"I told him that I didn't know any Jules Dunbar and that you and I were casual friends and that we had a business relationship, but I couldn't discuss any of our business issues with him. Then he asked the strangest thing; he asked if you knew my parents or the rest of my family."

"How did you answer him?"

"I told him the truth. We never discussed my family except for the polite questions that normally come up over a meal or during a game of golf. You know. "How are your mother and father doing?" Normal dinner table chit chat. We've never had a real dialog about my family."

"Well I wouldn't worry about it. He is just poking around trying to find something that he can use as justification for running up his billable hours."

"Yeah, you're probably right. But it's still disconcerting."

"Just give me a call if he shows up again."

While Fredrick and Paul were talking, Carl sat in his car thinking about what Fredrick had said and writing notes on the conversation. He paused after going over the conversation in his mind then reached the conclusion that he would visit Paul Hamit the next day.

CHAPTER 24

Carl walked into Hamit's office on Sansom Street, San Francisco. The secretary looked up, gave Carl a friendly smile and in a rather cheerful voice said, "Can I help you?"

"My name is Carl Lukin. I would like to see Paul Hamit please.

"Do you have an appointment Mr. Lukin?"

"No, but if he can give me a few minutes I would be most appreciative."

"Please have a seat and I'll check as soon as he is off the phone."

As Carl looked around the office he could see that there was a group of five or six businesses that shared one secretary. He assumed that it was hard to justify having your own secretary in the arms business. He didn't think it was the kind of business where you had a lot of walk-in customers.

After a few minutes the secretary looked up and said, "It looks like you're in luck, he's normally not here. Go right in."

Carl walked into a well-appointed office. A middle aged man wearing glasses and a blue sport coat and gold tie sat behind a large desk. As Carl entered, the man stood, came around the desk and offered his hand saying, "I'm Paul Hamit, what can I do for you Mr. Lukin?"

His personal appearance was that of a prosperous business man. His hair was graying at the temples and he was carrying a few pounds of extra weight. He had a solid handshake, his hands were smooth and he had manicured nails. His suntan indicated that had spent some time outdoors in the sun, probably playing golf. Carl judged him to be about four inches shorter than himself and certainly not as physically fit but not exactly a creampuff either.

"Thank you for seeing me Mr. Hamit, my name is Carl Lukin. I am a private investigator looking into an industrial espionage case that you might be able to help me with."

"I don't know what I can tell you Mr. Lukin, I mainly broker sales between buyers and arms manufacturers, or other parties wishing to buy or sell weapons. It's a small but lucrative business. I don't know much about industrial espionage. But I'll help you if I can. What is it that you want to know?"

"I understand that you are acquainted with Fredrick Lunemann?"

"Yes, I know Fredrick. He's an investment specialist that I use. He's very good. He has helped me from time to time with advice and financial transactions. Why do you ask?"

"Are you acquainted with the rest of Fredrick's family, Jake Lunemann, Hans or Callah Lunemann, or a Mr. Taos Kassini?"

"No, only Fredrick, I have never met any of his family other than Fredrick wife."

"Jake Lunemann, Fredrick's father, died in an automobile accident and Hans and his wife are under arrest for theft and murder. The theft occurred at Martin Munitions Company but Fredrick does not appear to be involved in any way. We are simply checking with anyone who knows him and who might have some information that could help shed light on the case.

"Do you know Jules Dunbar?" As Carl watched Hamits face he did not see any sign of recognition.

He went on, "The authorities are looking for Mr. Dunbar in connection with the theft. There was apparently some connection between the Lunemann family and Jules Dunbar."

"I am not acquainted with any person named Dunbar or other members of the Lunemann family. But I am in the business of selling weapons, and munitions, and other items needed by an army, and I do business with the Martin Munitions Company from time to time. I believe they are located in Ogden, Utah. Is that the company that you are referring to?"

"Yes, that's the company. One of the company's products is a heat seeking missile. The theft consisted of some electronic parts used in missile guidance systems. Did Fredrick ever discuss his father's work at the Martin Munitions Company with you?"

"Fredrick is a business acquaintance. We have had dinner occasionally. He may have mentioned his family in casual conversation, but I don't recall any specific conversations involving his family or a Jules Dunbar, and I'm sure I would have remembered a conversation about a man named Jules."

"Do you ever get requests for heat seeking missiles?"

"Yes, we receive inquires for missiles from time to time and we simply say no. We only broker conventional weapons, specifically items that are not controlled by the American government. Most of our sales are for ammunition and weapons, such as rifles, handguns, machine guns, mines, and grenades. Occasionally we will get orders for uniforms, boots, helmets and other dress items. I don't deal in items which the government has expressly forbidden me to sell."

"Who do you sell weapons to?"

"I won't discuss specific customers. But I will tell you that I sell to legitimate governments and to insurgent groups supported by the United States government."

"Insurgent groups supported by the Government? Can you give me an example?"

"An Example would be the Mujahideen that were fighting the Russians in Afghanistan. Or groups like the Afghan Northern Alliance that is now fighting the Taliban. There are a few other groups that the United States supports. I won't sell to any group that is not supported by our government. If I were to do so I would lose my arms dealer license. So I'm very careful who I sell to.

"Of course there is always the problem of a group that appears to be legitimate but are in reality only a front company. They solely exist to buy weapons, ammunition or other items on behalf of an organization on the restricted list. We try to identify them but we are not always successful."

"Somali pirates are not supported by the government so I suppose you don't do business with them."

"That's correct but keep in mind that there are hundreds of arms dealers around the world and I'm sorry to say some don't care who they sell to. That is not an area that people talk about and they certainly don't advertise so I can't give specific names."

"Have you ever bought missiles from the Pakistan government?"

"No, I haven't. But I am sure there are others who would do so given the opportunity."

"Thank you for taking the time to talk to me Mr. Hamit, if you think of anything that might be helpful please give me a call." Carl stood, shook hands with Paul Hamit, and left the office.

After leaving Hamits office Carl went into the coffee shop across the street from Hamits office building and bought a cup of coffee to go. Just as he started toward the door he could see Hamit leave his office building and walk down the street. Out of curiosity Carl picked up his coffee cup and followed.

Hamit went to Union Square and sat down on one of the steps leading to the park.

Carl stopped across the street watching and thinking about their conversation. "His answers were just too pat, it's as if he were expecting to see me. It almost as if he echoed Fredrick comments about the talks concerning his family."

Then there's Ian's comment that appeared to be a connection between Hamit and Jules. Hamit categorically denied even hearing of a man named Jules.

As Carl watched, Hamit pulled a cell phone from his pocket and made a short call. From the expression on his face it's obvious he was unhappy about something.

CHAPTER 25

A few minutes after Carl left, Hamit told his secretary he would be out of the office the rest of the afternoon and left. He began walking toward Union Square. He sat down on the granite steps leading to the park, and using a prepaid cell phone called Jules Dunbar at his home in Antelope.

When Jules answered, Paul was brief, saying "Jules we have a bit of a problem I'll tell you all about it when we meet. I'll meet you halfway. Can you be at Marie Calendar's, just off highway 80, in Fairfield in two hours?"

"Yeah, I can do that. See you there."

From across the street Carl could see Hamit placing his call. Hamit looked as if he was worried.

Paul retrieved his car from the parking garage under Union Square and drove across the Bay Bridge. He arrived in Fairfield an hour and ten minutes later. Since he was early, he entered the restaurant, sat in a booth, and ordered a slice of berry pie and a cup of coffee. When Jules arrived he slid into the booth saying, "Okay what is so bloody important?"

Paul shook his head from side to side and put his fingers to his lips, "Order some coffee and then we'll go out to my car where we have some privacy and talk."

After they finished their coffee and seated themselves in the car, Paul said, "I just had a visit from a private investigator who introduced himself as Carl Lukin. He said he was investigating a case of industrial espionage for the Martin Munitions Company. He asked if I knew Fredrick Lunemann and a man named Jules Dunbar. I told him that Fredrick is my investment advisor and that I only knew him as a business acquaintance, and that I didn't know a Jules Dunbar at all. This same investigator had been to see Fredrick the day before.

"On the drive here I had a call from Fredrick saying that the FBI had come to his office with more questions and a search warrant. They also had a warrant to examine my investment accounts with his firm. The damned fool called me from his office phone. I had no choice but to tell him that I had nothing to hide and to show the FBI any of my financial records that they wanted to see. If the FBI is in his office with warrants they probably have his phones tapped as well."

Jules said, "Fredrick doesn't know anything that can hurt us. His brother and father never discussed our arrangement with him. They made a point of letting me know that. I never told the Lunemann's or anyone else my last name. The investigator is just fishing."

Hamit, with an incredulous look on his face said, "Are you crazy? You must have slipped and dropped your name to somebody. If Carl Lukin has your name he probably has your picture, and he has probably shared the information with the FBI. Lukin didn't come up with your name out of thin air. He knows you're involved in the missile deal. Maybe not all the details of how you're involved, but it's not going to take long to figure it out. On top of that, Hans and Callah can identify you as the person who approached them and who set up this whole scheme. It won't be long until Lukin or the FBI shows them your picture and that will confirm your involvement.

As for Fredrick, When they start questing him in detail it won't take them long to figure out that he provided the information in bits and pieces to me, and that will tie me to you."

"Relax Paul you're not involved in anything. I am the one who talked the Lunemann's into getting me the circuit boards, bought the missiles from General Karim, had them modified, and sold them. The only thing you did was give me some information about Han's and his family, plus share in the profits. If anybody is going to get burned it's going to be me and I'm not going to let that happen."

"If the FBI takes a serious look at Fredrick they will come looking at me. If they arrest you they will eventually trace your activities back to me. I don't want to be an accomplice to murder."

"Don't be so naive Paul you're already an accomplice to murder. Every time we sell weapons to some African or Kurdish insurgent group so that they can go out and kill, or give missiles to pirates who then shoot down helicopters we become accomplices to murder."

"I'm just a merchant selling weapons to organizations that my government says it's okay to sell to. I don't pick the target or pull the trigger. I don't know how or when they're going to be used!"

"Don't kid yourself Paul you know those weapons are not going to be used as some avant-garde room decoration. They are used to kill men, women and children. So don't get squeamish on me now.

"I'm going to take care of Fredrick and the investigator. I'll make it look like an accident or a robbery that's gone bad. With both of them out of the way there is no way to connect you to me. Then I'll spend a few years moving around Europe and Africa until this whole thing blows over. We don't have any more circuit boards so the heat seekers we have in the warehouse are the only ones left. We can still sell other weapons and ammunition just like before. We'll be able to conduct business as usual except I won't be living in this country. As far as anyone is concerned there is no connection between us."

"I don't like it Jules, but if you're going to go through with your plan just make sure it looks like an accident. We don't want to stir up the police or the FBI any more than necessary."

CHAPTER 26

Uzun Vadisi Turkey The two men and one woman stood behind a large rock staring into the long narrow valley. They spoke in soft voices aware that their voices would carry in the cool morning air. The sun was coming up and the apple and pomegranate orchards on the valley floor were just becoming visible. While the mountains on the west side of the valley were in sunlight, the mountain side, where the three were trying to warm themselves, was still in shadows. Smoke was beginning to rise from the chimneys in the small village on the far side of the river that ran through the center of the valley.

The three were cold, sore, and stiff from sleeping on the cold hard ground. They stood behind some brush swinging their arms and stamping their feet to warm up. They badly wanted a hot cup of tea but that would not be possible until they left the valley and returned to Iran. "You two had better get under the netting and I'll take the first watch." The two covered themselves with a piece of camouflage netting, drank some water and ate a few bites of the food that they had brought with them. Every few hours they would rotate positions. The hours passed slowly.

It was nearly six in the evening when they heard the distinctive sound of a helicopter's rotors. The young woman removed the missile launch tube from the canvas bag and turned on the switch that would warm up the electronics and arm the missile. The men began folding the camouflage netting and putting their supplies back in their back packs. No matter what happened they would be leaving that night.

They watched as the helicopter entered the valley from the east. It was flying at about 2500 hundred feet above the valley floor, almost at eye level with the three people watching. The woman brought the launcher to her shoulder. As the helicopter passed their position there was a beeping sound from the launcher indicating that the missile had acquired a heat source. The young woman waited a few second more then pulled the trigger. There was a bright flash and the sound of the missile as it left the launch tube. Seconds later there was an explosion and a ball of fire as the helicopter disintegrated and fell to the valley floor. There were smiles as the three hugged and clapped each other on the back. The long wait had been successful. They would wait until it got dark then they would make their way home.

As the sun was setting they watched as villagers rushed to the crash site. Several men tried to extract the bodies from the wreckage but were only able to reach three before being driven back by the hot flames. The two remaining bodies were entangled in the wreckage and would have to wait until the fire died out and the metal cooled. They would not be removed until the army arrived in the morning and had a chance to examine the crash scene.

When it was fully dark the three PPK (Kurdistan Workers Party) members started back over the mountain and headed home to their Kurdish village on the Iranian side of the border. They had accomplished their mission.

The following morning three military trucks and a staff car drove into the valley stopping at the crash site. There were two villagers armed with rifles standing guard over the wreckage and the three bodies that had been removed from the downed helicopter. The Army Colonel in charge stepped from his car and thanked the two standing guard for their help. He then ordered a forensic team to examine the crash site and wreckage. Within a short time they reported that it appeared that an explosion had occurred in the engine, most likely from a missile strike. The Colonel turned to the two guards saying, "Did anyone see the explosion?"

One of the villagers said, "Some young boys were outside playing when the helicopter fell. They said that they saw a streak of light come from the mountain and when it hit the helicopter it exploded."

"Where are the children now?"

"They are in school, sir."

"Please come with me to the school and point them out."

When they arrived at the school the guard asked the teacher to send the two boys who had seen the explosion outside to talk to the Colonel.

The Colonel introduced himself then asked, "Did you see the helicopter fall?"

"Yes sir, there was a streak of light that hit the helicopter and it fell in a ball of fire."

"Did you see where the light came from?"

"Yes sir, it came from the side of that mountain." The boys pointed to a rocky area midway up the side of the mountain on the East side of the valley.

"You are sure that the light came from that area with all the big rocks?"

"Yes sir, we saw it clearly. It came out of the rocks then it hit the helicopter and there was a big explosion, everything was on fire."

The Colonel thanked the boys and went back to the crash site. He ordered a team of soldiers to search the area around the rock outcropping that the boys had described.

A few hours later a radio message from the search team said that they had found food wrappers, a weapon, and an area by some bushes that had been used by two or three people to relieve themselves. The soldiers were told to collect the evidence and return to the crash site.

When the search party returned to the crash site with the items that they had found the Colonel immediately recognized the weapon as a missile launch tube. In a low voice he said, "Dammed PPK!"

He ordered a Sargent and six men to follow the trail of the terrorists until they reached the border. They were to try and capture the terrorists, and if that was not possible, try to determine the village that the terrorists came from. He would send a truck back for them the next day.

He next ordered the soldiers to load the bodies and what was left of the wreckage onto the trucks and return to base.

On their return, the launch tube was photographed from every angle. Particular care was taken to photograph the lettering and serial numbers on the side of the launch tube. The Colonel prepared a report saying that the helicopter was attacked and downed by a missile, probably delivered by the PPK terrorists. He went on to say that the terrorists appeared to have gone east into Iran.

The report made its way to the Minister of Defense who sent copies of it to the Iranian and Iraqi Ministers of Defense, asking for their help in capturing the terrorists. Copies of the report and photographs of the missile launch tube eventually arrived at the CIA where the launch tube was recognized as being the same type as that photographed by Carl in Algiers. The serial number on the side of the tube was sequentially close enough to the launch tube in Carl's photographs to suggest that they both were probably sold by the same weapons dealer. The director sent a copy of the report to the FBI. Jean was made aware of the report and the probability that the weapons were sold to the PPK by the same weapons dealer that organized the theft from the Martin Munitions Company.

CHAPTER 27

Fredrick left his office late and headed home for dinner. He decided to stop at the Stop-N-Go liquor store for some Tequila. His wife was making a Mexican dinner and a couple of Margaritas would start the evening off on the right foot.

The parking lot for the liquor store was on the side of the building. The parking lot didn't have good lighting, on the other hand you could always find a parking space and it was convenient. On this night the lot was virtually empty. He had made his purchase and was returning to his car when he noticed that the car he had parked next to was gone and had been replaced by a blue Chevrolet.

As he fished in his pocket for his keys, a man wearing jeans and a black pea jacket got out of the Chevy and started walking toward the street. As he came around Fredrick's car he said, "Hello Fredrick, how are things this evening?" All of a sudden the man took two quick steps and was standing next to Fredrick.

Before he could say or do anything Fredrick felt something sharp stick him just below the sternum, instantly there was an intense pain and he couldn't get his breath. His mouth opened but he could not make a sound.

The sharp blade slanted upward penetrating his heart. The mugger twisted the blade so that it sliced through the heart muscle almost bisecting it. With the interruption of blood flow to the brain Fredrick immediately began to black out and slide to the ground.

His assailant pulled out the knife and wiped the blade clean on Fredrick's jacket. Bending over the body he removed a wallet from the inside pocket of the jacket, and pulled the wrist watch off of his left arm. He was in the process of removing a large gold ring from the left hand when he was bathed in bright light.

Mary had left her job at the real estate office and was driving home. Her mind was on the pasta dinner that she was going to prepare for her family; penne pasta, Alfredo sauce, Romano cheese, sliced chicken, asparagus, and a green salad. All that she needed was a good bottle of Chianti for her and her husband. The kids were going to settle for milk or water with their meal.

As Mary turned into the parking lot of the Stop-N-Go Liquor store her headlights fell on two men, one on the ground and the other bent over him holding his hand and trying to remove a ring. Mary slammed on her brakes and watched as the man stood and stared at her like a deer caught in the headlights before he ran to a parked car. With tires spinning he headed toward the exit. Mary had not fully completed the turn into the parking lot when she stopped her car which partially blocking the driveway.

The headlights of the Chevrolet switched to bright, blinding Mary. She heard a scrapping sound as the exiting car brushed against hers, ripping off the driver's side mirror.

She drove forward a few feet and could see that the man on the ground was covered with blood and was not moving. She called 911 telling the operator that she just saw a man being mugged and that he was on the ground bleeding. When the operator asked for her location she said, the liquor store at the corner Barton and Pine.

Within minutes she heard the wail of sirens as two police cars pulled up blocking the entrance to the parking lot. The fire department ambulance was not far behind. The EMT from the fire department checked the body for a pulse and listened for a heartbeat then shook his head. The policeman called for a supervisor and a detective to investigate a possible homicide.

One officer motioned Mary to a parking space then asked see her driver's license. "Can you describe what you saw?"

"I was turning into the parking lot when I saw this man bending over the man on the ground. It looked like he was taking the man's ring off. He was right in my headlights. He jumped up, ran to his car and tore out of here. He hit my car on the way out."

"Can you describe the other car?"

"It was either black, dark green, or blue. You can't really tell at night. And it all happened so fast."

"Was it a two door or four door car?"

"I think it was a four door. It could have been a two door, I don't know, I think four door."

When she had finished he told her to wait, "A detective will be here and he'll want to talk to you."

Badly shaken by the experience all she could think about was making dinner for her husband and kids. It was going to be pizza again tonight.

The forensic team and coroner soon arrived. They scraped paint samples off of Mary's car and picked up the side mirror as evidence. They took pictures of the body, Mary's car, and the victim's car, plus some general shots of the parking lot to provide some perspective.

After the detectives finished looking over the scene they gave the men from the coroner's office the okay to take the body. Within minutes the body was loaded onto a gurney to begin its ride to the morgue. Fredrick's car was towed to a storage yard.

Mary told the detective that she thought that between seeing the man in the headlights of her car, and the brief glimpse of him as he drove away, she could provide a rough description. He asked her to come down to the police station and describe the man to a police sketch artist.

A short time later the police left to handle other calls, everything had returned to normal except for the blood on the ground.

After describing the killer to a police artist, Mary was released to go home to her family. By the time she got home her kids had finished the pizza, done their homework and were in bed. Mary and her husband decided that a bottle of wine, any wine, was needed with their rewarmed pizza.

CHAPTER 28

The day after the incident at the liquor store, Carl and Ann decide to get away from the office for the afternoon and were on Highway One heading toward Half Moon Bay to have lunch and squander away the afternoon. Half Moon Bay is between San Francisco and Santa Cruz. About forty minutes from San Francisco it's a pleasant place to wander through antique and art shops or simply go to the beach.

Between San Francisco and Half Moon Bay, Highway One hangs on the edge of a cliff which drops one hundred and fifty feet or more to the crashing surf and rocks below. There are several overlooks for those who simply want to drink in the scenic view or watch for migrating gray whales.

A blue Chevrolet Impala started to pass Carl but as the Impala moved just slightly ahead of Carl's front wheels it suddenly cut hard right, hitting Carl's car turning it toward the edge of the cliff and the ocean below. Carl tried to stop but before he could react his tires were in the gravel at the side of the road and he was unable to stop.

The Impala did not swerve away but continued to push Carl toward the guard rail that separated the roadway from the edge of the cliff. Carl crashed into the metal barrier ripping one of the posts from the ground and bending the metal railing.

The blue Chevy sped away.

When Carl's car finally came to a stop it was hanging at a precarious angle over the edge of the precipice. If Carl or Ann tried to move, the car wobbled up and down sending dirt and rocks over the cliff to the rocks and ocean below.

The cars that had been behind Carl stopped to see what had happened. Some quick thinking drivers jumped from their cars and rushed to grab the rear bumper of Carl's car, adding their weight as a counter balance.

When the car stabilized Carl told Ann to slowly crawl into the back seat and go out the back door on the driver's side. Within a few minutes Ann was outside adding her weight to that of the men who were trying to stabilize the car. A semi-truck came over the rise and saw the car balanced over the edge of the cliff with people trying to keep it from completely slipping over.

The driver turned his truck until it was facing the rear of Carl's car. He tied a heavy duty cargo strap to his front bumper and the other end to the rear axil of Carl's car. He then backed the semi up to remove the slack from the cargo strap. With the car unable to move, Carl was able to crawl into the back seat and escape.

Carl and Ann held on to each other for several minutes. Tears flowed as Ann thought about how close she and Carl had come to death.

Within a few minutes a California highway patrol car stopped and radioed for a tow truck. Carl told the officer that it was not an accident. The driver of a blue Impala had deliberately tried to force him over the edge of the cliff. Several other drivers gave statements agreeing with Carl's version of the incident. The consensus being that the driver of the blue Impala was deliberately trying to kill Carl and Ann.

CHAPTER 29

Jean Peters called Carl on the afternoon of the attempt on his and Ann's life to tell him that Fredrick had been killed in what appeared to be a mugging. She went over the information that was known and ended by saying that the police were still not sure it was a mugging gone bad and they're still investigating. The facts were just not typical of that type of crime.

"I don't buy the part about a mugging either. Muggers are typically drug addicts looking to get enough money for their next fix, or some down and outer that is living on the street, not someone who drives a late model Chevy. I think the police will have to look in a different direction to figure this one out.

"One other thing, someone tried to kill Ann and me this morning while we were on our way to Half Moon Bay. The timing is too much of a coincidence to be unrelated. It has to be somebody involved in the Martin Munitions case since that is the only place where Fredrick and I intersect. I think it's more than chance that Fredrick is killed two days after I interviewed him and then someone makes an attempt on my life two days later. The day after I interviewed Fredrick I talked to Paul Hamit and within a day Fredrick is dead, then Ann and I are nearly killed. I don't know how you feel about it but I'm sure Paul Hamit had a hand in the murder and the attempt on our lives."

Jean thought about what Carl said for a few seconds and said, "From what I know about him Paul Hamit doesn't appear to be the kind of man that would have the balls to murder someone himself. But he could have easily hired someone to do it."

"I could only see the driver of the other car for a few seconds when he tried to push us over the cliff but I know it wasn't Hamit driving.

"I guess our best bet is to find out who owns that car or who rented it. I'll have people start checking rental agencies."

"Just watch your back a little more carefully Carl. When they find out that you're still alive they will want to take another shot at you."

A few days later Jean Peters called Carl again saying, "We located the blue Chevy that was involved with Fredrick's murder at a Hertz rental agency at the Sacramento Airport. When it was returned it had damage to the left side which fits with the report that Frederick's death is murder. Unfortunately it had already been sent out for repairs. Our crime lab people are checking it for fingerprints. The rental agency people could not describe the person renting the car or recognize the man in the police sketch. So at this point we have nothing but a police sketch."

Carl said, "I'm going to talk to Paul Hamit again. Maybe I can shake him up enough to make a dumb move."

The following day Carl visited Hamits office but was told that Paul had left the Country the week before and the secretary didn't know when he would be back. Carl did a quick calculation and reached the conclusion that Paul had left the Country the day before Fredrick's murder.

CHAPTER 30

Jean Peters and Carl were discussing the death of Fredrick over coffee at the Regency Hotel coffee shop. Jean was saying, "It's been a week since Fredrick was killed but the Police have not turned up anything new. We are keeping our eye on it but so far nothing other than finding the car has turned up. We didn't find any fingerprints on the car. It was apparently wiped down before being returned to Hertz.

"We've shown the police sketch to Hans and Callah and they both said that it looked like Jules Dunbar but we don't have solid proof that it was actually him. However the police and the FBI sure would like to talk to him.

"By the way the police have also concluded that Fredrick's death it wasn't a result of a mugging. The theft of the wallet and watch were meant to suggest a mugging gone bad but the use of a late model car by the killer doesn't fit. They are going on the theory that it was a murder."

"Do you have any new information about the missiles that the pirates used?"

"The only thing that we know for sure is that they were manufactured by the Pakistanis. The missiles are considered less than effective and are now used only for training purposes. The record keeping on their disposition is so poor that there is no way to tell how they moved from government control into the hands of some arms dealer."

"Okay Jean, please keep me informed if you can. Paul Hamit should be back from his trip soon. He has a home here and there is nothing to tie him to the murder, the theft of the missile parts, or the Lunemann family. All we have at this time is a theory. There is nothing to keep him from returning. When he returns I'll pay him a visit and see if I can shake any information loose."

Carl sat in a coffee shop across the street from Hamit's office building and watched. He finally dialed Hamit's telephone number. His secretary answered, "Mr. Hamit's office, may I help you?"

"Yes, I would like to speak with Mr. Hamit please?"

"I'm sorry Mr. Hamit is not in."

"When is he expected back?"

"He is not expected back for the rest of the week."

"Will he be back next week?"

"I'm sorry sir I don't have his schedule for next week."

Carl thanked her and hung up.

Carl was nearly done drinking his coffee and getting ready to leave when he saw Paul Hamit walk out of the office building and flag a cab. Carl left the coffee shop and managed to flag down a taxi quickly enough to follow Hamit to his apartment on Toledo Way in the Marina District.

Getting out of his cab, he paid his fare, then walked to a building across the street from Hamit's apartment and sat down on the front stairs. As he sat thinking about Paul Hamit and Fredrick Lunemann he considered how he would approach Hamit. He decided that the most effective way would simply be to knock on the door and confront him. Maybe Hamit would make a mistake and do or say something stupid.

Carl rang the doorbell and waited. When Hamit opened the door there was a look of surprise on his face which quickly turned to anger, through clinched teeth he said, "What the hell are you doing here?"

"I need to talk to you about Fredrick Lunemann's murder, and since your secretary said that you were not at the office I came here.

"Do you want to talk about this inside or out here in the hall where your neighbors can get an earful?"

Hamit thought for a few seconds then opened the door and stepped back. Carl stepped into the living room. It was nicely furnished, a large leather sofa, 50 inch flat screen TV, two black leather wing back chairs and a small coffee table. Through a pass through counter Carl could see a modern gourmet kitchen and a hallway that apparently lead to the bedrooms.

Hamit did not invite Carl to sit down, but closed the door and stood facing Carl with his arms folded across his chest.

"The police said that Fredrick died during a mugging not that he was murdered so why are you calling it a murder?"

"The police are reconsidering the evidence. They found the car that the murderer used and have an artist's sketch of the man who killed him. Two days later the same man tried to kill me. I find that to be too much of a coincidence to be simply random events.

"The only thing that Fredrick and I have in common is the case involving his family that I have been investigating. The industrial espionage involved the theft of heat seeking missile technology. The fact that you are an arms dealer and are acquainted with Fredrick and the Martin Munitions Company makes it an even greater coincidence. When someone tries to kill me I get angry and very curious."

"I don't know anything about Fredrick's death, the attempt on your life, or any missile part theft. I especially don't like you coming in here suggesting that I might have some involvement in a murder. I have been out of the Country for the past few weeks. If you want to talk to me in the future set up an appointment at my office. Now get the hell out of here!"

Carl smiled at Hamit and said. "Have a nice day." and left.

Carl went to the end of the block and waited in a doorway. Twenty minutes later, Hamit left his apartment and walked three blocks to a convenience store on Lombard Street. Although the store had ads for various products taped to the front windows, there was enough clear space to see him go to a pay phone at the rear of the store and place a call. After ending his call he bought a package of cigarettes and a bottle of Hennessey scotch then returned to his apartment. Carl watched the apartment for another hour then walked toward Bay Street where he flagged a cab.

CHAPTER 31

When Carl returned to his office he had a message from Jean Peters that said, "I just received a report that you might be interested in. It looks as if a missile using a Martin Munitions circuit board may have been used off the coast of Somalia again. You would think that the pirates would be worried about firing heat seeking missiles by now. I'll fax you a copy of the report."

"Thanks Jean, I'd like to read it. If I were a pirate I would be a little distrustful of both the missiles as well as the person who sold them."

The faxed report was sent a few minutes later; it said:

Greek Tanker Attacked by Pirates

The Greek tanker Athena steaming south through the Gulf of Aden on its way to Mozambique was attacked by Somali pirates. The attack was spotted by a French Destroyer attached to NATO Forces patrolling the Gulf of Aden which was able to foil the attack. As the pirates tried to escape, they fired what appeared to be a shoulder mounted missile but the missile prematurely exploded as it left the launcher, killing several pirates, injuring a number of others and severely damaging one of the pirate boats which later sank. NATO forces captured the escaping pirates four hours later. Before their capture the pirates threw weapons and scaling ladders overboard. The only remaining evidence was several rounds of rifle ammunition found in the bottom of one of the boats.

The pirates were detained for questioning and given medical attention. Because there are no formal procedures for the capture of pirates, and uncertainty as to which country was willing to prosecute pirates, they were given water and food and released.

CHAPTER 32

Ten hours after being released, the three remaining pirate fishing boats pulled into a small cove on the coast east of the town of Dhurba, Somalia. The cove was not big enough to support large ships but there was a small fishing village there. As the men jumped into surf, children on the beach danced around in excitement. The Older children ran into the surf to help pull the boats up onto the beach. The boat crew then carried or led three injured men to a group of huts with corrugated metal roofs. There was a lot of commotion from the villagers and then wailing from the families that had lost men on the raid.

A short time later Ahmed Yusuuf, the leader of the village and the leader of the pirate raiding party, jumped in a battered Toyota pickup and drove in the direction of Dhurba, until he came to Nur Hussein's compound, the warlord who controlled this part of Somalia. After telling Nur what had happened, Nur said, "That is the second missile that has blown up in our faces in the last few weeks."

Nur ordered that a missile launcher be tied to a tree and a long cord be tied to the trigger. The missile was then armed and the trigger pulled. There was an immediate explosion.

Nur's face burned hot with anger. He hated that he had been sold faulty equipment, and the notion that he had been cheated out of a great deal of money by Jules Dunbar cut to the core of his sole. His anger was made even worse by the thought of losing the ransom from two lost prize ships.

His pride had been severely damaged, he swore he would find a way to restore it. "If Allah is truly merciful he will allow me, Nur, to find Jules Dunbar and get my money back then let me have the pleasure of slowly killing him."

The question was, how would he get his hands on Jules? He could not send the villagers to find him, they had never been out of the village and would not be able to search out and find Dunbar in a large western city. Few had ever left the village or had the language skills that would be needed. For his villagers to go to a large western city, locate and kill a man would be like a fish trying to swim on dry land.

"I will have to think about this problem for a while. Do not use any of the remaining missiles, instead bring them all to me. We don't want anyone else to die because of that bastard Jules Dunbar. Allah willing he will be dealt with in good time."

Nur was a physically powerful man despite his nearing sixty-three years of age; an age that was considered elderly in Somalia.

He stood at five feet ten inches in height and weighed 198 pounds; his body was lean with firm muscles covered with very little fat. He had broad shoulders, short curly hair and very light bronze skin.

He had demonstrated his skills in diplomacy by steering the villages under his control away from any conflict with the British governing the Country at the time. The British began their governance of Somalia after the defeat of the Italians during World War II. Establishing a military governing body to rule Somalia until control could be given to a British civilian governing body in 1950. The Country was placed under British civilian administration by the United Nations until administrative control was turned over to the sovereign state of Somalia in 1960.

The Somali government had been largely ineffective and left much of the Country dependent on local warlords to provide administration and security.

Nur Hussein controlled a large area of the coast East of Dhurba. For the villagers within this area Nur represented the law. He could resolve local disputes, mete out justice, and provided the protection from other warlords as well as the marauders that roamed the countryside.

He spoke English with a British accent. Most people hearing him would have thought they had just stepped off a bus in Trafalgar square in London. He also spoke Arabic and a smattering of Italian. His formal education had consisted of attending the first few grades in one of the schools that the British had constructed in the Country. But when the British left, the educational system began to decay and Nur did not get any further formal training.

He took over as warlord at the age of twenty. At that age he had the audacity to challenge the existing warlord on one of the policies he thought to be unfair. The old warlord, feeling that he could not let stand the young man's challenge of his authority started to strike Nur, but to his surprise instead of cowering Nur struck back. The battle ended when Nur broke the man's neck. The villagers following custom acknowledged Nur as their new leader. In quick succession he was challenged by others who thought he was too young and inexperienced to be their leader. In each case he defeated the challenger. He demonstrated compassion by letting challengers live. In doing so he gained their loyalty and the respect of the villagers.

When the British left Somalia in 1960 there was a period of chaos while the new government tried to establish its authority. Bandits roamed many of the provinces in Somalia but they quickly learned that to attack a village controlled by Nur was a fatal mistake. In contrast Nur treated the villagers under his control with respect and fairness. The only thing that he asked was to be treated with fairness in return. As a result, within a short time, he received their loyalty. The one thing that he would not abide was someone who tried to cheat him; the prematurely exploding missiles labeled Jules Dunbar as a man who will cheat you.

Nur was not afraid of breaking someone else's law if the benefits were worth the risk. Pirating fell in this category. As long as the spoils of the pirating enterprise were shared with him he would support the pirates. Pirating was considered a legitimate profession that had been supported in this region of the world for hundreds of years. Nur simply capitalized on the idea and expanded the territory in which to hunt for prey to include those in the Indian Ocean. There were large profits to be made by ransoming the passengers and selling the ship and cargo back to the owners.

The passengers and crews of the ships that were taken were treated reasonably well. Nur realized that to harm prisoners was to invite a war, otherwise it was simply a business arrangement. It was much cheaper for insurance companies to pay a ransom than finance a war. After all, the cost of a ransom was passed on to its customers.

To continue his business he had to share some of the profits with those in government but he understood that was also the price of doing business.

As his pirating enterprise expanded and he needed more weapons, he called on a number of arms dealers, none of whom would deal with him until he was approached by a man calling himself Jules

Dunbar. As long as Nur had the cash, Jules was ready to supply the latest weapons, ammunition and other equipment.

Shipping arms and ammunition was always tricky. Many countries frowned on weapons passing through their territory for fear that some or all of it would fall into the wrong hands. The government of Somalia particularly did not like the idea of a warlord getting better arms than the government forces had for fear of being overthrown. To resolve this problem Jules would lease a plane as needed and fly the arms directly to the buyer. He also found it a lot cheaper than paying all the bribes that it would cost using commercial means of shipping. He and Paul eventually invested in their own airplane.

To move arms to Nur he would use an emergency landing strip that had been built by the British during the Second World War. The landing strip was conveniently close to Nur's compound which made moving the weapons and ammunition far simpler. The only dangerous aspect of flying in weapons was that over the years the landing strip had been used as a pasture for cattle, as a result there was the danger of a cow straying on the path of a plane trying to land.

CHAPTER 33

Carl sat at a small table in Starbucks on Grant Street waiting for Jean Peters. He thought about all that had happened in the past few months; the murder of Fredrick, the attempt on his life, and meeting Paul Hamit. In particular he thought about Paul's use of a public telephone in the grocery store after talking to him at his apartment.

While he was mulling over these thoughts Jean Peters walked in. After ordering Jean's coffee they decided to walk a block to Union Square for a little sunshine and a bit more privacy than Starbucks would afford.

After reaching Union Square they sat on the steps leading to the park. Carl began to fill Jean in on his meeting with Paul Hamit and ended by telling her about Hamit's unusual behavior. "He obviously thought his phones were tapped or he would not have felt the need to leave his apartment and find a phone. What did he have to say that made him afraid that the authorities might overhear his conversation. I think he was talking to Jules; telling him that the police now think that Fredrick's death was a murder not a mugging, and that I'm still alive.

"I guess my next question is: does your warrant to tap his office and home phone extend to any other phones he might be using?"

"The warrant is somewhat open ended to cover any phone he might be expected to use. We have a lot more latitude under the Anti-Terrorism act. We obviously can't record the conversation he made from the market but we can find out what number he called. With the development of cell phones not many people use a pay phone anymore, his call is probably the only call from that phone in days and since you know what time it was made it should be easy to find out who he called."

"Jean, I hope you're not going to get in any trouble providing me with information. I know that the FBI doesn't like to share information with non-law enforcement people like me in an ongoing case."

"I cleared it with Director Riley some time ago to provide you with information, but it's a two way street. Anything that you come up with you'll have to share with me. Director Riley recognizes the help you gave the FBI and more importantly you haven't overstepped any boundaries.

"Besides I have a personal reason for wanting to help you get to the bottom of this problem. I have a brother that flies helicopters for the navy and he's stationed on a ship in the Gulf of Aden trying to stop piracy. Having helicopters shot out of the sky by heat seeking missiles does not set well with me."

Jean called the next day saying, "The number that Paul Hamit dialed was to a cell phone. The cell phone had GPS but the GPS location was a Bel-Air grocery store in a small shopping center in Antelope, California. The cellphone is registered to Jules Dunbar. The GPS and cell phone tower location are about ten miles from Sacramento International Airport where the blue Chevrolet Impala was rented. Jules was probably shopping at a grocery store near his home. It's pretty obvious he used a pay phone because he didn't want anybody to connect him to Jules, the murder, or the attempt on your life.

"Now we know he is connected, but how do we prove it? If I call him tomorrow and the phone is near the same grocery store it's a good bet that he is in or near his home. I'll give him some excuse for dialing the wrong number."

"Okay, let's try at 8:30 tomorrow morning. That will give us time to make arrangements with the telephone company to get a location."

The next morning Carl dialed the number. After two rings a man answered, "Yes?"

Carl said with a questioning voice, "Is Helen there?"

The man answered in a voice with an English accent, "Sorry, there is no Helen here. You must have the wrong number." then hung up.

Five minutes later Carl's phone rang. When he answered, Jean said, "Be very careful Carl, that phone is very close to your office. If it's Dunbar he could be getting ready to finish the job that he started."

"I hear you Jean. The voice had an English accent, so it could very well be Dunbar."

"We know. We heard the accent. He did not say much but we may have enough for a voice print if we get lucky."

At noon, Carl and Ann left the office to get something to eat. As they walked through the heavy noontime crowd on Geary Street, a man coming from the opposite direction walked directly toward them. He was carrying a folded newspaper in his right hand and a paper shopping bag in his left. When he was about five feet from

Carl, his right hand came up and Carl recognized the a gun and it had silencer. Before he could react he felt as if somebody had hit him squarely in the chest with a sledge hammer. He staggered and fell onto his back. Ann screamed and bent over Carl. The man with the gun dropped the newspaper and the gun in his shopping bag and continued walking as if he were unaware of any problem.

When Jules reached the corner he turned left, walked another block then turned right, midway down the block he turned into an alley. When he reached a trash bin, he pulled the gun from the shopping bag, wiped it clean, returned it to the bag, and tossed the bag into the bin. He had already wiped each bullet clean when he had loaded the gun. The gun itself had been part of a group of weapons purchased in Russia and later sold to the PPK. It could not be traced to him. Leaving the alley he caught a cab and headed for the airport and a flight to London.

A man in the crowd that had gathered around Carl had called an ambulance and it arrived about three minutes later. Carl was lifted onto a gurney and placed in the ambulance. To the onlookers it looked as if Carl were dead. The front of his shirt was soaked in blood. When the ambulance doors were closed Ann leaned over Carl and said, "Are you okay?"

"Yeah I'm okay but I feel as if a mule kicked me in the chest."

With Ann's help Carl sat up, unbuttoned his shirt and tried to remove the bullet proof vest he was wearing, but he had difficulty "Damn this hurts."

As Ann struggled with the vest one of the packets that still had a little red dye continued to leak.

The ambulance attendant stared at Carl, his mouth agape; finally he regained his wits, "You may have a couple of broken ribs or at least one hell of a bruise. Better have a doctor check you out."

Carl called Jean Peters saying, "You were right, thanks for the warning. The guy in the sketch, at least I think it was him, it happened pretty fast, just tried to take me out with a couple of shots to the chest. Thanks to you I wore a bullet proof vest. I'm bruised and sore as hell but I'm able to get around. Ann's with me and we're on our way to the hospital to be checked out."

"I guess we know what Hamit's call was all about."

"I guess we do. Luckily whoever he was didn't come up behind me or decide to try for a head shot instead of my chest. I guess he wanted to see my face to be sure he got the right guy. The one good thing that came out this experience was that both Ann and I got a good look at his face. It's one face that I won't forget for a long time. Getting shot tends to engrave the shooters image in your memory.

"I think it was the same guy that tried to kill us by sending us over a cliff when were on our way to Half Moon Bay. I only saw him from slightly behind and in profile but I'm pretty sure it was the same guy.

"I'll check on Paul Hamit's whereabouts but I'm willing to bet he has been out of town since the day after he made that phone call."

Chapter 34

Carl and Ann were in their apartment talking about Jules Dunbar when Ann asked, "How are we going to find this guy? We only have a sketch, and we don't know where he lives."

"We know the location of the cellphone tower that was used when Hamit called him from the pay phone. As a start we can assume he is probably located within a four mile radius of the tower. Anything beyond that and you lose signal or are switched to a different tower. While I was in Algiers Ian mentioned that his friends, I assume he meant the CIA, thought he lived in a city named Antelope, they didn't have an address. If this tower is near Antelope it's reasonable to assume that it's Dunbar.

"As a starting point we can assume that he lives somewhere near the tower, if we are right we can find him by checking property assessment rolls for a Jules Dunbar. If he is renting he won't appear on a property assessment roll so we will also check with the local utility companies that supply services within four miles of the tower. Even if he lives in an apartment he will use electric power, water, telephone services, and probably natural gas.

"We not only have to check the cell phone company he uses, but he might also have a home phone. If we don't find anything we'll have to assume that he was visiting someone in the area, just passing through, or going by another name. I'm betting that he lives in the area and that he is using Jules Dunbar as his name."

"Why do you say that?"

"Everybody needs a place where they can be themselves and feel safe. Since he does business with a questionable bunch of people in Africa, Europe, and the Middle East countries I'm betting he would feel safer in a country on another continent. Canada, the U.S., Mexico, or South America, somewhere he doesn't have to be constantly on guard; where he can be a little more relaxed. Someplace like California. If I am right this is as good a place to start looking as any, besides this is where he got the call."

"I'll have Dan start checking with the phone company that issued that number; they have to send the phone bill somewhere. I'll also start checking utility companies that service that area. You, on the other hand, can rest for a few days and let the bruise on your chest heal. It will take us a couple of days to gather all the information anyhow, so just take it easy and read a book."

Later that Afternoon, Ann sat across the dining room table from Carl and said, "That was Dan on the phone just now. He said that AT&T had issued the number to a Mr. Jules Dunbar. They had a billing address for 10271 Poker Lane, Antelope, California; that's in the 95843 zip code area. He said it's less than two miles from the cell tower.

"I also found a Jules Dunbar with both the Sacramento Utility District and Pacific Gas and Electric Company with billing at the same address. His utilities have been paid in advance and have a substantial credit balance. It looks as if he planned to be away for a while and wanted to prepay for his services. He gets his Internet, T.V. and home telephone services from Surewest Communications in the nearby city of Roseville. Again with the same billing address but he canceled that service two days ago. I think it's safe to assume that we have the right address."

"I guess it's time to take a road trip and check this address out. It looks like he plans on being gone for a while. But we'll have to check it out in any case. Call Jean and let her know where we are going."

"What happed to taking it easy and reading a book?"

"Some other time, besides I'll let you drive."

As Carl's rental car went over the crest of the coastal range at Vallejo dropping into the Sacramento Valley, the outside air temperature jumped from a pleasant 65 to 101 degrees and the humidity dropped to 17 percent, a typical Sacramento Valley summer day; hot and dry. They made good time on highway 80, two hours and 15 minutes later they took the Antelope exit. Then west for two miles, then east on Poker Lane, a dead end country lane.

Antelope is a community of subdivisions in northern Sacramento County that completely surrounds a rural area of 271 acres consisting of small two to five acre farms. Most of the farms have modern homes, but a few parcels still have older farm houses. The address they were looking for on Poker Lane was an old white two story farm house that sat on a three acre parcel. Over the years the house had been renovated and landscaped. There was a detached garage, barn, and several other out-buildings. All in all, the property had taken on the appearance of an estate occupied by a wealthy gentleman landowner.

"I guess the only way we are going to find out if he's home or left the Country is to call Jean and see if the FBI can get a search warrant. If he is home the FBI can arrest him, if not he may have left a clue as to where he has gone. In the meantime let's go find a restaurant and get something to eat while we wait."

Three hours later Carl, Ann and two agents from the Sacramento FBI field office knocked on the door of Jules' home. When there was no answer they jimmied the door and entered the house. After a quick search it was quite clear that Jules Dunbar had left for good. There were no clues to indicate where he had gone.

CHAPTER 35

The following morning Carl sat in his office holding a hot cup of coffee thinking about what he would do next. He finally reached for the phone and called Jean Peters. Although she already had a report, he told her about the search of Jules Dunbar's house.

Carl said, "It looks as if he planned to kill me and then simply leave the area. I suspect he went directly to the airport, called Hamit, told him I was dead, and flew out. There is no telling where he is now."

"I think you're right. I already have people checking with airport personnel and looking at surveillance videos, maybe we can find out where he went." said Jean

"I have another idea that might tell us where he is. Can you still keep an eye on the cell phone number he called last time, even if it may be out of the Country now?"

"I can ask my friends at the CIA. Since this involves the selling of heat seeking missiles it's a case they are interested in as well, and will probably be willing to help. What do you have in mind?

"I'm going to call on Paul Hamit when he gets back to town. If Jules told him that I am dead, as I suspect he has, he is going to be in for a hell of a shock when he opens the door. Maybe he'll make the same mistake and call Jules at the same number as last time."

"That could be pretty dangerous for you Carl. Jules might be tempted to take a shot at your head using a sniper rifle, and a bullet proof vest won't be of any use."

"That's why I am going after him. A killer can just wait for an opportunity, then when you least expect it he can make his move. I don't want to spend the rest of my life looking over my shoulder and wondering when some killer is coming for me."

"Alright Carl, give me some time to set this up before you go see Hamit. I'll call you tomorrow."

The next evening Carl rang Hamit's doorbell. When the door opened Hamit looked as if he had seen a ghost. After a few seconds he regained his composure and asked, "What are you doing here? I thought I told you if you wanted to see me make an appointment at my office."

"Actually I'm not looking for you I'm looking for your friend Jules Dunbar."

"I told you I don't know any Jules Dunbar."

"I find that rather hard to believe. Every time I talk to you he tries to kill me two or three days later. The last time he came very close to succeeding. The next time you talk to him tell him that I'll be watching for him and he won't be so lucky." With that Carl turned on his heel and walked away.

From a position across the street Carl watched Hamit's apartment. Every few seconds he would see Hamit through his front window as he paced back and forth in his living room holding a cell phone to his ear. Finally the pacing stopped, the room lights dimmed, and Carl could see light and shadows flash in the room; Hamit was watching T.V.

As Carl watched Hamit's apartment his cell phone vibrated. When he answered it he heard Jean say, "Jules is still using a cell phone with GPS so we have an exact location but it doesn't help much since it turns out to be a pub in London. He was picked up on four cell towers so we can get close to a general location to where he is living, assuming he is in a pub near his home.

"Hamit must have bought a new cell phone. The call number is a new one, but we have it now."

"That must be why he made the call from his home rather than a public telephone.

"Thanks Jean, I'll catch a flight out tonight maybe I can get there before Hamit's phone call spooks him and he moves on."

CHAPTER 36

It was midmorning in London when Carl stepped off the plane at Heathrow airport. He had managed to get about five hours of sleep, then some coffee and a sweet roll on the plane just before it landed. Now looking rather sleepy he waited in line to go through passport control. When his turn came he handed his passport to the agent, and waited while he leafed through the pages. Finally he looked up and with a smile asked, "Are you here on business or pleasure Mr. Lukin?"

"Business."

The agent stamped his passport but retained it while he made an entry on his computer, then smiling, handed the passport back to Carl saying, "Enjoy your stay Mr. Lukin."

Carl thanked the man then walked down the corridor that led to the baggage area. He was standing in line waiting to have his carryon bags inspected by customs when he was approached by a man who identified himself as Avery Jenkins from the Secret Intelligence Service (SIS), more commonly known as MI6. Showing his credentials, Jenkins said, "Mr. Lukin please follow me Sir." He was led to a small room just off the customs area.

Carl asked, "Is there a problem, Mr. Jenkins?"

"Not that I know of Sir. I have been asked to escort you to our headquarters for a short meeting with my director. He will explain everything to you. Please follow me, I think we can bypass customs." A request that Carl had the distinct feeling it would be best to follow.

After a forty-five minute drive they arrived at a non-descript stone building that had the distinct look of a government office building. There was no signage anywhere to indicate which governmental agency occupied the building.

After showing his ID to a guard, Carl was led to a small third floor bureaucratic looking office and introduced to Mr. Harold Miller, head of a group focused on Anti-Terrorist Activities.

Government employment ran in the veins of the Miller family. Harold's grandfather, the first Harold Miller, had been head of the intelligence service that operated in India during British rule. One of his sons, John Miller, after a stint in the military in which he attained the rank of Colonel, was assigned to the British Diplomatic Service as a Military Attaché. One of his responsibilities was the acquisition of intelligence regarding the political, economic, and military conditions of the country to which he was posted. John was sent to Somalia in February of 1941, as part of the British Administration of Somalia when it was reacquired from the Italians during World War II.

Toward the end of 1941, while he was on leave in England, John married. He then returned to Somalia with his new bride. The couple had a son who was named after John's father. As the son of a diplomat, Harold had tutors for his early education. He was later sent to boarding school in England.

While in Somalia on vacations, his friends consisted of the children of other diplomats and local governmental administrators who were largely of Italian or Somali descent. One of his closest friends was Ahmed Hussein. Ahmed and Harold hit it off together, they were about the same age, had similar interests, liked the same athletic events, and enjoyed doing the same things; in short they enjoyed each other's company. The two boys spent a considerable part of their free time together either playing, exploring the local markets, reading, or simply watching people go about their daily business.

Each evening John would listen to his son tell of his adventures for the day. He would ask questions about what Harold had heard or seen that day, then ask Harold what he thought it meant. Many of these observations ended up in reports that John sent to England. Frequently Harold and his father would enter into lengthy discussions about one of the observations. What did it mean to the British? How would it affect the Somali people? Was it a good thing or a bad thing? Harold did not realize it at the time, but he was receiving training in how to be observant, how to relate small details in his observations, and how to interpret the information he received.

When Harold completed his formal education, he also joined the diplomatic corps and asked to be posted to Somalia. Because of his extensive knowledge about the Country and his ability to speak Arabic and a little Italian he got the assignment he requested. When the British returned the control of the County to Somalia, Harold stayed on in the British Embassy as the Director of Financial Aid to Somalia.

The reports that he sent to England were concise and contained insights not normally seen in field reports. As the information was passed on to the Intelligence services for analysis Harold's name became known and respected. Within a short time he was invited to a meeting with an organization called the Secret Intelligence Service (SIS), an organization that he had heard about in government circles but of which he knew almost nothing. At that meeting he was offered a job as an analyst, which he accepted. Although he had to leave Somalia and his many friends, he made a real effort to keep in contact with them. As with most long distant relationships, many would drift away with time, except his relationship with Ahmed with whom he kept in contact.

When Harold and his family went on vacation they occasionally visited Africa, invariably stopping in Somalia to see their friends, Ahmed and his family. They would have long discussions about the political direction in which the Country was moving. They both expressed concern about the various radical elements that were causing trouble for the Somali government.

Over time, Harold moved up in the SIS ranks, finally ending up in his current position in the SIS anti-terrorist unit.

"Welcome to England Mr. Lukin. I understand that you have been of assistance to the FBI in dealing with the heat seeking missile problem that concerns us both. We have been asked to give you a hand if we could while you are here. Would you care to fill us in on what led you to Merry Old England?"

"I'll be glad to give you what information I have which isn't much. I'm sure you are familiar with the missile attacks in the Gulf of Aden."

"Yes of course. We lost two helicopters to pirate missiles."

Carl went through the history of the theft of the circuit boards and the tracking of Jules Dunbar and Paul Hamit. He ended his briefing with, "We believe there are still twenty-seven viable heat seeking missiles unaccounted for. Undoubtedly some are still in the hands of Somali pirates. We have evidence that some were sold to the PPK but we're not sure how many, others may have been sold to other groups as yet unidentified. Jules Dunbar is probably trying to buy more missiles so that he can fill his orders."

Miller said, "We will of course assist you in any way we can. We are familiar with the pub Jules was in and will, along with MI5, be on the lookout for him. Do you have any further information as to Dunbar's location?"

"No sir. The last time we were able to trace him he was at the pub. We assume he is living near the pub but we haven't been able to pinpoint his exact location."

"I think that's a reasonable assumption. We talked to MI5 about putting their staff on the watch for him but he could be anywhere in a very big area. We have provided MI5 with the artist's sketch and an old photo from his military service. We may get lucky and spot him."

"I think I'll spend a few days watching the pub myself, maybe I'll spot him," said Carl.

"Perhaps Avery can accompany you. Since you have no law enforcement authority, Avery can make the arrest if you find him."

At 6:30 Avery and Carl entered the pub and looked around. Since they didn't spot Jules they took a seat at a corner table where they had a good view of the door and the majority of the bar. It was still early and the crowd consisted mostly of office workers getting ale on their way home. The waitress informed them that the local pub crowd would not be coming in until later in the evening, around 7:30 or so and stay until closing.

Holding up the sketch and photograph, Carl asked, "Do you recognize this man?"

"Yes, I think I have seen him before, but if he is the same man he looks older than this picture. He usually comes in about 8:30 and stays until 11:30 or so." She thought for a moment then said. "He's a good tipper. What's he done?"

"Thank you miss, this is not a recent photo. It was taken when he was much younger."

At midnight, Carl and Avery decided to call it quits for the night. They would try again the following evening.

The next night they arrived at 7:00, the table in the corner was again empty. Carl sat with his back to the wall facing the front of the pub, Avery sat with his back to the glass window and had his head turned to face the bar. The waitress came and took their order.

Before she got back Jules stepped out of the toilet and started to step back into the pub. He looked to his right and stopped immediately. He recognized Carl sitting at a table with another man who appeared to be a cop. Jules backed up into the hallway. The sight of Carl alive and sitting in his favorite pub startled him. He backed further into the hallway. "What the bloody hell! You're supposed to be dead. I know I put two bullets into your chest and saw you bleed. Bloody hell!"

With that thought he turned around and exited through the back door into an alley filled with garbage cans.

At that moment the waitress was walking back to Carl and Avery's table with two pints of ale. She placed the glasses down and said, "Did you get a chance to talk to your friend?"

Avery asked, "Which friend would that be?"

"You know the man in the picture, he was right here."

"What do you mean he was right here?"

Pointing she said, "Why, he was standing in the hallway not six feet from you a minute ago."

Avery and Carl jumped up, ran down the hall, and crashed through the door into the alley. Seeing no one they sprinted down the alley to the street but Jules had disappeared.

From a bookstore across the street Jules watched as Avery and Carl bolted from the alley looking for him in both directions. He watched them as they stood there talking then as they walked back to the pub.

CHAPTER 37

Jules continued to watch the pub. A few minutes later Avery and Carl left and walked to a car parked down the street. Avery had a cell phone to his ear and was talking rapidly.

After Carl and Avery drove away Jules left the bookstore going to an apartment building three blocks away. In his apartment he quickly packed a bag, put on an overcoat and a broad brimmed hat and left.

When he tilted his head down, his face would be unrecognizable to the surveillance cameras that provided coverage of a major part of London's business district. He left his apartment and made his way to a luggage shop, getting in just before they closed for the day. He bought a brief case, then stopped at a kiosk and bought a newspaper. He folded the newspaper and put it under the arm that was carrying the briefcase. With his small carryon luggage, briefcase, newspaper, and his head bowed under a broad brimmed hat he looked like one of many very tired businessmen heading home after a long day.

Jules took a taxi to the train station and bought a ticket to Paris. He made his way to the men's room, found an empty stall, and sat down to kill time until his train left. When he finally boarded his train and found his seat, he stored his luggage, then leaned back in his seat, pulled his hat down over his eyes and pretended to sleep.

Avery's phone call had triggered a beehive of police action in the area of the pub. Police fanned over the area showing Jules' picture to store owners, residents of apartment houses, and managers at rooming houses. By 1:30 the following afternoon they had zeroed in on an apartment building three blocks from the pub. The manager identified Jules as the man in apartment 3B. The police obtained a search warrant and rang the bell to the apartment. When no one answered they used the managers pass key to enter. To no one's surprise the apartment was empty.

Carl and Avery walked through the apartment, finally Carl said, "It looks as if he left in a hurry, probably within minutes of having seen me in the pub. Just threw a few clothes in a bag and left everything else."

Carl looked up as Avery came in from the bedroom and said, "Nothing but some odd bits of clothing in the closet, razor and shaving cream are gone, the only thing left in the bathroom was a bottle of aspirin."

The living room furniture consisted of an easy chair, sofa and coffee table. On the table was a paperback novel with a folded receipt from a Monaco casino for a wire transfer to mark his page. The wire transfer was for 520,000 dollars to an account in the U.S. An empty cup and saucer along with several hard core porn magazines were the only other things on the table. Lying on the sofa was an open French newspaper.

Carl looked around then at Avery and said, "I think he is headed for France. The newspaper shows he can read and probably speak French. He spends time in Monaco where French is the primary language, but who knows where he will go from France."

"We can check the surveillance cameras and see if we can find him. He has only been gone for about twelve hours, that's a pretty narrow window to search, we might get lucky."

While the apartment was being searched by a forensic team other police officers questioned shop owners, newsstands operators, and restaurants close to the apartment. The kiosk owner thought he might have seen Jules but he could not be sure when. He thought it might have been within the last day or two. The luggage shop owner was sure he had seen him the night before. "Not many people come in just minutes before closing and buy the first briefcase they are shown."

The shop owner was asked to describe the man who bought the briefcase. He said, "He was in a bit of a hurry. He was carrying an overnight kit, he was wearing a hat with a broad brim and an overcoat which I though was a bit odd since it's been warm. He paid me cash then walked out. He tried to flag down a taxi but it had a fare so he walked on down the street."

At police headquarters a group of three officers from the surveillance identification office were looking through video recordings attempting to match the sketch and photo to people on the computer screen. After an hour Sgt. Harris leaned back and looked at Carl and Avery saying, "You say your man is trying to escape, most likely in a hurry to get out of the Country?"

"Yes that's right." said Carl.

"Well in that case we ought to be looking for someone who doesn't look like the picture. What I mean Sir is that he is probably hiding his face with his hat or umbrella or something else. And you say he is wearing an overcoat and carrying a suitcase? Maybe a newspaper, flowers or something else in his other hand?"

"Yes, that about right"

"I think I may have seen your man. You can't see his face for a positive identification but I think he might have gone into the train station about a little after eight last night."

Carl looked at the pictures, for a few minutes then said, "It could be him but I'm not sure."

"There is a train out of there at 10:15 that connects with the Chunnel train and a fast train to Paris. If that is your man he is in Paris or moved on to another city by now."

"There's not much more that I can do here, I might as well head to France and see if I can pick up his trail. Maybe we will get lucky and he will use his phone again and we can get a new location to start looking."

CHAPTER 38

Carl called Jean Peters. He told Jean about his meeting with Harold Miller, Jules seeing him in the pub, and the futile search to find him. "All we know is that Jules took a shuttle train to France. We have no idea where he went from there."

"I'll put a request to the French police and Interpol for his arrest on murder charges. If he leaves France, Interpol might be able to locate him. He has got to surface sometime." said Jean."

"He's still in partnership with Paul Hamit and will have to communicate with him at some time in the future if they are going to continue doing business together. Although Hamit has a legal business he really has no need for Jules, he might just cut him loose. But I'm betting he will come across a deal that is not sanctioned by the government that's just too lucrative to pass up and he will get in touch with Jules. Greed is a powerful taskmaster and it will eventually get the best of him. Do you think we can continue to monitor all his calls?"

"I don't know the answer to that but I can find out. Having a killer on the loose who's willing to sell heat seeking missiles to anyone who has the money scares the hell out of me and I'm sure it's a problem that will scare a lot of other people as well. I'll call my director in the morning and I'll see what can be done."

"One other thing Jean, I'll be going to Monaco for a few days. When we searched his apartment we found a receipt that he was using as a bookmark. It was a receipt for a wire transfer to an account in the U.S. in the amount of 520,000 dollars. He might be going there or somewhere else but Monaco looks like a promising place to start looking.

"I doubt that a wire transfer from a gambling casino for that kind of money was from a legal weapons sale and there is no reason for Jules to send money he won gambling to Hamit. You may want to alert the IRS about it."

When Carl finished his call to Jean he called Ann Curlin saying, "I'll be gone for about another week. Jules got away and headed to France. He likes to gamble in Monaco so I'll start there." He told her about the receipt and asked her to contact Dan Nakamura and ask him to see if he could get a look at Hamit's bank accounts. He gave her the wire transfer number, the amount, and the account number to which the money was sent."

"Hurry home Carl I miss you, beside my feet get cold at night."

Carl laughed then said, "Oh great, now I'm only a foot warmer."

CHAPTER 39

After talking with her director, Jean called Aaron Kovak at the CIA to set up a short meeting. When she arrived at the CIA, a secretary led her to an office where Aaron was waiting.

Jean reviewed what has happened since their last meeting, "We estimate that enough parts were stolen to upgrade at least thirty-five heat seeking missiles possibly more; at least twenty-seven of them are unaccounted for. There may be more that we are unaware of."

Jean pointed out that Jules Dunbar had sold missiles to pirates as well as the PPK insurgent group and possibly other terrorist groups. "There is no evidence that he has sold them to an Islamic terrorist group as yet. But on the other hand he has demonstrated that he has not the slightest compunction about selling his weapons to groups who have no scruples about killing innocent civilians. I have no doubt that it is only a matter of time until he sells them to other terrorist groups if he hasn't already. He has already proven that so long as they have the money he will sell them whatever they want.

"Carl believes that Paul Hamit is the brains of the outfit and Jules is the salesman and facilitator. The business licenses are in Hamits name and he runs the business office. It is unlikely that

Hamit is the kind of guy that would do the dirty work himself, and would probably want to distance himself from any illegal sale. We believe he has the contacts in the weapons manufacturing industry and Jules is the person that meets with the contacts looking for illegal weapons.

"To date we only have evidence that they have sold modified Pakistani missiles. Now that we have shut down his source of circuit boards there is little doubt that Paul Hamit will identify other sources for missiles that don't require any modification. Once he has done that Jules Dunbar will be out there pedaling them to groups such as Lashkar-e-Taiba, al-Qaida, or Islam's Fire. Any terrorist groups would love to get their hands on such weapons and be willing to pay a good price for them. They could kill thousands and bring commercial air travel to a standstill.

"Jules Dunbar has murdered one man in San Francisco and attempted to kill Carl Lukin twice. When Carl told Paul Hamit that Jules had murdered Fredrick Lunemann and had attempted to murder him, Hamit said that he did not know anyone named Jules Dunbar. But thirty minutes later Paul called Jules in London.

"We were fortunate enough to get an approximate location for Jules in London. Carl flew to London and with the help of an MI6 man tried to find Jules. Unfortunately, Jules saw Carl first and managed to escape to France. We have asked the French Police and Interpol for help but haven't heard anything yet."

"How can we help Jean?"

"If you or NSA can monitor phone traffic and pinpoint Jules Dunbar's location, we may be able to nab him before he can sell the rest of his missiles, or if he has already sold them, we may be able to intercept them or track them down. We want them both for murder and industrial espionage and you want him for terrorism. Between us we may be able to stop him before he does any more damage.

"If there was any question about Jules Dunbar's connection to Paul Hamit we now have some pretty solid evidence." She went on to tell Aaron of the wire transfer receipt that Carl had found. "Half a million dollars is probably Hamit's cut from an illegal sale."

"How does Carl Lukin fit into this situation?"

"Carl will work with us if we let him or he will work on this independently if we don't. Carl doesn't want to be always looking over his shoulder to see if Jules is trying to kill him, he may get lucky the third time. He's a very capable and resourceful man. Carl will continue to look for Jules on his own if necessary. I think he can be very useful. As a result, my Director has agreed to a quid-pro-quo exchange of information between Carl and the Bureau."

"Our man in Algiers worked with Carl for the few weeks he was there. He was very impressed with Carl. Seems to think we ought to try and hire the man as a field agent. I'll see what we can do to help him.

"Aaron thought about the problem for a minute then said, "I'll bring this problem up to the Director and we'll continue to monitor calls to Mr. Jules Dunbar."

CHAPTER 40

It was 6:45 A.M. when Director Richard Rice arrived at the White House to go over the morning briefs with President Clyde Andrews while he ate his breakfast. They had just finished the briefing and were sipping their coffee when the President asked, "Is there anything else Dick?"

"Yes sir, there is one thing that I didn't include in the formal briefing because we have not developed sufficient information as yet, but I think that you should be made aware of it."

"Okay Dick, What is it?"

"As you know Sir, there have been a number of pirate attacks in the Gulf of Aden. The pirates use AK47s for the most part and rocket propelled grenades (RPG), however, we now have proof that on a couple of occasions they have used surface to air heat seeking missiles. Twice they have shot down helicopters and on one occasion fired a missile at a cruise ship killing three crew members. We believe that they have used SAMs on other occasions but we don't have any proof to that effect, they could have used RPGs which were mistaken for SAMs."

The President leaned forward and said, "The pirates are a significant problem for everyone. It will be difficult problem to solve short of starting a war in Somalia and endangering the lives of all seven hundred or so hostages that they now hold. I've had the Secretary of State contact the Somali Government to get them to put a stop to the piracy but they are unwilling or unable to take action against the pirates. It appears it is the latter. The Government has no control over the warlords who run the pirates, and in fact they appear to be fearful of them."

"Yes sir, if the government tries to stop the pirates, they could find themselves in the midst of a civil war."

"I didn't mean to interrupt you Dick, you were saying."

"Yes Sir. The American company that has a government contract to manufacture heat seeking missiles has had parts stolen that are used in their guidance system. One of these parts was used to modify a Pakistani made missile thereby making it accurate. That missile was fired at a cruise ship in the Gulf of Aden. The missiles are being modified in a small machine shop in Algeria.

"The FBI had been investigating this problem for some time but haven't been unable to find out how the parts were stolen or who used them to modify the missiles. The company, in an effort to protect its own interest hired a private investigator a Mr. Carl Lukin. The investigator discovered the thief, and how the parts were being smuggled out of the manufacturing plant. Working with the FBI they discovered how the parts are shipped to Algeria. Carl traveled to Algiers and found who was making the modifications, and how the missiles reached the Somali pirates.

"The CIA decided to keep an eye on Carl as well while he was in Algiers. Our station chief there stopped an attempted mugging of Carl and was able to form a working relationship that resulted in his sharing some valuable information concerning the missile problem.

Over the course of the a few weeks, Carl impressed the station chief enough that he recommended that the CIA hire him.

"In essence, Carl has been of significant help to both the FBI and the CIA. For those reasons we have chosen not to interfere in Carl's investigation but to instead keep a close eye on him and to provide assistance to him within the limitations of our authority.

"Our major concern is the weapons dealers who sold the missiles to the pirates. There is little doubt in our minds that they would be willing to sell heat seeking missiles to anyone who had the money, including terrorist groups. If terrorist groups get their hands on missiles we could have a major problem, particularly when the news media discovers that a component of the missiles is American made.

"We suspect the arms dealer, who is American, is selling the missiles to pirates, although at this time we can't prove it. The arms dealer has an English partner but that's not going to make much difference to the news media."

The President sighed and took a sip of coffee then said, "It sounds like this problem could get worse before it gets better. If those missiles get into the hands of terrorists and are used to shoot down passenger planes loaded with tourists it could have serious international implications.

"When it's discovered that an American sold the missiles, and the technology used was also American, the problems could escalate quickly. Please keep me informed on this issue."

CHAPTER 41

When Jules arrived in Paris he immediately switched to the Gare de Lyon station and bought a ticket to Nice. Train travel was slower than flying but it had one big advantage, you didn't have to give anyone your name or any other information to buy a ticket. Just open your wallet and take out money. You're just another person trying to travel, in most cases the ticket agent doesn't even bother to look at you.

He had an hour to kill before his train was scheduled to depart. He found a store near the station where he could buy a new cell phone. He made a single call to Hamit's home in Budapest, Hungry and left a message on the answering machine saying he would check the answering machine periodically for any messages. He then boarded his train. For now all communication with Hamit would be via the answering machine and only using a new cell phone for each call.

On arriving in Nice he hired a taxi for the eleven mile drive to Monaco. He asked the driver to take him to a small out of the way inn.

Before Carl left London he called on Harold Miller to thank him for his assistance. During the conversation he mentioned that he was going to go to Monaco to see if he could locate Jules.

"I'll call Agust Dupre, Director of Public Safety, which includes the police force, and let him know that you will be there sometime tomorrow. I'm sure the police will assist you any way that they can. They are very touchy about keeping unsavory characters out of the Principality."

After leaving Harold Miller, Carl boarded a British Airways flight to Monaco and by three in the afternoon he was at the Department of Public Safety.

"Welcome to Monaco Mr. Lukin. Harold called to say that you would be stopping by to see me. He gave me some of the facts concerning the man that you are trying to locate, we will of course help you find him if he is in Monaco. Do you have any idea where this man might be staying?"

"No sir I don't, I only have an old receipt from Le Grand Casino for a wire transfer. I assume he spends some time at that casino. If they have hotel facilities he might even stay there."

"No matter, we will find him if he is here. This principality is less than a square mile in size and only has a population of 33,000. Our police have a very close working relationship with the casinos, hotels, and shop owners. It is very hard for anyone to hide in Monaco. I will have Captain Rankin of the Monaco Police help you in your search."

Following introductions to Captain Rankin, Carl said, "Since I have a receipt for a wire transfer from Le Grand Casino to a bank in California that would be a good place to start. Jules Dunbar is wanted by the FBI for murder in addition to selling weapons to Somali pirates.

"In the past Mr. Dunbar has used the casino to wire money from illegal weapon sales to his accounts in the U.S. The casinos are a convenient way of laundering the money. If possible I would like to get a list of all the wire transfers he has made from the local casinos."

"The head of security for Le Grand Casino is Monsieur Patriess, I know him very well. I will give him a call to let him know we are coming. We can walk over if you would like, it is only a short distance from here.

"As to Mr. Dunbar's whereabouts, we received an inquiry from Interpol early this morning and I have already instructed my staff to make inquiries of the local hotels and Inns. We should have the answer to that question within a few hours. However, if he is not registered in a hotel it does not mean that he is not here. If he is staying on one of the yachts in the harbor we would not necessarily know about it until he stepped ashore. But we will inform the local businesses to be on the watch for him. Be assured that if he is in Monaco he will surface eventually."

The head of security for Le Grand Casino was waiting for them when they arrived twenty minutes later. When Carl showed the receipt to Patriess he said, "Yes, Mr. Dunbar is one of our high rollers from the United States. He comes in five or six times a year. He usually buys half a million Euros or more in chips and spends three or four days gambling. I was not aware he was sending so much money to his bank account."

"Can you tell me how many wire transfers he has made; the account numbers, amounts, and dates since he has been coming here?"

"Yes, of course, we keep very good records. Let me tell the head cashier what we need and we can have a cup of coffee while we wait.

It may take a few minutes if some of the records have to be retrieved from the archives."

Forty-five minutes, two cups of coffee and a pastry later, the head cashier approached their table with a list of the dates, account numbers, and the amounts wired. He handed Captain Ranking the list saying "We have researched our information for the past six years. We have found a total of fourteen transactions during that period.

Captain Ranking and Carl thanked Mr. Patriess for his help then visited the four remaining casinos explaining their need for information. By the end of the evening they had a list of twenty-six instances in which transfers had been sent to Paul Hamit's account.

"Captain Rankin, could you please send the lists of transactions to Special Agent Jean Peters of the FBI in Washington D.C.? That way the chain of custody will have been maintained by law enforcement since they were received from the casinos. I'll give her a call and let her know that it's coming."

Jules had arrived at the Inn several hours after the police had been in asking questions of the owner, but when Jules arrived the owner was out and his daughter checked Jules into a room. Since he had used a different name, and sketch and pictures were shown to the owner, not the daughter she did not know the police were looking for the man. It was not until the family sat down to dinner later in the evening and the discussion turned to the tenants, that the owner decided to call the police. Since he had not seen the new tenant he was not sure that it was him but thought he had better notify the police just in case. When the police showed Jules' pictures to the daughter she was not sure, the man she rented the room to looked older, but she said that it could be the man.

Jules had gone the Le Café de Paris casino for the evening and was standing at a craps table when he noticed two men walking toward the business offices. He instantly recognized Carl and moved behind a couple who were placing bets, "How the bloody hell could that bastard follow me here?"

When Carl and Captain Ranking entered the business offices Jules left the building. He found a taxi driver and asked to be taken to the airport in Nice. He didn't stop at the Inn to pick up his suitcase he could easily replace his clothes and personal items. When he arrived at the airport he promptly stole a car from the long term lot and drove to Paris.

After leaving Captain Rankin, Carl returned to his hotel room and called Jean, saying, "I think we have a solid connection between Jules Dunbar and Paul Hamit. The Monaco police will be sending you a record of wire transfers sent by Jules from Monaco casinos to an account in the U.S., I think the account belongs to Hamit. If the account is Hamits it will be interesting to see how he accounts for the money from gambling casinos when he wasn't there. I think the IRS will be interested in asking the same questions."

"Good work Carl, I'll be on the lookout for it."

"Have the wiretaps on Hamit's phones given us anything? Any clue as to where Jules went after leaving London?"

"Not yet, Jules hasn't made contact with Paul yet by telephone since the last time. And Paul hasn't placed a call to Jules, so we have nothing. He may have gotten a new cell phone and we haven't picked up his number yet."

"Okay, In that case I'll fly back to San Francisco tomorrow. I'll give you a call after I've had a chance to get a good night's sleep."

He next called Ann to tell her that he would be flying to San Francisco the next day.

"I've got a better idea, why don't I fly to Monaco tomorrow, we could swim in the Mediterranean and I could show you how much I missed you."

"That sounds great but could we skip the swim and get right to the showing me part? I really missed you. But if you came over here we wouldn't get anything done, I think I had just better come home."

Carl had just dropped off to sleep when his phone rang. "Yeah hello, who is this?

"It's Captain Ranking, I just received a report that a man matching Jules Dunbar's description has checked into an Inn this afternoon. I'm going over there to check it out. Would you care to come along?"

"You bet, where should I meet you."

"I'll pick up in front of your hotel in five minutes."

After rousing the owner of the Inn they were taken to Jules' room. Captain Ranking knocked but received no answer. Using the owner's passkey they entered the room. There was a suitcase on a bed that had not been slept in. The towels in the bathroom had not been used. There was nothing to indicate that Jules would not be back.

"Well Carl it looks like your man may have gone to the casinos for a while and may be back. What do you want to do?"

"I think we should just wait in this room until he returns."

It was a long wait. It was not until late the next morning that they found the taxi driver who had driven Jules to the Airport.

CHAPTER 42

Carl got a few hours' sleep with Ann in his arms before going to the office. The question on Carl's mind was what they could do to force contact with Jules Dunbar. Their problem was resolved when Hamit received a call from Jules who said, "Paul? Get a new prepaid phone, don't give anyone the number, then call my hotel, you know which one, ask the clerk for Mr. Miller's room." Then without another word he hung up. The call was made from a public phone at the train station and only lasted seventeen seconds but that was enough time for NSA's computers to recognize where the call originated from and record the message. By the time the call was sent to an analyst and a copy passed to Jean Peters, forty-five minutes had elapsed.

After Jules had hung up, Paul Hamit immediately left his office to go to a store where he bought a new prepaid phone. He put the phone in a charger fifteen minutes later. After two hours it was ready to use.

Since Jules' call came from France, a CIA analyst reviewed all calls made from the San Francisco bay area to Paris, France using a cell phone. From the time Hamit received his call from Jules only nine cell phone calls had been made to France within the following eight hours. Of those calls only one was made to a Paris hotel. There was little doubt that the call was made using Hamit's new cell phone. The new phone's ID number was added to the watch list.

Aaron Kovak placed a call to the American embassy in Algiers asking the operator to locate Ian Macintyre. The operator tried his office and when no one answered she tried his apartment. The very sleepy voice of Ian McIntyre answered the phone, coughed twice then said "Yeah, who the hell is this?"

In the background Aaron heard a female voice ask, "Who's calling you at this hour?"

Aaron said, "Good morning Ian, this is Aaron Kovak. I apologize for waking you and your friend at this hour but I need you to go to Paris immediately."

In a voice that was much more alert Ian asked, "Okay, I'm up, what is this about?"

"Go to the Paris embassy. There will be a message waiting for you with the details, and tell your girlfriend that you'll be away for a few days."

"Okay boss, I'll be on my way in about twenty minutes."

He hung up the phone then looked at the clock, "Christ only 4:10" he lay back then rolled over to give the woman a hug and said, "Sleep in honey, I've got to go but I should be back in three or four days." In response he received a grunt then the sound of soft breathing as she drifted off to sleep.

Ian took a quick shower, forty-five minutes later he was at the airport booking his flight to Paris. By mid-morning he was in a Parisian cab headed to the American embassy. After checking in, he went to the message center where he found an email waiting for him.

The message provided basic information about Jules Dunbar along with two photographs. One of police the sketch, the other appeared to be an ID photo. The attached message said that Carl Lukin was on his way to Paris, and provided his flight schedule. He was given instructions to provide assistance to Carl if needed, and to keep surveillance on Jules Dunbar.

Next Ian went to the office of the resident CIA Station Chief where he picked up a camera with a long lens, a pair of binoculars, and a small Berretta 9000 pistol. If he wanted to look like a tourist he had to have a camera.

He called the Le Bristol Hotel and asked if they had a Mr. Dunbar registered. The clerk said "No, we have no such person registered."

He then asked if they had a Mr. Miller registered. He could hear the clerk typing on the computer keyboard and then say "Yes, Mr. Miller has checked in, should I put your call through to his room?"

"No I'll just come over and surprise him."

He had four hours to kill until Carl's plane landed so he might as well make good use of the time. He went to the hotel and sat in the lobby pretending to read a newspaper, watching guests come and go. Just before he had to leave to meet Carl's plane he saw Dunbar, alias Miller, step out of the elevator alcove into the lobby. Dunbar walked into the dining room and sat at a table. He looked like he would be at the hotel for a while. It was time to go to the airport and meet Carl.

Jules watched Ian get up and leave the hotel. He had noticed the man when he entered the lobby. He may have been just reading the newspaper but after his experience in London and Monaco he was nervous and his instincts said this just didn't feel right. When the man left the lobby and walked out of the hotel he got up and went to his room and lay back on the bed. But he continued to have that nagging feeling in his gut that the authorities had found him again.

Intellectually he considered his gut feeling as irrational but it was persistent and it had kept him alive in the past.

After an hour he finally decided to move to a different hotel. He picked up his new travel bag that had the new clothes he bought when he reached Paris. Going to the bathroom he picked up the few toiletries he had and threw them in his travel bag. He made his way to a door marked employees only. Pushing the door open he entered an alcove and saw doors to a freight elevator on his left. Once in the hotel basement he exited the building through a door that led to a loading platform.

He had paid the hotel for five days in advance. Hopefully that would keep whoever was following him occupied watching the hotel for a while. He was still nervous and decided to go to a corner bar across from the hotel and have a couple of drinks. He sat at a table with a window that had a view of the hotel entrance and ordered a brandy.

Ian was waiting outside the customs area for Carl to exit. "What are you doing here instead of living the good life in Algiers?"

"I told you, you have friends in Washington. They asked me to keep you out of trouble which I said would be very difficult but that I would do my best."

"So I guess you know why I am here?"

"Unlike you Carl, I was jolly on the spot just hours after receiving the call to make sure that you did not get in trouble. I had hours to kill before you arrived so I went to the hotel to insure that your query was indeed registered there. About an hour and a half ago I was sitting in the lobby reading a newspaper when your man stepped out of the elevator and went into the dining room. I had to leave about ten minutes later to come and collect you, Dunbar was still in the dining room."

"Great let's check in with the local police. They can make the arrest. Jules is nervous; he won't stay in one place long. The quicker I see him in cuffs the happier I'll be."

"If you don't mind Carl, I would rather not go with you to the police. They will ask who I work for and I would rather not tell them. Clandestine service and all that, you know what I mean. I'll go back to the hotel and pretend to read my newspaper while keeping a vigilant eye out for our friend."

Two hours and four brandies later the butterflies in Jules stomach had begun to seattle down. He began to think about returning to his room or finding new lodgings for the night. He rationalized his feeling of unease as the result of the close calls in London and Monaco. As he continued to watch the hotel he saw a police car pull up in front. He started to finish the last of the brandy in his glass as he watched three men get out of the car. The brandy glass stopped midway to his lips when he saw Carl, he muttered, "Bloody hell, he must be part bloodhound." as he watched the men entering the hotel. When the men were out of sight, Jules left the bar, walked across the street to a taxi, and directed the driver to take him to an out of the way hotel where he would not be asked to many questions.

The following morning Jules rented a car and drove to Berlin, Germany. From there he boarded a plane to Budapest, Hungary, where Paul Hamit had a house and where they kept a warehouse for weapons that they had bought but had not sold or had yet to be delivered. The warehouse was located at a small airport where they kept an old C-130 cargo plane that they used to move large loads of weapons.

The C-130 was an excellent plane for this purpose. It could carry a hefty load and land on short and unprepared landing fields. A handy capability when making deliveries to Africa or South America.

For small shipments they would use commercial transportation if it was feasible. Jules and Paul did not keep pilots on the payroll but they had a few retired pilots who they could call on short notice if they needed the plane.

All mail or telegrams for the business were delivered to Paul's Budapest home. Jules left a short message on the answering machine telling Paul the phones were compromised and to change his cell phone and erase the message from the answering machine after every call.

Jules next went through the accumulated mail. Most of it was junk or mail that pertained to Paul's legitimate business dealings. However one piece of mail caught his eye, it was postmarked from Somalia. When he opened it he saw that it was from Nur Hussein, the Somali warlord who had bought a number of heat seeker missiles and other assorted arms. It said that Nur had brokered a deal with several other pirate leaders for a large order but that they wanted to meet him in person before committing so much cash to the purchase. It occurred to Jules that this would be a good time to visit Somalia for a short while and get that bloody investigator off his trail. But first he had to see General Karim in Pakistan.

CHAPTER 43

General Karim walked into the restaurant and immediately saw that there were only a few customers. Jules Dunbar sat at a table near the rear of the restaurant. On seeing the General enter Jules stood and waited for the General to approach, "Good afternoon General, how have you been? There's a small room in back that we can use for a private conversation."

The General followed Jules to a room normally used for private dinner parties or discreet meetings. After seating themselves, Jules moved an empty cup in front of the General. The restaurant owner seemed to materialize from nowhere with a hot pot of tea, a small pot of honey, a small bowl of nuts, and a plate of halva.

"It is always a pleasure to see you Jules. I can see that you are doing well."

The General continued to eye Jules saying, "What brings you to my part of the world Jules?" Never taking his eyes off the man sitting in front of him he reached for his cup of tea adding honey to sweeten it.

"I am on a shopping trip and thought I would stop and see if you had any bargains that I could use. I am particularly interested in AK-47's, two hundred and fifty thousand rounds of ammunition, RPG's, SAM's, claymore mines, semtex, SAMs, and hand grenades. You know, the usual items."

"Ah, Jules my friend evidently you have not heard that there is a war going on in Afghanistan between the Americans and the Taliban? Those weapons are in great demand and are becoming harder to get. As always, when there is a war weapons are more expensive."

"I have heard that the Taliban are looking for weapons but are they willing to pay your price, and more importantly, do they have the money? I understand that the Americans have been destroying the poppy fields and the supply of heroin is significantly lower than usual. Without a crop to sell how do the Taliban intend to pay your exorbitantly high prices?"

"Of course the prices of the items that you want are going up but that is not the only consideration. I have the weapons that you want in large quantity and I have the SAMs that you want but would have difficulty getting elsewhere. So the question is, are we going to do business or simply enjoy lunch?" After an hour eating and haggling over the prices they reached an agreement.

The General said, "Half of the AK47s are new, the rest are not but they are in good working condition. The RPG and grenades are Chinese made as is the ammunition." He explained that his inventory of the heat seeking missiles was running low therefore he could only spare twenty.

Jules sighed and said, "Too bad about the missiles, but I'll take what I can get. I will come to the usual location tomorrow at 7:00 P.M."

The following evening Jules and two men in a large truck drove up to a locked gate near a cluster of warehouses. There was a man standing there who opened the gate, then jumped on the running board of the truck giving the driver directions to one of the warehouses. When they arrived he told the driver to back up to the loading dock.

Waiting there was an officer and three enlisted men. As soon as the truck stopped, the man jumped off the running board and joined the other three in loading boxes into the back of the truck. Thirty minutes later Jules and the truck full of weapons drove out of the gate and headed in the direction of Karachi. About ten miles from the camp they came to a small airport used by both civilian and military aircraft.

The truck drove directly to the tarmac area where a Hercules C-130 Cargo plane was parked with its ramp down. The truck backed up to the loading ramp where four men waited to unload its contents into the plane's cargo bay. When the cargo had been moved the men pulled a cargo nets over the load of weapons and tied it down to floor cleats. Jules paid each of the men who then quickly disappeared.

Jules and the pilots inspected the cargo net to make certain that it was secured to the floor cleats properly. When they were satisfied, the engines started and the plane moved toward the runway.

Nine hours later the C-130 landed at a small airport near Budapest, it moved toward a group of three warehouses on the edge of the airport. Boxes of new AK47s were offloaded and replaced with boxes of older used but serviceable weapons. The boxes of claymore mines, semtex, 50 thousand rounds of ammunition, and ten missiles were also offloaded. Pirates had no need for mines and semtex and had only asked for missiles, more rifles, and ammunition. In this business there were always groups who would be willing to pay a high price for the remaining weapons stored in the warehouse.

This was a growing business. There seemed to be and endless supply of customers willing to kill to get what they wanted.

Now that he had everything that Nur wanted, Jules told the pilots to have the plane fueled and ready to go then get some rest. He had some business to conclude. They would be leaving in the morning.

With the profits from this sale, Jules planned to take a long vacation, probably Cuba or Bora Bora. So long as it was warm and had beautiful women he wasn't too picky.

General Karim also planned to leave the army and travel, probably to France or Spain, he hadn't decided yet. Although he had a wife and three children, two girls and a boy, they had grown apart. The children had long since married and had families of their own. He seldom saw them. His wife had grown very heavy over the years and had acquired a waspish manner in dealing with her husband. He would miss his daughter and son but he did not plan to live in Pakistan. Instead he would occasionally make trips to see his children and grandchildren; that is, whenever it suited him.

Over the years he had acquired a nice nest egg from his less than legal business dealings. In addition he had acquired a taste for young women who knew how to please him. Now that he was near retirement he could live a good life in some country near the sea, where the sun was warm and the women scantily clad.

CHAPTER 44

Nur received a message from Jules saying that he would arrive at the landing strip near Nur's compound the next day with the order he had asked for. He gave Nur a price, saying that the price was not negotiable. Jules took off with a flight plan giving their destination as Al Adan, Yemen.

The plan was for the plane to be on the ground in Al Adan only long enough to be fueled. From there it was only a short hop to the landing strip near Dhurba, Somalia.

The landing strip consisted of a flat grassy field close to Nur's compound. The only danger in using the landing strip was cattle which were often pastured there. With any luck at all Jules was hopeful he could finish his business and be back in the air within a few hours.

When they arrived they had to circle the landing strip twice to give the herders time to move the cattle. When Jules stepped off the plane he was met by a pickup truck and six armed men. Jules was told that the meeting was to be held at Nur's compound and the guards would stay with the plane to insure that nothing happened to the cargo. Jules did not like this development, but it didn't look as if these men would take a refusal lightly.

The leader of the group said that he was instructed to inspect the cargo before he was to take Jules to the meeting. Jules was not happy with this demand either, and started to refuse when he heard the click of rifle safeties being moved from safe to fire. He could see the barrels of the weapons begin to come up. After voicing his discontent loudly he relented and invited the leader to board the plane to inspect the cargo. When the inspection was completed they returned to the truck. Four guards remained with the plane, and Jules, two guards, and the leader drove off.

They drove to Nur's compound and parked near a large building. When they entered, Jules saw Nur and two others seated in chairs. Two women hovered nearby with pitchers of water and bowls of what appeared to be fruit and nuts. The two guards remained directly behind Jules, their weapons at the ready.

Jules said, "I hope we can conclude our business soon so that I can get back in the air."

Nur nodded at the men behind Jules. Jules started to look around but before he could move he was knocked to the floor by a blow on the side of his head. Within seconds his hands were tied behind his back. He was pulled to his feet and thrown onto a stool. His head throbbed and his vision was not fully clear but he was rapidly regaining his senses.

Nur sat some feet away staring at him. Jules knew he was in serious trouble. Finally through a weak voice, he said, "Why am I treated like this, I brought you everything that you asked for?"

Nur sat quietly for a moment before speaking then said, "The last shipment of missiles were defective, they killed many of my men and wounded many others. I do not like to be cheated. I paid you good money for those missiles, and I expected them to work properly. Now I cannot trust them to work properly so I cannot use them. I do not trust men who cheat me; you will not have the opportunity to cheat me or anyone else again."

"I did not know they were defective. I will return your money; just take me to a bank! I will have the funds wired anyplace that you want."

"You have already brought me my money. All I need to do is sell the cargo that is on your airplane; you are not a man to be trusted and I have heard enough of your lies."

Nur nodded to the two men standing next to Jules. Jules was jerked to his feet and taken to an open area outside the compound where his clothing was stripped off. They tied him between two trees with rope. As he pulled, trying to break free from his bonds, the rope grew tighter on his wrists. The ropes holding his wrists were tied high in the trees preventing him from sliding to the ground. His only option was to stand. His guards walked away and squatted on the ground watching him. Soon a woman walked up to the guards bringing them water. They did not offer any to Jules.

Jules yelled to Nur that he wanted to talk but no one paid any attention to him. Within a few hours his voice became horse. His throat dry, red and sore; he finally had to rest his voice. He asked his guards for water but they continued to ignore him.

At sundown Nur approached the guards and told them to give the prisoner water. He wanted Jules alive when it was time to received his punishment.

In the evening insects swarmed over his body, stinging and biting, until his body was a mass of sores. He gained some relief from the night insects when the sun came up, but they were replaced by insects that forage during the day. When the sun went down again different insects would begin their incessant stinging and biting.

For two days he remained tied between the two trees. The guards changed, but the new guards were no more sympathetic to him than the first two. By the second day he gave up asking for Nur. From time to time the guards gave him enough water to keep him alive but not enough to satisfy his great thirst.

If he tried to sleep he would slump forward and the rope holding his wrists would cut further in, and his body weight would pull on shoulder joints, further adding to his pain.

His body was covered by insect bites, he was bloody where his rope bonds had cut through his skin, and his eyes had been swollen shut by insect bites. He was barely able to stand. By midday on the second day he was badly sun burned and dehydrated. This time he was given sufficient water to satisfy his thirst. The water quickly revived him.

On that day people came to the compound walking, riding in carts, or in the back of trucks. The women and children carried sticks and bats. The men simply watched and drank a home brew that looked like beer.

Two men gave him more water to drink and threw buckets of water on Jules to further revive him. After a few minutes his head came up and he struggled to open his eyes but the insect bites would only allow his eyes to open to slits. His head and his body both ached with pain. He could not understand why they were doing this to him, he had brought everything that Nur had asked for. And he was willing to reimburse Nur for any product that did not work properly.

Finally, Nur strode into the clearing and stood next to Jules. In a loud voice he said, "This is the man that sold us the faulty weapons that blew up when used. He sold us the weapons that killed your fathers, husbands, and sons. This is the man who prevented your men from capturing the ships that provide you with the money that you need to buy food to feed your families."

In a loud voice that roared over the murmuring crowd, he said, "If you believe he has committed a crime against our people it is your right to punish him."

Jules knew enough Arabic to understand what was being said. When Nur stopped speaking and walked away there was silence, then one older woman walked up to Jules and started beating him with a stick. He cried out with pain. Soon there were many woman and children beating him with sticks and bats. It was not long until he lost consciousness.

Still they continued to beat him. The skin was flayed from his body and he bled from every wound yet they still continued to beat him. With each blow, blood splattered on those standing near. When it was obvious that he was dead, and those beating him were exhausted and losing interest, men came forward to cut him loose from the tree. His body was dragged to an open field and left for the scavengers. By the end of the following day there was nothing left of Jules Dunbar but bones.

Nur had seen enough of the punishment meted out under Sharia law to learn that punishment was an excellent way to teach, and from his point of view it made the point that no one cheats Nur Hussein without retribution.

When the pickup truck had driven away with Jules, the two pilots were removed from the plane at gun point and shot. The cargo of weapons was moved to a nearby building where it could be more closely examined. The airplane was then towed to a far corner of the landing strip and covered with brush. The plane and its cargo would be sold. Cattle were again allowed onto the landing strip to graze. From all appearances everything was normal.

CHAPTER 45

Following Jules' death, Nur made a trip to Boosaaso, a port city to the west of Dhurba, to visit Ahmed Hussein, a cousin who worked for the Interior Ministry. Ahmed was in a position to know people that might be interested in buying the weapons and the cargo plane that Jules had brought with him. Of course Ahmed would be expected to be paid for his services but that was customary, the only question was how much?

The guide books say that Somalia is predominately a Muslim country but that it is tolerant of other religions. Ahmed had worked for the Interior Ministry since he was a teenager but it did not take him long to realize that those who moved ahead in the Ministry practice the Muslim faith. In order to insure his advancement as well as his survival he had quickly converted to the Muslim faith. It was not many years after his conversion that he began to advance in the Ministry.

Somalia has a central government, but it is extremely weak and ineffectual, in some parts of the country it is virtually non-existent. Governing of some provinces is left entirely to the local warlords and their militias. Nur was the warlord in the northern coastal area of

Puntland, province, commonly known as the Horn of Africa. The warlords provide security and enforce some government programs. The level of enforcement and the programs to be supported are left to the discretion of the local warlord. As long as they willing to give a share of their income to government officials, the warlord is left to his own devices.

After they had lunch Nur asked Ahmed a question. "Do you know of any anyone that would interested in acquiring AK-47s, ammunition, grenades, heat seeking missiles, and a used cargo plane?

"If you know of such a person or group and a sale results, you can be sure of a nice commission."

"I might know of such a group, but it will take a little time to see if they are interested. Give me two weeks and I will let you know if there is any interest."

Ten days later Nur received a call from Ahmed saying, "There is a group that has expressed interest in your weapons. This Islamic group is engaging in defending the faith in several western countries. They would like emissaries to inspect the articles that are for sale. As soon as a date for the inspection can be arranged I will notify you.

"But I must ask you cousin, what do you have in mind as a commission? I am taking considerable risk in arranging for a sale of weapons."

"I think that ten percent is more than generous for such a simple task cousin."

"Ten percent is indeed customary for most business transactions cousin. But arranging the sale of weapons has a great deal of risk and very high penalties. There is considerable personal risk from both the Somali government if the sale occurs or from the prospective buyer if it does not. In my opinion, the risk is worth at least twenty percent." After a great deal of arguing back and forth they settled on sixteen percent.

Two days later Nur received a call from Ahmed saying, "The interested party will come to Dhurba next week to inspect the articles that you have for sale."

On the appointed date, two vehicles drove up to Nur's compound. Ahmed and three Arabic speaking men approached Nur. After the appropriate greetings and refreshments they asked to see the weapons that he was selling. Nur took them to the building where the weapons were stored. The buyers spent some time thoroughly inspecting the merchandise. As they looked at the weapons their eyes virtually glowed when they saw the surface-to-air missiles. The number of missiles had grown now that they included the thirteen that had been returned to Nur by the captains of the pirate boats.

The visitors were impressed with the C-130. They explained that they might not be able to take all of the goods since they did not have anyone who could fly the plane, but they were definitely interested in the weapons, particularly the heat seeking missiles.

Nur explained that it was an all or nothing deal. The man who the others deferred to asked "Why do you not sell the missiles to the local pirates."

"I did sell missiles to the captains of the pirate boats and they used the missiles on several occasions with great success. But their use had the same effect as stirring a hornet's nest with a stick. The result was that the western nations had then sent warships into the area to protect the shipping. With naval war ships nearby, fewer commercial ships could be taken, which in turn meant less income to their villages and to me. The missiles yielded very little benefit but cost a great deal, I wished we had never seen them."

The explanation seemed to satisfy the buyers, and they said that if they could find a pilot to fly the plane they would return.

CHAPTER 46

Although Ahmed had been a young man when the British turned the governing of Somalia over to the Somalis, he retained many of the British ideals. So it was natural that he should maintain contact with his close friend Harold Miller when the British pulled out of Somalia in 1961. As the years passed, Harold's SIS career advanced as did Ahmed's in the Interior Ministry. From time to time Ahmed would pass his friend bits of confidential information, nothing big, but tidbits about governmental or economic problems that Somalia was wrestling with. In return, Ahmed would receive a small amount of money for his trouble, not enough to offend propriety but enough to help in offsetting the poor salary that the Somali government paid its employees. Besides, taking money for extra special services provided by a government employee was a well-established and accepted way of doing business in Somalia.

On his return home from Dhurba, Ahmed sent a message to Harold explaining the sale of the airplane, missiles, and assorted weapons to a Muslim group. Although he was not sure who the buyers represented, he thought they might be associated with the terrorist group called Islam's Fire. The weapons were to be moved using a Hercules C-130 aircraft that they had also bought from Nur.

He did not have a specific date of departure, but thought it would occur within two weeks. He described the location and the landing strip near the town of Dhurba. He also mentioned the weapons dealer who had brought the weapons to Somalia. The weapons dealer, who went by the name of Jules Dunbar, had been killed because he had previously delivered faulty weapons which had resulted in deaths and injuries to a number of the pirates. The local warlord felt he had been cheated and took his revenge out on Jules Dunbar.

When Harold Miller received Ahmed's message, he immediately forwarded a copy to the CIA.

The message landed on the desk of Aaron Kovak who immediately notified the Director. Aaron Kovak also asked that a satellite be tasked to fly over the northern part of Somalia, with a focus on the town of Dhurba and surrounding villages. Photo analysts were directed to look for possible landing sites that would support a Hercules C-130.

Nur had never been up in an airplane and it never crossed his mind that the brush used to cover the airplane might have a different appearance when seen from the air. By the end of the day, photo analysts had identified a possible landing strip. They were confident of their analysis when they saw a pile of brush at one end of the landing strip that was piled in the shape of an airplane.

Following his national security briefing to the President the next morning, the Director told the President about the information provided by the British and that CIA photo analysts had located the landing strip and the airplane.

"Okay Dick, we can't let those missiles get in the hands of terrorists. If they're used against commercial aircraft they would kill thousands, and cripple the entire air transportation industry. What can we do to destroy the missiles without starting a war with Somalia?"

"Our people believe that we can keep an unmanned reconnaissance drone over the area to let us know when the plane is ready for takeoff. If we put an Aegis destroyer in the gulf between Dhurba and Al Adan, they will be able to knock it down. If they try to move the plane before we can position an Aegis Destroyer, we can use fighter planes based in Bahrain. The use of planes will draw a lot more attention because we will have to keep them in the air 24/7. The F-15s are based too far from Somalia to wait until the C-130 takes off."

"Whatever it takes Dick, but don't let those missiles get into the hands of terrorists."

Within hours the USS Ramage, an Aegis destroyer was sailing at high speed from the Persian Gulf to the Gulf of Aden. To allay any suspicions of why the USS Ramage was being moved, American partners in the region were informed that the Ramage was being sent to the Gulf of Aden because of increased pirate activity. The Ramage took up station midway between Dhurba, Somalia and Al Adan, Yemen.

A pair of Global Hawk unmanned drones fitted with surveillance equipment began keeping a close watch on the landing strip and the camouflaged C-130. The electronic feed from the surveillance aircraft was sent both to Langley for review by analysts, and directly to analysts on the Ramage.

On the eighth day following the sale, two pilots that had retired from the Pakistan International Airlines Corporation (PIA) were convinced by Islam's Fire to fly the C-130 from Somalia to a remote valley in the northern part of Pakistan. Both pilots held fundamental Islamic beliefs and were willing to help. The high wage that they were offered for their effort helped in strengthening their desire to assist in protecting Muslim faith from the West's corrupting influence.

The two well-dressed Arab men who had met with Nur before, two pilots, and two armed guards, arrived at Nur's compound shortly after noon. They were served refreshments, money was exchanged, and the pilots were taken to the landing strip where they inspected the plane. After a brief examination, they said that they could be in the air by nightfall if the brush was removed and the cargo loaded quickly.

The circling Global Hawk recorded the removal of brush and the towing of the C-130 to the end of the landing strip. It watched as the cargo was moved from the storage building and loaded on the plane. The drone also photographed six crates being placed on one of the pickup trucks instead of the plane. Just before seven in the evening the loading had been completed and the plane prepared for takeoff. Herdsmen could be seen removing the cattle from the runway. The four turbo prop engines were started and appeared to be running smoothly. The brakes were released and the plane was soon off the landing strip and on a course for Al Aden.

The plane maintained an altitude of 500 feet and the pilots planned to stay at that altitude for the entire flight. At that altitude they could stay undetected by radar until ready to land at the airport where the plane had supposedly ended its flight some weeks earlier. There they would refuel then they would simply file a flight plan for Islamabad, Pakistan. To anyone watching they would appear to be a legitimate commercial cargo flight on the way home.

Twenty-eight minutes later they appeared on the radar screens of the tactical command center of the Ramage. Within thirty seconds weapons rose from their protected cargo hold and swiveled into firing position. The C-130 continued on a course to Al Aden. The pilots were not aware they were a sitting duck for the Rampage's weapons. Six seconds after the order to fire, there was an explosion, and a large fireball plunged into the sea.

The Ramage filed a report that they had seen a fireball that appeared to be an aircraft that had exploded, approximately twenty miles due west of their current position. They gave their position and said that they were going to investigate. A subsequent report said that the Ramage did not find the cause of the fireball and did not find any wreckage to indicate what might have happened.

CHAPTER 47

During the following morning's security briefing, Director Rice was saying, "The plane, with most of the missiles and all the weapons and ammunition is now at the bottom of the Gulf of Aden. The destroyer will stay on station for another two weeks ostensibly to deter piracy, then move back to the Persian Gulf.

"Unfortunately, the reconnaissance photos also show that six large creates were loaded onto a pickup truck instead of the plane. From the size of the crates, the analysts think that they contained missiles. They did say that seventeen other boxes of the same dimensions were placed on the plane."

The President looked up and said, "So the upshot of this is that the terrorists have gotten their hands on at least six missiles. And we have no idea how many the arms dealer has stashed in a warehouse somewhere."

"That's not quite accurate Sir. We know that the PPK also has some missiles but we don't know how many or where they might be."

"That not quite our problem, that's a problem for Turkey. The PPK has not declared war on anyone else, only Turkey. Their fight is for independence from Turkey, and the formation of their own state. We provided helped to the Kurdish people when they helped us bring down Saddam Hussein. Let's hope they remember that aid and not use those missiles against us. However, I believe that heat seeking missiles in the hands of any insurgent group is a danger to everyone."

"I suggest that we help Turkey all we can. Provide all the information that we can to the Turkish government but be discrete about it."

"I agree Dick, I think you'd better muster the troops to find those six missiles and destroy them. Six missiles used to shoot down American passenger planes are enough to cripple the entire airline industry."

"Yes sir, I have already made that a priority task for the agency."

CHAPTER 48

Carl was back in San Francisco when he received a call from Jean Peters saying, "I just wanted to let you know that you don't have to worry about Jules Dunbar anymore."

"Yeah, why is that?"

"He was killed in Somalia a short time ago. He must have gone there shortly after his visit to France. We are still trying to track his movements. Interpol tracked him to Budapest, Hungary but from there he disappeared. The British found out that he had been killed because the pirates thought he had cheated them by selling faulty weapons that kept blowing up when they tried to use them.

"The belief is that he had a plane just outside of Budapest and flew to Pakistan and back a few days later. Later a flight plan was filed from Budapest to Al Adan, Yemen. There was no flight plan to indicate that he ever left Al Adan. He probably flew to Dhurba, Somalia without filing a flight plan, which is reasonable, since our source says that Dunbar was killed near Dhurba about that same time. Dhurba is only about 350 miles from Al Adan, Yemen. It's doubtful anyone would have taken any official notice of a plane leaving Al Adan or one landing in or near Dhurba."

Carl considered what Jean had told him then said, "His boss, Paul Hamit, is the person behind the theft, he's the one that sent Dunbar to kill me, and he is the one selling weapons illegally to insurgent groups and pirates. Jules Dunbar was his employee not the one making the decisions. Now that Jules is dead he could easily send someone else to kill me. I am not going to stop until Paul Hamit is behind bars."

"How do you propose to do that?"

"Maybe I can spook him into making a dumb move."

"Maybe the information you gathered in Monaco will help. It's been turned over to the Internal Revenue and there is no doubt that there will be a fraud investigation soon. We're also alerting the ATF (Bureau of Alcohol, Tobacco and Firearms) to what looks like shady arms deals.

"Also our forensic CPAs have been going over his finances and it looks like he has been engaging in a money laundering operation which is a violation of the Anti-Terrorism Act. So our own agents will be involved at some point. Since we're dealing with foreign securities it will take a little longer than normal to unravel that mess. The raid on his offices won't take place for about three or four weeks, I'll have more information on that later. It will take time to gather the information from other countries. Some of the countries are not exactly cooperative."

"Thanks Jean, please let me know when you or the IRS are ready to raid Hamit's office. After the raid I would like to add to the pressure by telling him about Jules being dead. I want to see the expression on his face now that he doesn't have Jules to do his dirty work."

"Go right ahead Carl, I think you have earned that privilege, just don't mention where you got that information."

"Jean please keep an eye on his phone calls. He may be pissed off enough to want to take another shot at me. If he does it would be nice to know who he is sending. Besides that, it will be interesting to see who he calls after the raid."

"I understand. I'll see what I can do."

CHAPTER 49

Three incidents involving commercial airlines happened within a few days of each other that caused the people at the Anti-Terrorist unit and airline executives, to cringe. Anti-Terrorist unit analysts, because they were aware that terrorists had acquired six heat seeking missiles. And Airline executives because they knew that any airliner that crashes makes the flying public more reluctant to fly, and that affects their bottom line.

The first incident occurred in Russia, when a plane crashed while making an emergency landing at Vnukovo International Airport in Moscow. For days, the rumors were rampant that the Tupolev's Tu-154M had been shot down by Chechen rebels. The media worldwide carried the story, including many of the rumors that it had been shot down.

Russian investigators were able to recover the flight and voice recorders, and determine that the crash had resulted from an interruption of the fuel supply to two of the plane's engines, causing them to shut down while the plane was trying to land. The plane skidded off the runway where it then broke apart.

Anti-terrorist analysts gave a sigh of relief when it was finally determined several days later that it was not hit by a missile. But rumors about Chechen rebels shooting the plane down had already begun to circulate. The government tried to quell the rumors but they persisted.

Five days later, a Spanair MD 82 heading for the Canary Islands from Barajas International Airport, Spain, crashed into a wooded area at the end of the runway during takeoff and burst into flames. Of the 172 passengers and crew, 153 died, and only nineteen survived. It was Spain's worst airline crash in twenty-five years. A short time later, airline executives announced that the crash was an accident

It was not until a week later when the wreckage had been removed to a hanger and a closer examination had been completed, that it was determined that an external explosion from an unknown source had actually caused an engine to disintegrate. In addition to the loss of an engine the shrapnel from the disintegrating engine had severely damaged flight controls in the wing. Further examination of engine parts revealed a chemical residue that is commonly used in explosives. Chemical analysis determined that the residue was PETN an ingredient in Semtex, an explosive commonly used in missile warheads.

Some boys playing near the end of the runway found the missile carrying case and the launch tube. Not knowing what they were they took them home to their parents who in turn turned them over to the police. The serial number on the side of the launch tube indicated that the missiles where close in sequence to the serial numbers on the missiles the Carl had photographed in Algiers and had probably come from the same source.

The information regarding the PETN was not circulated to the press for fear of the panic it would cause in the airline industry. Although efforts were made to keep this information quiet, within a few days it was leaked to the press. The finding of the carrying case and the launch tube hit the newspapers about the same time as the leak about finding the PETN on the engine parts. The result was an additional worldwide six percent drop in passenger air travel.

A third incident occurred in a small wooded area near Heathrow Airport, in England. The wooded area was within a quarter mile from the end of the Heathrow Airport runways. Heathrow is one of the busiest airports in the world. Planes are either taking off or landing about every ninty seconds.

This day, air traffic seemed to be heavier than usual. Shift change at Heathrow had occurred some hours before, so there was not a lot of foot traffic entering or leaving the employee parking lot. A car with two men had parked in a space against the back fence, adjacent to a small wooded area. The men waited in the car for a few minutes. They looked around for several minutes to make sure they were not being watched. Yahya, a young man in his early twenties, got out of the car carrying a heavy duty bolt cutter. Kneeling at the back of the car he was able to cut a hole through the chain link fence without fear of being seen.

When he finished cutting the fence, he slapped the truck lid twice. Saleh, the driver, pulled the release lever and the trunk lid opened. Yahya reached in and pulled out a canvas bag. Saleh got out of the car, and the two went through the fence into the wooded area.

The area was heavily wooded around the perimeter with only a few trees in the center. Air traffic leaving Heathrow Airport flew directly over the area. Saleh opened the canvas bag and removed a heat seeking missile. He turned on the electronics and lifted it to his shoulder. Yahya began watching for aircraft leaving the airport. He was able to distinguish a cargo plane from a passenger aircraft by the windows along the fuselage.

He waited until a large 747 finally came into view and said, "This one."

Saleh pointed the launcher toward the aircraft and waited until it had passed overhead. When the missile was able to detect the heat coming from the engines it gave a beeping sound indicating that the heat sensors had locked on to a heat source. When he heard the beeping, Saleh pulled the trigger. There was an immediate blast as the warhead prematurely exploded, killing Saleh and severely injuring Yahya. The blast also started a small grass fire. The 747's passengers and crew flew on unaware of how close they had come to being killed.

Within minutes, fire equipment and police were on the scene. While the fire was being extinguished, emergency EMTs started giving medical aide to Yahya. Police called for an ambulance, a coroner, and investigators.

A newspaper reporter who had been listening to a police scanner arrived on the scene before the investigators. One of the ambulance drivers told the reporter that there was one dead and one badly injured. He also said that there was what looked like a shipping case for a missile launcher.

When asked how he knew the case was for a missile launcher, he said that he was ex-military and had seen similar equipment. Before the Investigators arrived, the reporter had already called his story in to The Sun, England's largest tabloid. He had his scoop.

Within twenty minutes, there were more than a dozen reporters on site clamoring for information. Although a perimeter had been set up some distance away preventing reporters from getting a look at the scene, they pestered anybody they could for any scrap of information.

Without hard information to report, the story of the Spanish airliner that had been shot down took on a new life. With only rumors and very little hard information, stories that were filed were peppered with empty phrases such as: *similar to airline attack in Spain*; *it may have; it could have been; possible terrorist attack;* et cetera. Within hours headlines throughout the world screamed: **Attempted Missile Attack on passenger airliner at Heathrow, one terrorist killed.**

The following day the Anti-Terrorism Unit planted a story which said that a second man in the attack at Heathrow had died of his wounds after arriving at the hospital. In fact, Yahya had been place under heavy guard in a private room in the jail ward of a psychiatric hospital.

In the days that followed the incident, there was an additional fifteen percent drop in air travel. Airline executives were screaming at their respective governments to do something to stop these terrorist attacks and calm public fears.

The President was deluged with calls demanding that the government do something before the airline industry went bankrupt. They were told that all federal law enforcement and intelligence agencies were working to identify and apprehend the terrorists who had tried to carry out such cowardly acts against innocent civilians.

The White House suggested that the airlines should consider installing missile detection and infrared counter measure devices on each aircraft. Airlines explored the cost for such devices, and found out that the cost exceeded 400,000 dollars per aircraft, plus the maintenance expense. The screams from the industry became even louder. They asserted that the cost would break the financial back of the airline industry.

In England, MI5 were working in cooperation with MI6 to identify the missile that had exploded, and the men who had been killed or injured. Photographs of the carrying case and what was left of the launch tube were transmitted to the CIA who quickly identified them as one of the missiles that had a modified circuit board and Carl Lukin had photographed in Algiers.

The American, British, and Spanish, governments demanded that Pakistan find out how their missiles where ending up in the hands of terrorists. General Bahir Karim could see the political storm cloud coming in his direction and decided it was a great time to retire. He went to his headquarters and made it known that he was going to retire to the French Rivera. He was tired, and after many years in the army had earned a chance to relax.

He was only gone three days when he received a call telling him to return to Pakistan. There had been a major fire at his old headquarters and all of his records had been destroyed. His knowledge of his old command was necessary to complete a vital audit of all military units. When he read the message he smiled, he would give his men a well-earned bonus. He replied that he could not return as requested, he had suffered an illness and had been advised not to travel. Instead he packed his bags and went to the Costa del Sol in Spain, using a different name and passport. He left nothing to indicate where he had gone.

Two of the leaders of Islam's Fire met at an apartment in Islamabad to discuss the airline crisis and were jubilant at the chaos they had created. The air travel industry had experienced a twenty-five percent decline in travel, which translated into a severe economic problem for both the airline and leisure travel industries. The loss of the men in England was regrettable but did point out the need for additional training.

In light of this experience the decision was made to send two of the four remaining missiles to the United States and keep two in Europe that would be used in attacks in France and Germany.

While the missiles were being distributed, they would conduct some basic training on how to successfully fire the missiles.

Training in aircraft recognition and proper use of the missile launcher would prevent further accidents and insure a greater success with the few remaining missiles. The effect on air travel would be dramatically increased if there was a high body count during a second wave of attacks. Confidence in air travel be would totally destroyed.

Two of the missiles were repacked in boxes labeled machine parts and delivered to a shipping company, where they forwarded to friends in Chicago, Illinois, and Seattle, Washington. The remaining two missiles were shipped to friends in France and Germany. Each cell had been instructed to wait for further orders. The missiles would not be used until the attacks could be coordinated. The effect on the public would be greater if planes were shot down at the same time in both the United States and Europe.

Chapter 50

Both men were identified as British citizens. Saleh had immigrated to England from Yemen; the other, Yahya, had been born in England to Yemeni immigrants. Both attended the same Mosque in London. Neither one had been in trouble with the law before but they were being watched by the London Anti-Terrorism unit because they were often in the company of the imam.

Both men frequently attended lectures by an imam who had been preaching the legitimacy of using jihad against anyone or any country that did not fully support the teachings of the Muslim faith. He preached that jihad was a legitimate means of protecting the faith. He encouraged his followers to visit Islamic countries, and consider joining a group that advocated the use of jihad in holy war. He failed to mention that some groups only used protecting the faith as an excuse for getting recruits to their cause. In reality, their use of jihad was simply a spiritual justification to attack perceived western imperialism or nationalistic goals.

Additionally, the imam had been actively engaged in efforts to have English courts adopt sharia law instead of English common law when any Muslim was charged with a crime; a proposal that the English judiciary firmly rejected. The failure to take his proposal seriously gave the imam impetus for more radical rhetoric, until it reached the point that it came to the attention of the Anti-Terrorist unit. Although this was a land of free speech and the imam had not broken any law, it did not mean that law enforcement did not consider the imam a threat. So they carefully watched him and those that associated with him.

When Yahya's wounds had healed sufficiently to allow interrogation, he was questioned by Anti-Terrorist investigator Sgt. Mathews. Mathews started off the interrogation by asking questions that would put him at ease such as the young mans name, "My name is Yahya Hamidaddin," he answered in a resigned voice.

Sgt. Mathews continued asking non-threatening question, "Where do you live Yahya, Where did you go to school," etc. With each question Yahya became more relaxed. Finally, Mathews started to address the attack at Heathrow.

"Well Yahya you are in some serious trouble. From what we can tell you have never been in trouble before, you have a job, a girlfriend, and you still live with your parents. Your friend, Saleh is dead and we found the remnants of the missile launch tube. We know what you were trying to do. If you tell us what we need to know the courts will take your cooperation into consideration when you are sentenced. Can you tell me how you got involved with terrorism?"

Yahya realized that they had all the evidence they needed to put him in prison for a very long time. He also knew they would continue to investigate until they knew everything. In a low resigned voice, Yahya, said, "When I told the imam that I intended to visit Yemen in order to get acquainted with my relatives he gave me a letter of introduction to an imam in Al Adan. The Yemeni imam and I got along well, and after a short time he encouraged me to attend a military training camp for three months. After I got there I found out it was run by an organization called Islam's Fire. I did not like the idea, but I thought, I'm here, why not, who is going to know?

"In the camp I met two men from Somalia who bragged how they had bought tons of weapons and ammunition from a Somali pirate and a large airplane to transport it. Can you believe it? They had got their hands on an airplane! Unfortunately, the airplane was old, and on its way to Al Adan, it crashed into the sea. The Somali's said that Allah had been kind to them and had advised that they keep six of the most important weapons safe in Somalia. They were waiting for instructions from their leader, who in turn was waiting for instruction from someone else. We all thought that they were just bragging, but later we started to believe them.

"At the end of training I was told to return home and to expect an important assignment."

"What was the important assignment?"

"They wouldn't tell me, they said that I would be told later."

"Who was going to give you the assignment?"

"They wouldn't tell me that either, only that I would recognize the messenger and the assignment when I received it. Eventually the imam of my mosque called me into his office and gave me the address for a private home. I was told to be there at 9:00 P.M. I was told when I arrived at the home I was simply to walk in and wait."

"Did you go?"

"Yes. I walked in but there was nothing there; no one, no furniture, nothing. It was completely empty. But there was a light on. So I sat on the floor and waited. A few minutes later another man came in. He introduced himself and sat on the floor next to me. We had been told the same thing by the imam; go to the house and wait."

"What was the name of the man who came in after you?"

"His name was Saleh."

"What happened then?"

"We waited. After about half, an hour a man entered and introduced himself as Mohammed."

"Can you describe this man, Mohammed?"

"He was 40 or 50 years old, he had black hair and eyes, he was thin and tall, he spoke good English but with a slight accent."

"What did he say to you?"

"He said that he had an assignment for us. He asked if we were prepared to fight for the faith, to carry out orders without question. We said yes, but my insides were shaking.

"He said that we were going to attack the airline industry by convincing passengers not to fly. He then went to a closet and brought out a canvas bag that contained a large metal case. He said the metal case contained the weapon we were to use.

"Mohammed showed us what we had to do to use it; it was not difficult. For the next hour he gave precise instructions. He gave us street directions, what day and time to be at the airport, where to park, how to operate the weapon, and what type of airplane to look for. He had us repeat the instructions several times to make sure that we understood them. Then he said good night and left"

"Did you follow the instruction?"

"Yes. We arrived at the right time and cut a hole in the fence as instructed then entered the wooded area. I watched the airplanes as they passed overhead. When a large passenger plane came over, Saleh aimed the weapon and pulled the trigger, and then the weapon exploded. I don't remember anything else after that.

"I am tired, can I rest now?"

"Just one more question. Did Mohammed tell you what kind of airplane to choose?"

"He said to pick a large airplane, preferably a 747 that had windows all along the side.

"That is all I know. I am very tired can I go to sleep now?"

"Okay Yahya, you can rest now. We will be back tomorrow with more questions."

As promised, Inspector Mathews was back the next day with more questions. "Good morning Yahya, did you rest well?"

"Yes, thank you."

"I have a few more questions for you. When you were in Yemen, where was the training camp?"

"I don't really know. I was taken there at night. I only know that we traveled about four hours in a car. I think we went north of Al Adan, but I'm not sure. Occasionally I would get a chance to see the stars but we made so many twists and turns I'm not really sure of the direction. We stopped at a camp that was in the mountains. In the camp I heard several others talking about going to Ma'rib for some real food, but I never did leave the training camp and neither did the others."

"Describe the camp in detail."

"We slept in tents, there were three of them. The tents were tan in color and were covered with a net that was designed to hide them. The commander had his own tent. He kept the radio, maps and other records in his tent. The other two tents were for those who did the training, and for the students.

"Close to the tent there were five water barrels, and a little further down the hill was a place that we used to practice firing rifles and pistols."

"What were the names of the people you trained with?"

"I only know their first names. We were told that it was a matter of security to know only first names in the camp."

"Did Mohammed say to which cities he was sending the other missiles?"

"No, only that the United States and Europe would feel the vengeance of Islam's Fire."

"Did he mention any city, state or airport?"

"He only said the United States and Europe, nothing more."

Copies of the interview were sent to the CIA and to the security services of European countries. Intelligence photos had shown a total of six missiles being loaded onto a truck and were now presumably in the hands of terrorists, two of which had already been expended. That left four missiles unaccounted for.

The reaction was immediate. Custom searches at border crossings became much more intensive. Boxes that would normally have gone through customs inspection with only a cursory look were now closely examined or opened.

FBI and local law enforcement became more intense in their questioning of those suspected of being involved with foreign or domestic terrorist organizations. Local police and sheriff's officers began patrolling areas surrounding major airports looking for anything that was out of place or unusual. After a few weeks of law enforcement on high alert, things began to settle down and local police spent more time resolving the everyday crimes that were beginning to rise with the relocation of law enforcement to the outlying areas near major airports.

CHAPTER 51

After reviewing the transcript of Yahya's interrogation the CIA tasked a satellite to photograph the area surrounding Ma'rib, Yemen. Photo analysts were instructed to look for any evidence of a training camp in the nearby hills. There was a lot of data to review. The area within a five mile radius of Ma'rib encompassed 78.5 square miles and would dramatically be increased if the distance from Ma'rib were to be increased.

Then there was the problem of finding something to see. If obvious camp activities at the time that the satellite passed over were being held under cover or in a cave, there might not be visible signs of a nearby camp. If tents were camouflaged, or if vehicles were elsewhere, then the analyst might miss seeing the camp. Nevertheless, it is hard to hide all the small details that human habitation leaves. There are always traces, such as worn foot paths, ruts that could pass as a road, or discarded trash. However, it does take a very sharp analyst to focus on the detail in the photograph in order to tease out the existence of a camp.

On the third pass, the satellite photographed what looked like twelve men lying on the ground in a prone firing position.

Some distance from the men were what appeared to be targets. In subsequent photographs, a puff of dust could be seen from the bullet passing through the target and hitting the ground behind it.

Closer examination of the surrounding area disclosed what might have been tents that could easily have been missed because they were of the same dull brown color of the desert, and covered by camouflage netting. But at the time of day that the photographs were taken the sun was at a low angle to the horizon which resulted in the tents casting shadows on the ground that were very visible. Once a few details were discovered many more details came into focus.

A barely passable tract, wide enough for a pickup truck, could be seen leading away from the camp to the only road to Ma'rib. In the immediate camp site were small blackened spots that were probably ashes from campfires, and hidden among the rocks could be seen the water barrels that Yahya described. As the various elements of the camp came into focus there was little doubt that this was the terrorist training camp where Yahya had stayed.

Since the camp leader had told Yahya of a forthcoming assignment and the Somali recruits had mentioned the use of special weapons, probably the missiles, the decision was made to send in a Special Forces team. The goal of the team was to capture the camp leader if possible, if that was not possible, to collect as many maps, documents, personal papers or other information as possible and eliminate the camp. Hopefully, the intelligence they found would provide a clue to where the remaining missiles had been sent.

A Special Forces team was flown from the U.S. to a carrier that was stationed in the Persian Gulf. On landing, they reviewed maps of the terrain, looking for approaches to the camp that would give the team the greatest advantage. The also looked for sites where sentries would likely be placed.

Finally, the team double checked the equipment that they had brought with them, replaced old batteries, insured the 30 round magazines for their Heckler & Koch MP5 SD's were fully loaded and ready to go, and radios were checked to ensure they were functioning and set to the proper frequency. Anything that could rattle was removed or taped together. When all the equipment had been checked they went to the mess hall for a big meal, the last hot meal until they returned. While they were in the field they would only eat high energy protein bars. Then they were given a bunk for a few hours rest before they left.

A short time later they boarded an MV-22 B Osprey that would fly them to the drop site. From there it was a five mile hike in the dark to the training camp. The Osprey would be refueled in the air and orbit the area until they received a message that the operation was complete and it was safe to land at the camp.

As they approached the campsite the team used night vision glasses to scan the surrounding terrain for guards. The first guard was spotted on a slight knoll that overlooked the ruts that barely passed for a road to the camp. He sat with his back to a large rock his rifle propped against the rock. Every few seconds a cigarette glowed red when he took a puff. The team leader, Sgt. John McRae raised his MP5 and fired two rounds hitting the guard in the head. The guard simply slumped over, not making a sound. A second guard was found in the camp walking between the tent area and the latrine area; he too was dropped without a sound. Moving silently, the team spread throughout the camp going through the tents killing the terrorists as they slept.

When they opened the flaps to the commander's tent he rolled over on his bunk, his hand came up holding a pistol. He did not have time to pull the trigger before a bullet went through his left eye and exited through the back of his skull. Sgt. McRae let out a soft curse, there would be no prisoners this day.

Six minutes after killing the guard watching the road, the terrorist camp ceased to exist. The team quickly began going over the bodies, taking pictures of each terrorist, personal letters and any other scrap of paper the man may have been carrying. Photographs would later be examined in an effort to identify each person. Sgt. McRae and one other team member then began gathering up maps, paperwork, and a laptop computer from the camp leader's tent.

Finally, they destroyed the generator, tents, water barrels, and other equipment. They left the bodies in the clear area in front of the tents. The jackals and scavengers wound pick the bones clean before the end of the day. Anyone entering the camp would find only remnants of clothing and bones and no clues as to who had caused the destruction, only suspicions.

Sgt. McRae radioed the Osprey to come in for a pickup. The laptop computer, maps, photos, and papers that had been found at the camp were in the process of being reviewed by analysts at CIA headquarters in Langley, Virginia twenty-two hours later.

The camp commander was identified as Kalil Assad. A well know terrorist that was last thought to be in Germany. He was considered to be in the middle management ranks of Islam's Fire and had been suspected of being instrumental in planning the attack on the American Embassies in Tunis, Tunisia and Nairobi, Kenya.

Khalil's computer proved to be a treasure trove of information. Aside from the email correspondence, it also had the decryption program and a file that contained the decryption key. A sixteen character key composed of randomized upper and lower case alphanumeric characters. Since the encryption key is difficult for many people to remember they often write it down and try to hide it by burying it in a report or some other innocuous document, but that seldom works. Some try to hide the key in a Quran not realizing a Quran is one of the first places an analyst would look. Normally it does not take long to find the hidden key. Even without the key an encryption code can be broken using a super computer. The process of using brute force to break an encryption code can often take so long that the information it contained is useless.

A message was decrypted that instructed the missiles be taken to an address in Cairo. The address belonged to a shipping company. The information was passed on to the Egyptian Security Police, and within hours the shipping company was raided. A thorough search of the shipping company did not locate any missiles.

During the period between the arrival of the missiles and the subsequent investigation by security personnel, twenty containers of cargo had been dispatched. Four of which went to the United States, two to France, two to Germany, three to England, one to Austria, one to Japan, one to Italy, two to Russia, one to Australia, one to Israel, one to Spain, and one to Turkey. All containers had reached their destination except the one bound for Japan. The Bills of Laden listed for the containers indicated cargos such as carpets, textiles, machine parts, and household goods. The shipping company at the destination port would unpack the container and distribute the contents to the intended recipients listed on the manifest.

The contents of the boxes were rarely inspected by the shipping company or by the customs officials. There were simply too many items and not enough inspectors. With existing manpower, customs would only inspect about one percent of the containers. When a container had a mixed cargo, the customs inspectors would randomly select and open a few of the boxes to verify the content. If everything was as stated on the manifest, the cargo was released. If a cargo was not as stated on the manifest it was almost a certainty that the shipping company would be included in the one percent that was always inspected.

Occasionally, a shipping company employee would be bribed to place a box in a container that was not as described on the shipping manifest. If found the company would pay a heavy price from there on. The result was that employees were carefully watched.

The security organizations of each country to which a container had been shipped were alerted to the possibility of a shoulder launched missile being included in the shipment. If the contents of each container had already been distributed to the recipients, authorities had no choice but to check each person or organization that had received part of the container cargo.

In the United States the recipients of all cargo had been checked except two organizations, one in Seattle, the other in Chicago. The two companies had each received one case of machine parts, neither company could be located, they didn't exist.

CHAPTER 52

Carl sat at his desk reading a security report when his intercom rang. He picked up the phone and heard Ann say, "Dan on line two."

Before she could hang up he asked, "Dinner tonight at Des Alps?"

"Are you planning to ply me with wine and good food then take me to bed?"

"Absolutely."

"That sounds good to me."

He pushed the button for line two and said, "Hi Dan, how are you?"

"Excellent, I think I have the information that you wanted. From time to time Hamit would send money from a bank in Budapest to a bank in France. Judging from the activity on the Budapest account it looks like it's a personal account rather than one used for business purposes. However there were a few interesting expenditures that caught my eye. The first was for a warehouse near Budapest, and the other for purchase of a villa just outside of Budapest. The villa is in the name of Hamit Enterprises. I'm sending a Google Earth picture of the villa and the warehouse, and maps to both.

The name on the French bank account is Jules Dunbar. Dunbar's account was used for a number for things; travel, car rentals, and purchases from European arms manufacturing companies; the normal things that you would expect a weapons dealer to buy. But there were a couple of special interest transactions, a transfer of $755,000 to a company that sells used airplanes. I followed up on that and it was for an old Hercules C-130 that was delivered to an airport just outside of Budapest. The other abnormality was the number of transfers over the last few years, totaling well over three million dollars, to an account owned by a Bahir Karim."

On the General's account the major activity, other than the deposits, were inquiries as to the balance. Since the inquiries were made shortly after each wire transfer it looks like someone was checking to see if the money arrived. I followed that thread and found out that the account is owned by a Bahir Karim who happens to be a General in the Pakistani army. That makes me suspect that the General was selling the military's equipment.

"I also tracked down some information on General Karim. In addition to his bank accounts in Paris, he has several other accounts that he uses. One account in Pakistan, as you would expect, and a second in Zurich Switzerland, which is a bit unusual. The Pakistan account is used for normal expenses. The Zurich account is used only to stash money, very little activity other than deposits. I hope this information is of some use to you."

"It will be Dan, thank you for the help."

Carl called Jean Peters. After the exchange of a few pleasantries he asked, "Do you have any connections in the Department of Defense? Someone who would have information on a Pakistani General named Bahir Karim?"

"Maybe, why do you ask?

"Because General Karim is the likely source of Hamit and Dunbar's heat seeking missiles, plus other military weapons."

"How do you know that?"

"I can't give away all of my private eye secrets. Let's just say I have a reliable source that has followed the money. Over the years Hamit and Dunbar have given over three million dollars to General Karim. The only reason that I can see for a large payoff to a Pakistani General is that he is the source of the missiles and other weapons."

There were a few seconds of silence then Jean said, "What kind of information do you have?"

"My source is sending me the information, when I get it I'll pass it along to you. Hopefully, it will give your accounting people some clues about where to look for evidence that they can use in court."

"Okay Carl, I'll see what I can find out for you, it will probably take a few days."

A few days later Jean called back. "I have the information that you wanted. General Karim is in charge of training. He is an administrative type, very little field experience. Our people say he is more of a bureaucrat than a field commander. He is in charge of a facility which provides infantry training, advance tactics, air defense, and several other disciplines. It is believed that he is a political appointee that has been in a position where he can't do much harm. He has a good cadre' of officers that are responsible for the training and day-to-day operation of the camp and he's smart enough to keep out of their way.

"Pakistan uses older weapons for training, usually captured weapons, or in some cases older weapons that have been eclipsed by newer equipment, such as the heat seeking missiles. In most cases the weapons are serviceable but are not issued to the field troops.

"When weapons are sent to the training camp there is very little record keeping on them. The General could have sold some of the stuff off and accounted for the reduced inventory as unserviceable and destroyed, or expended during training exercises. No one would be the wiser.

"It is quite possible that Hamit or Dunbar have made contact with the General and convinced him to sell some of the equipment that was slated for training purposes. That could account for the wire transfer of funds to the General's personal account.

"To pull off a deal like that, the General must have a group of men working with him. How else would he move tons of equipment to civilian trucks or a warehouse somewhere?"

"Thanks Jean, I have the information that might help your forensic accountants figure out what is going on. I'll send it right over to you."

CHAPTER 53

"Carl, I just wanted to let you know that the IRS and ATF will raid Paul Hamit's office tomorrow morning. I suspect they will take two or three hours to go through the process once they enter his office. If you still want to confront Hamit with news of Jules Dunbar's death, you can do that tomorrow evening."

"Thanks Jean, I'll do that and I'll let you know what happens."

The next morning six men walked into Paul Hamit's office. The agent in charge announced that they were IRS Fraud Investigators and that all financial and banking records would be seized. Any and all bank statements, correspondence with his accountants, stock brokers, or financial advisors were now under seal pending further investigation by the IRS.

When the IRS finish their announcement, An ATF agent said that Hamit's Arm's Dealer license had been confiscated and records pertaining to the sale of arms or munitions, would be seized including all correspondence dealing with weapon sales.

When the Agents walked out of Hamit's office at four that afternoon there was not a scrap of paper, calendar, computer, or backup file that had not been confiscated. Paul Hamit was effectively out of business.

Carl was waiting for Paul when he arrived home that day. When Paul saw him his anger flared. His hands bunched into fists and he took a few menacing steps toward Carl. He stopped before reaching Carl, his fists relaxed, and in a tense voice he asked, "What are you doing here?"

"You sound angry Paul, having a bad day? Don't bother asking me in for a beer, I really don't have time. I just wanted to let you know that your business partner, Jules Dunbar, is dead.

"He was killed in Somalia by some angry clients, and in spite of his being killed, he is still under investigation for fraud and violations of the Anti-Terrorism Act."

The color drained out of Paul Hamits face. He stared blankly at Carl for a few seconds, then without saying a word opened his door, stepped in, and slammed it behind him.

Carl said, "Have a nice day." Although it is doubtful that Paul Hamit heard him.

Carl dialed Dan Nakamura and found him in his basement computer lab, working on the computer code necessary to gain access into the latest Unisys operating system. "Dan, I need your help again. Can you get in Paul Hamit's financial data and his personal files?"

"I think that's possible. What are we looking for?"

"I want to know who sold the heat seeking missiles to Paul Hamit or Jules Dunbar, as well as the other weapons that they sold. I am particularly interested in dates, and descriptions of the items they bought from General Karim. By the way, be very careful, Hamit's office was raided today by the IRS and ATF, all his records were sealed as part of their investigation."

Three weeks later Carl called Jean, "I think our friend Paul Hamit has left town without telling me. I went by his office, and his secretary said that she hadn't seen him since the IRS raid. He hadn't told her when he would be back, or left any instruction for her while he was gone. He missed a couple of meetings and wasn't answering his phone. I checked his apartment, and he isn't there. I think our boy was scared off by the IRS raid and skipped town."

"Yeah, he probably skipped. He's out of business. He might just as well go fishing."

"I think I may know where he might have gone. I'm going to take a trip to Budapest. Hamit has a villa there, and a warehouse that I think he and Dunbar used for storage of weapons. He's probably holed up in his villa. I also want to check out his warehouse to see if he is storing any more missiles. If so, I want to be sure they are confiscated or destroyed before they can be shipped anywhere."

"I'll let a few friends know what you are up to. Have a safe trip."

Carl walked into the passenger exit area at Praque Airport. He felt a hand touch his shoulder. He turned to see Ian Macintyre standing there. "What are you doing here? Following me?" Carl put down his carryon bag and shook hands. "Good to see you Ian."

"I told you, you have friends in high places. We can talk in my car."

On the drive, Carl filled him in about Hamit's warehouse on the outskirts of town, and the possibilities of more missiles stored there. "Aside from the missiles, I still have a personal matter to settle with Mr. Hamit."

"Come on Carl, just because he tried to have you killed twice, don't make it personal." Ian had a big grin on his face "Let's see if your man is in town, then we can check out the warehouse."

They stopped at a tourist information center and picked up a street map of Budapest and the surrounding area then drove to Hamit's villa. The villa was on a country lane on the outskirts of the city where a number of expensive homes were located. As they drove past, they could see lights on in a room in the front of the house, a blue Mercedes was parked in the drive. There were no other indications that anyone was at home. After watching the house for fifteen minutes they decided to leave and find the warehouse.

The warehouse was one of three located at a small airport. It was made of red brick, and had a red tile roof. From the road they couldn't see any doors or windows. All entry to the warehouse was from the airport perimeter road. The entire airport was enclosed with an eight foot chain link fence.

There were two entrances to the airport, one near the small terminal building and the other on the opposite side of the airport from the terminal building. That gate was guarded by a rather bored looking man in an ill-fitting gray uniform. This entrance led to some hangers for private aircraft, an aircraft parking area, and the three warehouses, located about 100 yards from the gate.

They decided to come back after dark and see if the guard was gone for the night and if the gate was locked. The road on the back side of the airport did not have any traffic. It looked as if it was only used by delivery trucks, or people going to private planes. Since deliveries are normally made during the day, and private pilots rarely fly at night, the road as well as that part of the airport should be relatively quiet at night.

CHAPTER 54

They drove by the villa again but now the lights were off and the blue Mercedes was still parked out front. "I sure would like to get a look in that house." Carl said, "It looks like he's in for the night. Let's go have dinner and we can catch up on what has been happening."

After a great dinner and a good bottle of wine, Carl and Ian returned to the hotel. Carl called Jean's office; it was just after nine in the morning in California. "I just wanted to let you know that I found Paul Hamit. He's in a small villa just outside of Budapest. We located his warehouse and we'll try and get a look inside tomorrow."

"Who is "we", Carl?"

"You remember I told you about Ian. He is the guy that saved my ass in Algiers. He won't say, but I suspect he works for your friends in D.C. It's getting late here Jean, and I'm wiped out with jetlag, I'll call again tomorrow after we have had a chance to take a look in the warehouse."

Carl and Ian had been watching Hamit's house since early morning, About 9:10 they saw Hamit come out carrying a suitcase which he stowed in the car's trunk. When he drove off, they followed him to an apartment in a complex in the center of Budapest. A few minutes later he came out carrying another suitcase which he put in the trunk. He was accompanied by a very attractive woman who looked considerably younger than he.

Ian said, "This is indeed our lucky day, it looks like he will be gone for several days. I say we follow him for a while to make sure he is on his way then head back to his villa."

"Sounds like a plan, with any kind of luck I can be headed back home tomorrow and you can rejoin your lady friend in Algiers."

They drove past the house, parked on a side road then walked back to the house. They decided to disconnect the telephone wires just in case Hamit had a burglar alarm, and hoped that he did not have a modern one with a built in cellphone. Ian knelt down, and within a minute had picked the lock on a side door. When they entered they found an old alarm system in the entrance hall, but it was unarmed. Ian, with a rueful smile on his face, said, "Trustful bugger isn't he, or he was in such a hurry to see his girlfriend he forgot to set the alarm. In either case good for us."

The house was plainly furnished, nothing much worth stealing. They checked the bedroom but found nothing of interest. The study held a desk, an answering machine, a bookcase full of books, and a couple of chairs. They listened to the messages on the answering machine, nothing much of interest, except a message from Jules telling Hamit to buy a new cell phone, and a few messages from customers wanting to buy rifles and ammunition. The desk held nothing of interest.

Carl said, "I can't believe that there is nothing pertaining to his business. That is not normal for a business man. Let's go over this place again." This time they looked under rugs, behind pictures, and checked the baseboards. Ian finally pulled back a small rug and noticed that there was a small curved scratch on the floor at one corner of the bookcase. He examined the bookcase carefully and found that the bottom cleared the floor by about a sixteenth of an inch. The fact that it did not touch the floor would not be noticeable if you did not see the scratch on the floor or were specifically looking for a moveable bookcase.

The bookcase would not move simply by pulling on it. "There must be a latch behind one of the books." As they began pulling out books they could see a metal ring lying flat against the back of the bookcase. Ian reached in and pulled the ring. The bookcase moved out smoothly. Behind was a safe door. Instead of a numbered dial there was a numeric keypad.

Carl leaned in and examined the keypad closely, using a flashlight held at a slight angle. After a few minutes he said, "Look at the keypad closely Ian. Does it look to you as if the paint on the 9, 6, and 3 keys is just a touch more dull than the other keys? The other keys have a shiny surface as if the paint is brand new, but the 9, 6, and 3 look a little dull as if they have been used."

"Oil and acids from the finger will sometimes change the surface of the paint just enough to make them look different under close examination. I have seen keypads where the paint is completely worn off from use. In this case, only three numbers show any signs that they have been touched. We should be able to figure out the combination, there are only 24 possible combinations using those three numbers.

"Many keypad locks are four number combinations, often one number is pushed twice so that only three buttons are used. Usually people will strike one key twice in rapid succession, for instance 9, 9, 6, 3 or 9, 6, 6, 3. I once visited the West Wing of the White House. Our tour guide pointed to a door and said, "That's the door to the Situation Room." Just then the Mike Dever, the President's Chief of Staff, approached the door and rapidly keyed the cypher lock. After he had gone in I looked at the lock, the last three keys were absolutely shiny because all the paint had been completely worn off, the other keys still had paint and were dusty, it was clear they had never been used; so much for Situation Room security."

"There is only one way to find out, give it a try Carl."

Carl tried twelve different combinations finally hitting the right one with 9, 6, 3, 3. They both heard the click as the latch snapped back. Carl twisted the handle and pulled the door open. Inside there were stacks of hundred dollar bills and a ledger book, plus three manila folders. The ledger held the names, dates, and amounts paid to people and their account numbers. Two of the folders held the details of purchases and sales. Who bought what, when, and how much they paid. Another folder held a list of names, and the weapons they were willing to sell. Looking down the list, Carl saw the name, General Bahir Karim. The list of weapons included SAM's. Carl said "This is what we are looking for, let's close up and head home."

Using a plastic bag from the kitchen, they took everything from the safe, including the cash. After locking the safe, and moving the bookcase back against the wall, they checked to make sure everything was back in place. Finally, Ian asked, "There must be close to a quarter of a million in cash, what are you going to do with it Carl."

"Hamit had Dunbar kill Fredrick Lunemann because we were getting close. I think it is only fair that he should pay for the Lunemann's kids' education, don't you?"

"Indeed I do, a grand idea."

Just as they were about to step back into the hallway they heard a key being used on the front door. Carl and Ian pressed themselves on either side of the study door. They heard the click of a woman's shoes on the tile floor. Whoever it was went straight to the kitchen. They could hear her making a pot of coffee then the sound of a radio. Carl mouthed "house keeper" and pointed to the short hall leading to the side door. Ian nodded and carefully made his way to the side door, Carl right behind him. They quietly eased the open and stepped out. Carl quickly reconnected the telephone line.

When they were away from the house Ian said, "That was close I don't fancy spending time in a Budapest Jail."

When Carl returned to his hotel room he called Ann, saying "I have a job for you and Dan. I want you to clean out Hamit's and Dunbar's bank accounts, all of them. Move the money into Mrs. Lynn Lunemann's account, say it's 'from Jules.'"

"Won't police be looking for that money in order to convict Hamit?"

"Don't worry Ann we have enough evidence to put him away for a very long time. Without the money from their accounts."

Next Carl called Jean Peters saying, "Jean, I have Hamit's journals saying where he bought the weapons and who he sold them to. Also, account numbers that he paid money to and a list of contacts for buying and selling weapons.

"That's great news Carl. Now the only missiles we have to worry about are in the hands of pirates and the PPK."

Carl and Ian returned to the warehouse at 11:30 P.M. They parked on a side road that looked as if it was used for agricultural purposes and walked to the airport gate. Using a set of lock picks, Ian opened the padlock and swung the gate open.

Carl found a telephone box fixed to the side of the warehouse, opened it and disconnected the telephone line. They didn't see any exterior alarm boxes. Carl said, "Let's hope that's the only alarm connection, I doubt if there are any more. If he has a bunch of weapons in there, I doubt he would want cops snooping around if he had false alarms." They picked the lock on the personnel door and entered the warehouse.

It was totally dark, using flashlights they glanced around. The warehouse was one large cavernous room with a small office near the door. Cases of AK 47 assault rifles and cases of ammunition were stacked against one wall; legitimate items for an arms dealer to have in inventory. Other items included land mines, claymore mines, and half a dozen light machine guns. What was not legal for them to have was the twelve crates containing surface-to-air heat seeking missiles.

In the office area there was absolutely nothing, not so much as a scrap of paper.

Carl and Ian stood there looking at the missiles, finally Carl said, "We can't just leave these missiles. What if Hamit has other partners or employee's that will pick them up? I think we ought to get rid of them now. We have enough explosives here to do the job. What do you think?"

"I agree. It won't take ten minutes to start a nice little fire."

"Okay, let's get started." Carl picked up the crowbar that they brought with them and started opening the cases of claymore mines. They soon had enough wood and packing material that could be used to start a fire. Next he started to break open a few of the crates for the missiles and stacked the wood over the packing material.

Twenty minutes later they had a pile of wood and packing material ready to go. Ian came over carrying a box of rifle bullets. He dropped the case on its corner. It split open, spilling its load of cartridges. Next he picked up an AK 47 and a hand full of cartridges. He put a bullet in the muzzle end of the rifle, and pried down until the bullet became loose enough to remove from the case. Removing the bullet he poured the gunpowder on the packing material. He repeated the process until he had a small pile of gun powder. After a few minutes, Ian said, "That ought to start a nice little blaze."

To finish off their little bonfire, they stacked boxes of claymore mines and grenades on top of the crates of missiles.

"One problem, how do we light the gunpowder?"

"Not to worry Carl, I have some matches."

"I didn't know you smoked Ian."

"I don't, but I always carry matches. You never know when you will be sitting in a bar and some beautiful young lady will ask for a light. I like to be prepared."

After laughing at Ian's comment, Carl said, "I'll check and see where the guard patrol is." He opened the door and looked out and saw a pickup truck with security patrol written on the door stop at the warehouse next door. "Hold on Ian, now is not a good time; the guard is at the next building." Carl eased the door shut and locked it. A few minutes later they heard the guard rattle the door knob. They waited fifteen minutes and carefully opened the door. The pickup truck was gone. Carl looked across the airport and could see a pickup truck pull up to the terminal building. "OK Ian, light that sucker and let's get out of here"

Two minutes later they closed the gate and replaced the chain and lock. They were almost back to their car when there was an explosion. When they started their car and started to drive away they heard another loud blast followed by a number of other explosions as mines, missiles, and grenades became hot enough to detonate. Then they heard popping sounds of the ammunition cooking off.

The walls of the brick building came down and the roofing timbers ignited along with anything else that was flammable.

As they raced down the perimeter road they heard the wailing of police and fire sirens coming from the airport fire department.

By the time they reached the main highway to the city, they could see city fire equipment coming in their direction.

As they neared the city, Carl said, "You know Ian, being an arsonist is a hell of a lot more fun than investigating."

When they reached the hotel, Carl called Jean saying, "We had a look in Hamit's warehouse. It was full of rifles, ammunitions, land mines, claymore mines and twelve SAMs, unfortunately the warehouse caught fire. Everything was destroyed, including the twelve SAMs."

Jean's only comment was, "Oh darn, that's too bad."

CHAPTER 55

It was almost three months since the incident at Heathrow, and rumors concerning air travel had begun to subside. The public had not totally forgotten its fear of flying, but passenger traffic had almost returned to levels reached prior to the incidents in Spain and England. Airline executives had started to breathe easier as revenue returned to near normal. Business related to travel in both Europe and the U.S. improved as tourism picked up.

Security services had interviewed those that were suspected of Islamic extremist activities and had not gotten a lead or even a hint of any activity, or rumors of any group targeting the airline industry. This is not to say that there was not the usual railing against western arrogance and imperialism, and the Jewish State; there was, a great deal of it. That level of extremist noise continued undiminished. But there was nothing that would point security personnel toward a plot to shoot down commercial aircraft. The air travel industry began to relax a little.

Local police that had been put on alert to keep a more watchful eye on airports and the surrounding areas were beginning to receive criticism from the public for putting much needed resources in the less populated areas surrounding airports, rather than in the cities where the crime rate was much higher. After three months, police commanders began to reduce the numbers of police patrols assigned to less populated areas, and reallocate scarce resources to high crime areas in cities. The apprehension over a possible attack had not disappeared but had significantly diminished.

In Germany, Nasim and Wadi parked their car on a dirt road which was partially concealed by woods. They walked into a small clearing and put their canvas bag on the ground. The approach to Tegel airport was almost directly overhead. The men quickly opened the canvas bag and extracted the launcher case. They opened the case and removed the launcher, turned the power switch to the "on" position and waited. At this time of day a plane landed about every minute and a half. They only had to wait until a large passenger plane came into view.

A police car was moving down the same road that the terrorists had used, before turning onto the dirt side road where they had parked. It had been a very quiet evening, and Officer Albert Tavin was relaxed, thinking about his girlfriend when he saw a streak of light shoot up and strike a large aircraft that was coming in for a landing. There was an explosion under a wing and the airliner seemed to tilt up and then veer to the left and down. Within seconds there was a loud explosion as the plane crashed in a large ball of flame.

Officer Tavin pushed the transmit button on his radio and told the dispatcher that he had just seen a missile shoot down a large plane at Tegel airport. He was asked to repeat the report and his location. Just as he finished, he saw a car come out of a side road moving in his direction at a high rate of speed. As it passed he saw two men in the front seat, both men appeared to be laughing.

He made a "U" turn, and with the red and blue lights on, and siren wailing, took up pursuit. Tavin radioed that he was chasing a blue Audi with two men who he believed had just shot a missile at the plane. The two cars sped toward Berlin, seven kilometers away. At the rate of speed they were moving they would be in the outskirts of Berlin in less than five minutes. Two other police cars joined the chase. City police moved to block the Audi from entering the city.

It did not take long for Nasim and Wadi to realize that they were being blocked from moving into the city, where they might have had a chance to escape. Nasim looked at Wadi, and said, "Allah Akbar" (God is great.) With that, he pressed the accelerator as hard as he could and aimed the Audi toward a concrete bridge abutment. The car seemed to explode; metal parts flew in all direction. Both men died instantly.

Following the crash, Officer Tavin led police investigators to the side road where he had first seen the Audi. Within a short time the police found the clearing, the canvas bag, and launch tube. The launch tube was later identified as being of Pakistani manufacture.

The airline had 256 passengers and crew on board, none of whom survived the ensuing crash and subsequent fire.

The media carried both accurate information and rumors. In the electronic age the news of the attack was spread worldwide virtually instantaneously. The public was inundated with the message whenever the television was turned on or a newspaper picked up. Terrorists had surface-to-air missiles and were shooting down passenger planes.

Two days later, a missile hit a plane that had just taken off from Seattle-Tacoma airport in the State of Washington, killing 236 passengers and crew. Another dozen people were killed on the ground when the plane crashed into a residential subdivision.

Police forces in every city with an airport went into high gear, sweeping up every suspected terrorist for questioning, and searching homes. Imams were asked for permission to search mosques, which they vehemently denied, which only brought the entire congregation under greater scrutiny and resulting in increased questioning and the issuance of more search warrants.

There was a public backlash against anyone who was Muslim or suspected of being Muslim. The Muslim community felt besieged and fearful. Muslims or people who looked Middle Eastern were afraid to leave their homes unless they went out in a group, and still they were nervous. There were a few random killing of Muslims, or people of darker skin who were thought to be Muslim. In California and Texas a few Sheiks were attacked or killed because they wore turbans.

As the police investigated the tips that came in, one in particular looked promising. The tipster provided the names of two men and an address. The tipster explained that the two individuals had expressed strong views against America. And that the American Muslim community had to stand up and fight for their religion by weeding out the bastards that were giving all Muslims a bad name.

The police officer taking the tip thought this was just one guy busting the balls of two people he didn't like, but like all tips it had to be checked out.

Using good police practice, the two detectives sent to investigate the tip stood to the side rather than directly in front of the door. When they heard someone approach the door they waited but the door did not open. One of the detectives yelled, "Police, open the door." Two shots splintered the wood door. They could hear footsteps running toward the back of the house. One detective called for backup while the other ran around of the house to the back yard arriving just in time to see a man getting ready to jump a fence. He yelled for the man to stop, when he did not, he shot, hitting the man in the shoulder.

Two men were arrested. The wounded man was taken to the hospital for medical attention, the other to the police station for questioning. Neither man would talk, they simply stared straight ahead. When the house was searched, instructions for the missile attack were found, along with a stash of explosives. When confronted with the evidence, both men said, "We are soldiers in a holy war. We demand to be turned over to the military."

For a second time within a week, newspapers, radio, and TV rehashed the incidents in Spain, England and Germany and now Seattle. With the renewed media assault, passenger air travel fell by more than seventy percent. The only people that were flying were businessmen who could not get out of their planned trips. Airlines began cancelling flights because they could not afford to fly planes that were nearly empty.

When two men were killed near O'Hare airport in Chicago because a missile had prematurely exploded, the pressure on Congress, the President, and the Muslim community reached a fever pitch. Anybody that was Muslim, wore a turban, or spoke Arabic was a target of distrust, and occasionally one was in the wrong place at the wrong time and was killed.

The airline industry announced that they were installing anti-missile defense systems on all their aircraft at a cost of half a million per aircraft. What they did not say was that fitting all aircraft with such a system would require several years. They asked the Federal Government to share in the cost since they simply could not afford it on their own, particularly in light of the lack of passenger travel.

hardest hit was the tourist industry worldwide that depended on air travel to bring them business. The only industry that began to thrive was cruise line travel, it is much more difficult to sink a cruise ship, but getting to the ship often presented a problem for vacationers who refused to fly.

The last incident occurred in Paris, when a missile was fired at a passenger plane that had taken off from Charles de Gaulle Airport. The guidance system failed to operate properly and the missile narrowly missed the aircraft. The missile was observed by the pilots of the aircraft as well as a number of people on the ground. As far as terrorists were concerned the ensuing news coverage accomplished the same result as if the attack had been successful; people became even more fearful of flying.

A dairy farmer lost three prize dairy cows when the missile finally dropped to earth. Again the news media focused on all of the attacks, rehashing each incident in excruciating detail. The front page of one French newspaper in an attempt to lighten the situation by carrying pictures of three dead cows with the headline that said **"Christian Cows attacked by terrorists."** The headline only served to anger farmers, animal rights activist, and religious groups.

Aircraft companies could see the handwriting on the wall and it was not good. Even if the perpetrators of the attacks were arrested the next day, it would many years before the number of airline passengers would return to the same level that existed before the attacks. Airline executives began to make plans to sell aircraft where they could. Many airlines decided to store aircraft in the Arizona desert storage facility.

Lenders were contacted to begin the process of realigning their portfolios or force airlines out of business altogether and risk losing a great deal of their investment. Orders for new aircraft were canceled and aircraft manufacturers began the process of laying off workers. Buyers in other countries took advantage of chaos to increase their aircraft fleets at bargain prices.

CHAPTER 56

The President called the Directors of the CIA and the FBI to a meeting. He began the meeting by saying, "These attacks on the Airline industry have, in three days, brought the entire industry to its knees. If we don't have some good information soon we won't have an airline industry by the end of the week. So what can you tell me Dick?"

"We have had a man in Hungary working with Carl Lukin and they have found enough evidence to indict the arms dealer who sold the missiles. We have also uncovered the chain of events that placed missiles in the hands of terrorists. We identified the person in Pakistan who sold the weapons to the arms dealers we have identified the buyers who bought the missiles. We have initiated legal proceedings to bring the arms dealer, Paul Hamit to justice. His Partner, Jules Dunbar, was killed in Somalia by an unhappy customer."

"Isn't Carl Lukin the man who uncovered how electronic guidance systems were being stolen form the manufacturer?"

"Yes sir, the same man."

"Okay, bring me up to date."

"Carl suggested a modification to the guidance systems that would cause the missiles to explode prematurely as a way of discouraging the

Somali pirates from using them. A couple did explode prematurely, causing the death of a number of pirates. The pirates apparently wised up to the trick. They lured one of the arms dealers, Jules Dunbar, back to Somalia on the pretext of buying more weapons. The pirates added their remaining missiles to the cargo that Dunbar brought with him and proceeded to sell the whole lot including the airplane to a terrorist organization called Islam's Fire.

The two pilots were killed because it was simply expedient to do so whereas Dunbar was killed to satisfy Nur's pride. No one cheated Nur and lived.

"Using intelligence gathered by satellite and drone aircraft, we were able to tell when the weapons were moved out of Somalia, and brought the plane down. Its entire cargo is now at the bottom of the Gulf of Aden.

"We later found out that the Islamic group that had bought the weapons had retained six missiles for their own use. It appears that the six missiles that were retained are the ones recently used to shoot down commercial aircraft. The missile that prematurely exploded, killing two terrorists in Chicago were apparently part of the group that had the guidance systems re-engineered."

"Are you telling me that if Carl had not suggested modifying the guidance systems we would have had two more airliners blown out of the sky?"

"Yes sir. I guess I am."

"Okay, go on."

The director of the CIA picked up the story, "Before Hamit could be arrested; he skipped the Country. Carl managed to trace him to Budapest. Carl and our man did a little breaking and entering, and found all the evidence we need to prosecute Hamit. Before they left Hungary, they also broke into a warehouse owned by Paul Hamit finding rifles, land mines, ammunition, and twelve more heat seeking missiles. Fearful that if they waited until the authorities could take action one of Hamit's associates might remove the missiles, they decided to destroy them. They managed to start a fire that destroyed all the missiles as well as everything else in the building."

"It sounds to me as if we owe a debt of gratitude to Carl Lukin and that agent of yours."

"Yes Mr. President, I quite agree."

Director Rice continued, "We are in the process of analyzing the evidence to insure that we have enough to extradite Hamit from Hungary, and persuade the Pakistani government to take action against those involved in the sale of government property to Jules Dunbar; Hamits partner. It seems that Dunbar purchased more than fifty missiles. We are currently examining the records taken from Hamits home to determine the number of missiles bought and sold, and to whom they were sold."

"Are you telling me that there are more missiles in the hands of terrorists?

"Yes sir. We know that an unknown number of missiles were sold to the PPK, but as far as we know only one has been used against the Turkish army. We hope that the evidence that Carl and our man found will tell us how many missiles were sold to the PPK. We will of course pass along what information we have to the Turkish government. Hopefully, they will be able to recover the remaining missiles before they can be used."

"Thank you gentleman, I am going to have to report to the American people or we are going to lose our airline industry and put a lot of people in the airline industry and tourism business out of work."

That evening during prime time the President outlined the attack on the airline industry and what has been done to stop them:

"The airline industry has been under attack by a few terrorists who believe that they can cause great harm to the world economic system by attacking air travel, thus hurting all the businesses that depend on it. In the process, they have caused the deaths of approximately 700 innocent civilians, men, women and children, who were on vacation, on their way to visit family, or to business meetings. They have not succeeded in destroying the airline industry, but they have damaged it.

"Our intelligence services have identified those responsible for manufacturing the missiles, those who sold them, and finally the terrorist organization that used them. We will bring all of those involved to justice, regardless of how long it takes.

It is easy to blame a whole group of people for the actions of a few. To point a finger in blame or hate, condemning a whole ethnic or religious group for the actions of a few is just plain wrong. Doing so only increases the divide between religious groups and increases the determination of the terrorists. Pointing the finger of blame or hate will not solve the problem of terrorism. Instead it will only increase mistrust and hate, which feeds the terrorists desire to continue.

There are over 1.5 billion Muslims in the world, but only about 10,000 terrorists. If we condemn those who practice the Islamic faith, or any other group for the actions of a few, the terrorists will have won.

Be assured that our intelligence and law enforcement people are going to bring those responsible to justice. We know who they are, and we are going after them. It will not happen instantly but it will happen. If you let terrorists change your travel plans they will have won. If you let terrorists dictate how you conduct your business, they will have won. If you let terrorists dictate how you live your life, they will have won.

I urge you to do the things that you have planned. Take that vacation, visit friends, and conduct your business as usual. Don't let terrorists guide your lives."

Chapter 57

Carl and Ian made copies of all the documents they had taken from Hamit's villa. Carl intended to take the originals to Jean Peters to be used in the investigation and prosecution of Paul Hamit when he was extradited. Ian would send the copies to Langley for analysis.

Both Ian and Carl left Hungary that night flying to Heathrow airport in London. In addition to the documents, Carl carried the $243,000 in cash from Hamit's safe.

When they reached Heathrow Ian purchased a ticket to Algiers. As they waited for Ian's flight to be called, Carl said, "I have a feeling that we will be seeing each other again in the not too distant future. Take care of yourself and that girl friend of yours, and if you get married let me know so that I can attend the wedding."

"I'm afraid you might have a long wait before you get a piece of wedding cake, but do keep in touch. It gets awfully dull attending all those embassy parties, eating all that good food, and being forced to dance with all those beautiful women. But you know how it is, when duty calls you just have to suck it up and head for the dance floor. As I've said before it's been fun." With that, Ian headed for his plane.

Carl had three hours before his flight so he went looking for a bank; he found one at the far end of the lobby in the main terminal. He told the teller that he wanted to wire money to Mrs. Lynn Lunemann, in California. He gave her the account number and passed across a shopping bag with the money.

The teller looked surprised when she opened the shopping bag then called over her supervisor. They closed the teller's window and asked Carl to step into a conference room where they counted the money. They asked Carl for his name for the transfer form. He said his name was Jules Dunbar. The teller gave him a receipt and assured him the wire transfer would be sent within the hour.

With a little over two hours to kill, Carl went looking for a Starbucks coffee shop. Finding one he bought a newspaper and started to catch up on world events while he drank his coffee. The headline screamed at him "*Spanair Passenger Plane Shot Down.*" The story that followed said that Spanish aviation inspectors admitted the evidence indicated the plane had been hit by a missile while taking off. The missile hit the left engine destabilizing the plane to such an extent that it did not have a chance to recover. All 189 passengers and crew had been killed. The paper went on with a few more details and then said, "Authorities speculated that the weapon used to shoot down the aircraft appeared to be a military heat seeking missile." There was a great deal of speculation as to who might have fired the missile, but no further facts that pointed to a particular terrorist group.

He finally sat in the lounge and ordered a beer and became lost in his own thoughts. "It looks like my involvement in this affair is over. The thefts at Martin Munitions had been solved and the members of the Lunemann family either arrested or killed. Hamit is going to be arrested and tried, Jules is dead, Taos is on the run, and Paul Hamit will unknowingly be paying for the education of Fredrick Lunemann's daughter. It looks I'll be back to reading security reports in the office."

CHAPTER 58

Paul Hamit Returns To His Villa

When Hamit returned home from his long weekend with the very young brunette he was relaxed. It had been a delightful and very entertaining weekend. Ellena was not only beautiful but also very energetic.

Everything was as he had left it. He poured himself a drink and thought about the coming week. He had to get back to work and generate some income. He was rich enough to afford taking a year or two off, but if he did he would lose many of his business connections. This was one business where you had to maintain your contacts. Besides, he was already tired of just sitting around. Although Ellena was a nice distraction he was not sure he could keep up with her appetites. But if the truth be told he was getting a little restless with nothing to do, he would start making calls in the morning.

The next morning, after he had a light breakfast, he went to his study, moved the bookcase aside and opened the safe. He stood there unable to believe his eyes. His journal, contact list, and buyer history were gone, as was the money, close to a quarter of a million dollars.

He could report the theft of the money to the police but not the journal and other folders. If they went after the thief would they also find the other items? If so, he could face time as an illegal arms dealer. His American licenses had been confiscated by the ATF, and the French license that he and Jules used was in Jules name not his.

He went back to the kitchen and poured a cup of coffee then retreated to his study to think about the problem. The loss of a quarter million dollars was serious, but he had other accounts that he could draw from. He had accounts in Germany, Saudi Arabia, Hungary, and another in England. The bank accounts in England, Hungary, and Saudi Arabia were in his name. The bank account in Germany was jointly held by Jules and himself. A plan began to form in his mind. He would go to the Raiffeisen Zentralbank and draw out some cash for his day-to-day expenses while he was in Budapest, then he would buy an airline ticket to England and take care of his banking problem from there.

While he was in town he stopped at a kiosk and bought a copy of the Herald, an English language newspaper and a cup of coffee. The headline story about the Spanish plane crash jumped out at him, his chest tightened. He relaxed as he realized that Jules had only sold missiles to pirates in Somalia and the PPK in Iran. Neither he nor Jules had talked to Basque Separatists (ETA or Euskadi Ta Askatasuna) in Spain. When he realized that the weapons that he had sold had not been in involved in shooting down a Spanish plane, his body visibly relaxed. "I guess the break-in at the house and now this has left me a little jumpy." With that thought he finished reading the article and drinking his coffee then walked into the bank.

Walking up to a teller at a window he presented her with a check for 100,000 FT, a little over $5000 U.S. Dollars. The teller looked up Hamit's account on her computer then with a very sober face said, "Mr. Hamit, I cannot honor this check the account has a zero balance."

Hamit stood in shock for a few seconds as the teller's message sunk in, he finally sputtered, "There must be some mistake I have had that account for years and it has over a million U.S. dollars in it".

Looking at his computer screen again, the teller said, "I am sorry sir but the account has a zero balance."

"Let me speak to a supervisor, now!"

The teller locked his cash drawer and walked over to a desk where he spoke to the man sitting there. After a few seconds the man typed in his computer and studied the monitor. Then he got up and approached the teller's window, "I am sorry Mr. Hamit but there is no money in your account, the balance is zero, we cannot honor your check."

In a very angry voice, Hamit said, "Dammit! Tell me what you have done with the million dollars that I deposited in your bank."

"I am sorry sir but you must have withdrawn your money, the balance as of this date is zero. Our records indicate that it was drawn out in cash two days ago. Is there anything else I can do for you?"

Hamit stared at the man in frustration, "I'm going to get a lawyer then I'm going to sue this bank for everything it has." With that, Hamit stormed out of the bank.

Back at his home he used his computer to access his bank in France. When he put in the number of his account he received a message saying. "Banque de France Nationale. Votre équilibre est: €0.00" Hamit reentered the account number several times always receiving the same answer, "Banque de France Nationale. Votre equilibre est: €0.00"

He tried his accounts in England and Saudi Arabia. The same thing happened; he was told that the bank accounts all had a zero balance. Next he entered the account number for Jules Dunbar's account but it also had a zero balance.

He sat in his study dumbfounded by this turn of events. He was broke except for the money that he could draw against his credit cards and the value of his properties. But the property would take time to sell. If he put everything on the market immediately at rock bottom prices they would still take time to sell. He could probably survive on his credit cards until they maxed out. How the hell could this happened, who could have done this to him.

Trying to work in Europe would be very difficult; he was not a citizen of any European country. He could not get work unless he was willing to take a menial job as a janitor or dishwasher in a second-rate restaurant. He could always broker deals between weapons manufacturers and buyers, but it often took many months for a deal to come through and he did not have enough money to survive that long. The problem was even worse if he went back to the States, he would end up in jail for twenty years or more.

In California, Lynn Lunemann had just picked up her mail. Discarding the advertising flyers she looked at the two letters from friends, and the bank statement. She quickly read the letters from her friends and smiled. It was always enjoyable to hear from them. She next read her bank statement and blinked in disbelief. Her balance had increased from a little over $10,000 to well over twelve million dollars. Obviously something was wrong. She would check into that tomorrow.

The following day she visited her bank and said that there had been a mistake. When the bank checked into the problem, they told her that the money had been wired to her account by a Mr. Jules Dunbar, the money was really hers.

CHAPTER 59

When Carl reached his office he placed a Call to Jean Peters and was told that she was in Washington D.C., and that she would return to San Francisco the next day. He left a message for her to call him. Then he set about catching up on the job of running his consulting firm.

The following afternoon, when Jean returned his call he asked for a meeting at her office as soon as she was available.

She asked, "What's it about?"

He said, "I have a present for you that I think you are going to like."

"Now you have me curious, how does four this afternoon sound?"

"Great, see you then."

At four, Jean met him at the reception desk and led him to a small conference room. After they were seated she said, "I know you're not hitting on me, so what is this gift that you've brought me?"

Carl opened his briefcase and handed her the journal and the file folders that he had taken from Hamit's safe.

"What are these Carl?"

"They are Hamit's business records, times and dates of transaction, account numbers, and people who he and Jules bought weapons from, and who Jules sold the weapons to."

"How did you get these records?"

"I would rather that you didn't ask.

"You'll see that Hamit and Jules sold the heat seeking missiles to a man named Nur Hussein, in Dhurba Somalia. Nur is the warlord that controlled the pirates that operated around the Horn of Africa. His pirates used the missiles to kill three sailors on a cruise ship and bring down two helicopters. In my book that makes Hamit an accomplice to murder."

"You probably don't know this, but Nur sold all the weapons that Jules brought with him to an Islamic terrorist group. We believe Nur added all the missiles he had, including those that had modified circuit boards, to the weapons that Jules brought.

"One of those missiles blew up just outside of Chicago's O'Hare Airport, killing the two who fired it. Another blew up outside of Heathrow airport, killing one of the two men sent to bring down a passenger plane. The suggestion that you made to modify the guidance system not only stopped some piracy, but it also saved two passenger planes from crashing and killed a few of the terrorists who were trying to shoot down them down. Those modified circuit boards saved the lives of a lot innocent people.

"I'll get this information to the right people and talk to the Attorney General's Office about starting the paperwork to extradite Hamit from Hungary. In the meantime we'll ask Hungary to pick up Hamit and hold him for murder."

"Jean, you should know that the CIA has a copy of these records, but I have no idea how they are going to use them."

The President poured himself another cup of Coffee, looking up he said, "How about you Dick, more coffee?"

"Yes please. The documents that were recovered from the arms dealer have been given to the FBI and they are pursuing legal action against Hamit. The Justice Departments has initiated extradition proceedings and will and he will be prosecuted in federal court for illegal arms sales, money laundering, and murder.

The CIA also received a copy of the documents. We have completed our examination and identified who sold the missiles. We were also able to determine how many missiles were sold to the PPK. At this time we believe we can account for all the SAMs.

What is equally important is that the records identified the person who has been selling the weapons to Hamit and his partner. It seems that the person who originally sold the missiles was a Pakistani General named Bahir Karim. Our staff is currently preparing a report for the Pakistani government. Hopefully they will take on action those involved."

"Give copies of the report to Spain, France, Germany, and England. They can help in putting pressure on the Pakistani government to take care of this General Karim."

CHAPTER 60

The report provided the details of the sale of weapons to Jules Dunbar and traced the history of the missiles to Somalia, Yemen, Cairo, and eventually to the cities where they were used to shoot down airliners. It detailed the steps that were taken to find the missiles and the loss of life that had resulted from their use.

When the countries that had experienced the damage caused by the missiles received the report, they placed calls to the Pakistani Ambassadors to their respective countries and informed them that there would be significant political and economic consequences if they did not take the appropriate action against General Bahir Karim.

Seeing the seriousness of the issue, the Pakistan President ordered the army to arrest General Karim and resolve the problem. The army tried to lure the General back to Pakistan on the pretext that he was needed in the investigation of a fire at his old headquarters. General Karim had not responded to their request for help, in fact he had disappeared.

The General was enjoying the sun and beach at Málaga on the Spanish Costa del Sol. Although he professed to be Muslim, he enjoyed his beer in the afternoon. In particular he enjoyed the sight of scantily clad young women sun-bathing on the beach. He did not fear the pangs of retribution from Allah. He may not attain the perfection of Allah's paradise with his 72 virgins but he was close enough here in Spain. He was living the good life and he was going to enjoy it.

The realities of living the good life on the Costa del Sol was that it required money, lots of it. The cash that he had brought with him was rapidly running out. He would soon have to transfer finds from his account in Paris.

When the General finally called his Paris bank to arrange for a transfer of funds, the CIA was waiting and watching.

The French bank officer watching the account made a call to a number at the American Embassy. When the call was answered he told the answering party where the money had been sent, the name of the bank and the account number. Two days later the Bank officer received an envelope with $2000 in cash.

When the General went to his local Spanish bank to pick up some of the cash that had been transferred, there was a man ready to follow him to his home.

Three days later, two men knocked on the General's door late in the evening. When he opened the door, a fist slammed into his face knocking him backwards onto the floor. Before he could cry out or move, a piece of duct tape was placed over his mouth, and he felt the sharp prick of a needle in his neck. Within moments his muscles went slack and he slipped into unconsciousness.

A Gulf Stream-V jet landed at the Málaga airport earlier. It had, it had been refueled and was ready to leave. A black Mercedes pulled up to the passenger door and two men helped an obviously ill man board the plane. Eight hours and forty minutes after takeoff, it landed at Islamabad, Pakistan, where two army officers and four enlisted men were waiting.

The next morning the General woke up with a slight headache and a nauseous feeling in the pit of his stomach. Looking around he found himself in a bare room with bars on the window. Outside he could hear men being drilled; the drill sergeant was barking orders in Urdu. As the fog began clearing from his brain, the realization that he had been kidnapped and was back in Pakistan in a military camp dawned on him. He had memories of being in his apartment hearing a knock on the door and being hit when he opened it, but nothing after that until waking up in this bare room.

Sometime later, an officer entered his room, followed by an enlisted man carrying a tray of food, hot tea, and a bag containing a clean uniform. The officer said, "General Karim you have been placed under arrest and will face a Courts Marshal this afternoon at 3:00 on the charge of selling government property for personal gain."

At 3:00, two men came to his room. He was taken from the room where he had awakened to another room where he was confronted by six army officers. The General leading the tribunal said, "You have been charged with selling military weapons that were later used to kill civilians in Germany, Spain, and the United States and you will be tried by military Courts Marshal. Do you have anything to say in your defense?"

"I know nothing of the crimes that you say I have committed."

The prosecuting officer for the Courts Marshal was asked to read the entire indictment, He said, "On March 5, 1995 you sold 20,000 rounds of ammunition and 200 AK47s to a Jules Dunbar. Again, on December 4, 1997, you sold 50 grenade launchers, 100 land mines, 100 AK47s to the same Jules Dunbar." The prosecuting officer continued reading the list of sales that Karim had made to Jules.

When he finished reading his list of weapons that General Karim had sold he said, "The missiles that you sold were later used to shoot down three passenger airliners, killing 695 passengers and crew members, in addition to twelve people on the ground, and the shooting down of three military helicopters. The small arms have been used by Somali pirates in the taking of ships and hostages in both the Gulf of Aden and the Indian Ocean."

"I don't know anything about that list of weapons! Why are you reading it to me?"

The General nodded at an officer standing at the back of the room and said, "Bring Captain Mehal."

When Captain Mehal entered the room flanked by two soldiers, it was obvious he had undergone a severe interrogation. General Karim looked at him, and knew that his life was over. They knew everything.

The General leading the Court looked at General Karim and said, "Shall we go on?"

General Karim shook his head and in a low voice, said, "No."

"Do you deny these accusations?"

"No."

"You have stolen from the army and your Country. You are a disgrace to both the army and to Pakistan. The weapons that you have sold have caused the death of hundreds of innocent people and you have brought shame on the army and Pakistan. This court has ordered that you pay for your crimes by execution before a firing squad tomorrow morning at eight. This court stands adjourned."

General Karim was returned to his room. He sat and thought about his life, his wife and his children. He ignored the food that was brought in. He just sat staring at the wall thinking. Occasionally he would drink a little water then return to staring at the opposite wall or the floor.

Late that night he pulled the sheets from his bed and ripped them into long strips. He then wove the strips into a rope. He stood his bed against the wall and tied one end of the rope to the metal frame. He tied the rope around his neck. He used a portion of the rope to tie his hands to the bed frame so that he would not be able to use them to escape should he lose his resolve. He stood there for a minute then hooked his feet on the bed frame and fell forward.

The next morning the guard came in early to bring the General his breakfast. He found General Karim dead.

On the same day Captain Mehal and four enlisted men were tried, convicted and sentenced to twenty-five years each for assisting General Karim in his illegal activities.

A week later, each country that had logged a protest received a letter saying that the General had been tried, convicted, and the sentence of death had been carried out. The letter did not give any specifics about General Karim's Death.

CHAPTER 61

Hamit had just purchased a ticket to Tunisia. He chose Tunisia because it did not have an extradition treaty with the United States. As long as he did not commit a crime there he would not be deported and he could not be extradited. Without the worry of an arrest he would have time to figure out a way to resolve his personal financial problems and legal troubles with the IRS.

If the records were stolen by someone who was only after money, the theft may even have helped him, particularly if the thief destroyed the journals and folders as having no monetary value. On the other hand, if the records were to reach the FBI, his problems would be significantly worse. He would be convicted of laundering money and much more.

He still had some cash left over from his trip with Ellena, and his credit cards had not been maxed out yet. At least he had enough cash to get something to eat while he waited for his plane. After his meal, it was time to board his flight to Paris where he would transfer to a flight to Tunisia. When he approached the gate he showed his ticket to the agent who looked at it saying, "Welcome aboard Mr. Hamit." He felt a pair of hands grab each of his arms and a voice say,

"We are the police. You are under arrest. Please come with us quietly Mr. Hamit." He was led to a small conference room.

Hamit said, "Why are you arresting me, what are the charges?"

One of the arresting officers said, "You are under arrest for possession of illegal arms."

"What illegal arms? I don't have any. I'm a weapons dealer and the weapons that I have are legitimate for me to have."

"Surface to air missiles are not legitimate for anyone to have except the military."

"I don't have any surface to air missiles, what are you talking about?"

"Your warehouse at the airport had a number of heat seeking missiles. Heat seeking missiles can only be bought and sold by the Federal government not an arms dealer. Your warehouse caught fire, but our investigators were able to identify the illegal weapons that were stored there."

All that Hamit could think of was that Jules must have bought more missiles from General Karim without telling him.

"We have also been asked by the United States government to hold you for extradition. You will receive a hearing to determine if extradition should be granted. The hearing should be held within the next three or four weeks, then American Federal authorities will send someone to pick you up. Until then you will enjoy the hospitality of Hungary."

While he was being booked he asked the booking Sergeant for a lawyer.

The booking Sergeant asked, "Who is your lawyer?"

"I don't have a lawyer yet I want to hire one who can help me fight extradition."

A young man who was standing near the booking desk overheard the conversation and walked over said, "Perhaps I can help you."

"Are you a lawyer?"

"Yes, I specialize in criminal law. Why are you being held?"

Waving at the booking Sergeant, he said, "I've been arrested and am being held pending extradition to the United States for a crime I did not commit."

"What crime are you being held for that you did not commit?"

The booking Sergeant handed the attorney a sheet of paper. It was the indictment, which listed the crimes Hamit was being charged with in the request for extradition. Listed, were Federal Tax evasion, illegal sale of firearms, murder, and violation of the Anti-Terrorism Act.

"This is quite an extensive list of crimes. You are very lucky I am a very good attorney and my rates are very low, nevertheless it will be very expensive to defend you. Do you have any money?"

The booking Sergeant picked up Hamit's wallet and handed it to him. He opened it and counted the cash. He looked up and said, "I have $540 in cash, do you take credit cards?"

A smile briefly crossed the attorney's face, "I am afraid I do not. Do you know anyone who will lend you the money?"

"No. Not in this country."

"No? Then I suggest that you wait until you return home, then either borrow the money, or if you do not get the necessary funds, ask the courts to appoint you a lawyer for free.

"Please excuse me Mr. Hamit but I have other clients waiting for me." With that he walked away.

For the next two weeks Paul Hamit sat in a Jail cell and waited. He thought about how he came to be in this position. He finally reached the conclusion that it was not his fault. Everything would have been alright if it had not been for that private detective nosing around looking into things that were none of his business.

Two federal marshals flew into Ferihegy International Airport in Budapest. After an evening resting, they returned to the airport where they picked up their prisoner. Hamit was handcuffed to one arm of a Marshall, and the second Marshal followed closely behind. The three made their way to the plane before the other passengers were permitted to board. Eighteen hours later they landed in San Francisco.

Chapter 62

When the Prime Minister of Turkey received a copy of the CIA report he became very angry. The thought of the PPK with eleven heat seeking missiles was outrageous and could not be tolerated. No military or commercial aircraft in Turkey would be was safe.

He called the Chief of the General Staff, Işi Koşanerk, saying, "I just received a copy of a CIA report that documents the sale of heat seeking surface to air missiles to the PPK. The report said the PPK was originally sold twelve missiles. Since they have already expended one missile shooting down a helicopter they still have eleven in their procession. We cannot tolerate the existence of the PPK with any missiles, let alone eleven. It's like having a dagger held at our throat. Our entire air transportation industry is at stake. Come up with a plan to find and destroy the remaining missiles."

The Chief of the General Staff in turn, called the Commander of the Army and asked that he prepare a plan for an excursion into Iran to root out the PPK, and find the eleven SAMs. Using satellite photos of the border region with Iran provided by Americans and the trail left by the three PPK members that shot down the helicopter when they returned to Iran, it was thought that the most likely area where the missiles were stored was the town of Khvoy, or one of the surrounding farms. The army formulated a plan to engulf the area in a pincer movement and then search every house, barn, or cave until the missiles were found. The greatest risk to the plan would be a war with Iran.

The plan was presented to the Prime Minister and approved. They would notify Iran of their plan one hour before the troops crossed the border. Notifying Iran sooner would likely mean that people in the town of Khvoy would be warned about the operation and have an opportunity to move their missiles before the troops could surround the area. If Iran believed them, they might be allowed to complete their operation and be out of the area before Iran mobilize their forces and reached Khvoy. They would express their regrets and apologize after the operation was finished and troops had returned to Turkey. For this operation to succeed secrecy was paramount.

The CIA was told of the operation. They provided Turkey a steady stream of satellite data of the area and any other intelligence that came their way.

Well before dawn on the appointed day, 6000 troops streamed across the border and surrounded the Khvoy area. Taking precaution to avoid any conflict with Iranian troops in the area or law enforcement that might be in the area, they began to search homes, farms, grain silos, or any other buildings that could conceivably be used to store the missiles. They were four days into the operation when they reached a farm wherein they found what they were looking for hidden under the floor of a shelter that was used to house goats. All eleven missiles were accounted for.

The army immediately began their pullout from the area and returned to Turkish soil. The following day photographs of the cache and an apology for the incursion that was necessary was sent to the Iranian government.

Turkish troops were kept on alert in the event that Iran did not accept the apology and felt the need to retaliate. The Iranians did not retaliate, and after a few months the tension between the two countries subsided.

The owners of the farm, a young woman, her father, and a cousin were taken back to Turkey when the troops evacuated the area. Under interrogation they admitted that they had fired the missile at the helicopter. Their confession was appended to the apology that was sent to the Iranian government. The three were sent to prison for life.

CHAPTER 63

After seeing his wife and children on a plane to Paris where they would meet up with her aunt, Taos Kassini caught a plane to Rio de Janeiro, Brazil. He hoped to lose himself in that country until things cooled down and he could reunite with his family.

Once he reached Brazil, Taos took a bus to Natal, a port city more than 1200 miles north of Rio de Janeiro. He could have flown there, but he knew that it would be easier to trace him if he bought another plane ticket.

For Taos the problems of remaining hidden was very challenging. Although he was an Electrical Engineer by training and had the ability to run a machine shop, trying to use those skills in a country where he was not a citizen and could not speak the language was difficult. There was no demand for anyone who could speak French or Arabic. It was especially difficult to find work if you didn't have a work permit or any identity papers. The only jobs Taos could get was as a janitor or dishwasher in a Chinese restaurant.

One night after washing the last of the dishes, and woks, he swept the floors and left for the night. It was usually late when he left the restaurant and made his way toward his rented room. On this night he had the bad luck to be mugged by four men at 2:30 in the morning. Thinking he was a tourist, they closed in around Taos. Stopping in front of him they said, "You're out late old man. Give us your money and we'll see that you get home safely."

Taos was not sure what they said but their intent was clear. Smiling he said "Eu não falo português." He repeated the sentence, "I don't speak Portuguese" in French.

The largest of the four men smiled and said, "He's a tourist, they always have lots of money." Without another word he struck Taos in the face knocking him backward. The other three men immediately jumped in and began beating him. One of the men pulled a knife and stabbed Taos' in the side. When Taos slumped to the pavement they kicked him a number of times. They only the stopped beating when Taos stopped moving or trying to ward off any more blows and simply lay there unconscious.

After going through his pockets and taking his wedding ring, watch, pocket change, and passport, the leader of the gang said, "This crazy bastard doesn't have any money." They left him lying in the street. It was nearly two hours before he was noticed by a police car moving through the area. By the time he reached a hospital he was nearly dead.

He lay in a hospital bed for nearly a week fighting an infection, slipping in and out of a coma. In his delirium he would ask for his wife, speaking in French, and occasionally in Arabic. When the staff asked his name he would say only his first name; Taos. They could not get a nationality from him. It was almost as if he was afraid to say. The police believed he was a tourist, but without a name or any indication as to where he came from they could only take his fingerprints and give them to Interpol and ask their help in the identification.

When the delirium passed and he was able to talk coherently, the police began to question him. The police officer speaking French said, "I'm a police interpreter. We need a little information from you. Can you answer some questions for me?"

In a weak voice Taos answered, "I will try but I don't remember much."

"Who are you and where are you from?"

"My name is Taos Kassini and I am from Calais, France."

"Why are you here in Brazil?"

"I am just a tourist here on vacation."

"Where are you staying? Which hotel?"

Looking a little uncomfortable Taos said, "I'm not staying at a hotel. I have a room at a rooming house."

"You say you are a tourist, but you stay at a rooming house? That is a bit unusual isn't it?"

"No, I don't have much money left and I wanted to stay as long as possible."

"Can you tell me who attacked you?"

"No, I just remember that there were four of them, but I don't remember anything else until I woke up here."

Two days later, Interpol responded with a request that Taos Kassini be held in custody. He was wanted by the United States on terrorist charges. The police soon received a second communication from the United States Justice Department saying that they would file the necessary paperwork for extradition of Taos Kassini to the United States on charges of terrorism and murder. When Taos awoke the following morning he found his left wrist handcuffed to the bed. When the French speaking police officer returned with more questions, Taos asked, "Why am I handcuffed to the bed? I am not a criminal I have done nothing wrong."

"You are under arrest."

"On what charge?"

"You are considered a fugitive and are being held for extradition to the United States. They will be here to pick you up soon."

Taos closed his eyes and sank back in his bed.

The paperwork requesting his extradition was promptly approved by the court after a short hearing. After all, he was not a Brazilian citizen, and there was not much interest in keeping him in Brazil. Let the American's take care of him.

CHAPTER 64

Nur Hussein called a meeting of the village elders to discuss the problem of the hostages and the possibility of attack by the nations whose ships they had captured. He knew the patience of the maritime nations was beginning to wear thin.

The elders from the villages were gathered around in a semicircle. Hundreds of villagers stood behind the elders listening intently to the discussion.

Finally Nur said, "We have over 700 hostages that we must take care of until they can be ransomed. Some have gotten sick and others have died. They are expensive to feed, which only takes food away from our own people, but most of all they are an emotional problem.

"If we take a ship and deal with an insurance company for the ransom of the ship, that is a business arrangement. But when we take hostages, particularly those that have no commercial value, we incur an emotional response from the rest of the world. They demand that their governments take action against us, and if they do we will be in a war that we cannot win.

"To avoid a war I propose that we release all the hostages, retaining only those necessary to operate the ships."

There was much discussion among the elders but no one answer emerged as a clear course of action.

Nur continued, "Then there is the problem of the ships. We have thirty ships at anchor waiting for the insurance companies to pay the ransom. Freighters, tankers, and yachts all have been taken and are being held. The crews for the large ships are being held aboard their ship. They and their ship will be released when the insurance company pays the ransom. The crews and passengers of the smaller ships and yachts have been taken ashore and are being held captive at our villages in the highlands. If their families can pay the ransom they and their ship will be released. If their families cannot pay the ransom they will continue to be held; but for how long? And then what? Do we kill them or release them without being paid? In the meantime we must feed and take care of them.

"The hostages are not accustomed to living in the conditions that we are able to provide. They are not use to the food that we feed them. They are not immune to the many diseases that our people have built resistance to over the centuries. The one truth that cannot be escaped is that a dead hostage is worth nothing. To the contrary, in death they are even more of a liability.

"For the commercial shipping it is only a matter of haggling with insurance companies over the price. They know that they will have to pay sooner or later. For an insurance company it is a matter of paying the least possible amount. But as we gained experience in dealing with insurance companies our ransom demands have increased. But we know that the insurance companies will pay. They know that if they failed to pay, they would lose the ship, crew and cargo which would cost them much more than the ransom. Besides, any money that is paid in ransom would be made up by increases in the premiums that the shipping companies will pay for insurance. For the insurance companies it is only a business relationship.

"For insurance companies it is good business to prod their governments to take action against us. If their governments send in their navies and armies, and stops us from taking ships the insurance companies will not have to pay ransoms and they will become even more profitable.

"In the meantime, we must go further and further to find a ship to take. We now have to go more than six hundred miles from our coast to find a ship. In the meantime there are warships trying to stop us. They now patrol the Gulf of Aden and Indian Ocean with warships, but that is a huge body of water with many fishing boats and local traders. Trying to identify us is not easy.

"Our people have grown used to the easy money. It would be difficult to give up such a lucrative business. But we must do something different, we cannot continue as we have in the past.

"I propose that we release all hostages, they are more trouble than they are worth."

There was a great deal of discussion among the elders. But again they seemed unable to reach any kind of a consensus.

In the surrounding crowd a young man stepped forward and challenged Nur, saying, "What you are proposing is foolish. It will significantly reduce our income and send the wrong message to the insurance companies. The navies of the countries from which the hostages come will never dare attack us out of fear for the safety of the hostages. If we release the hostages we will no longer have that safeguard. I have come to believe that you are losing your courage."

Nur could not let the young man's challenge to his courage and his authority go unanswered. Nur started forward toward the young man but when he swung at him he hit nothing, the young man had ducked the blow. Instead of cowering as Nur expected, he struck back, surprising Nur.

The battle raged for many minutes, finally ending on the ground as a wrestling match. After several minutes the dust settled. One man finally stood. The other lay on the ground with a broken neck. Nur was dead the clan had a new leader.

PREVIEW
OF
ISLAM'S FIRE

1

Simon Rossman was eagerly waiting for the phone call that he knew would consume the rest of his life, possibly ending with his death.

He was at home in Sacramento, California, playing with his two sons when the phone rang, answering it he heard the excited voice of Ken Barkley.

"It's done. The program worked. We're rich!"

"Where are you?"

"I'm in Washington at a fishing resort."

"Be specific, I want to come up and see you."

"I'm at the Ferguson Fishing resort, Cabin 12, just a few miles north of Belfair, just off State Highway 300--can we talk?"

"No. Not now. Not over the phone. I'll fly up this afternoon, just sit tight, don't talk to anybody, and don't call anybody. Got it?"

"Yeah, I got it."

Between the plane flight and the drive from the Seattle/Tacoma airport, it was late that evening before Simon drove onto the grounds of the fishing lodge.

When Ken had arrived at the fishing resort earlier he had asked for a cabin toward the back of the resort grounds saying he was a writer and wanted privacy. After he had parked and taken his one bag into the cabin, he used his cell phone to call Simon. Since then he had been pacing his room like a nervous cat.

By mid-afternoon hunger got the best of him. He had to get out of the cabin that seemed to be closing in on him. He made a quick trip to a convenience store for junk food. Returning he resumed pacing the floor, watching game shows on TV, and munching on snacks. Finally, just as the 10 P.M. news came on he heard a knock at the door.

"Come on kid, open the door, it's me, Simon."

Ken yanked the door open and stood there with a wide grin on his face staring at his visitor. He reached out his hand to shake but Simon pushed past him and stood looking around the room.

Simon was in his late thirties, tall, with light brown skin and a strong muscular build. He had a well groomed appearance but he was not what you would call memorable in appearance. Yet there was something about him that made people uncomfortable. His dark eyes seemed to bore right into you.

He carried a twelve pack of beer into the kitchenette and placed it on the short counter. He took off his hat and black leather coat, threw them on the bed and looked around, his eyes taking in every detail. The room was clean with a rustic décor you would expect at a fishing lodge.

He pulled two cans of beer from the carton, and smiling, tossed one to Ken. After putting the remainder of the beer in the refrigerator, he popped the tab on his can and took a drink. "Alright Ken, let's hear all about it."

"What do you want to know?" Ken asked, after opening his can, taking a drink, and slumping into a chair.

"Everything Ken. Start from the beginning and don't leave anything out," said Simon, taking a sip from his can of beer.

Ken began telling Simon about the computer program he had written and how he had recruited a friend, Al Genovese, from the production review section to run the program through the bank's testing procedures, and then install it in the Wire Transfer System.

At the mention of Al Genovese Simon grew tense but did not interrupt Ken.

As Ken gave his detailed account, Simon kept the supply of beer coming. After another two beers, Ken described how they could transfer the money from the account in Panama to anyplace in the world that he and Simon wanted to go. They would have all the money they would ever need.

Simon was familiar with the account at Banko de Panama since he had established it. He had already left instructions with the Panamanian bank to re-transmit the funds to an account he had set up in Bahrain. Ken would never know about this part of the plan. He forced himself to relax and let Ken continue telling his story.

Simon patiently listened. He got Ken another beer and when he finished his story Simon began asking questions.

"Tell me more about this person, Al Genovese?"

"He's the bank manager in charge of the production Wire Transfer System. He's the guy who has the password that you need in order to upload a program into the production stream. I couldn't make this work without his help."

"Is Genovese the only one at the bank who is helping you?" asked Simon in a tight voice.

"Yeah, he's the only one. Nobody else knows about this plan or the program I put together."

"How much did you promise to pay him?"

"I promised him ten million dollars when we finally get settled someplace."

Simon studied Ken with unyielding eyes that sent shivers up Ken's spine. Then he said, "I hope this guy can be trusted."

For the next two hours Simon asked questions, and prodded for details when Ken faltered. He took notes, asking more questions when necessary. He verified the account number Ken had sent the money to, and the bank's location. As the questioning continued, Simon encouraged Ken to drink more beer.

When Simon felt sure that he had an understanding of the banking details and how the system worked he went on to other subjects.

"So exactly where does Genovese live? Do you have his address?

"Yeah, sure," replied Ken as he scribbled Genovese's address on a note pad and handed it to Simon.

"How about we have one more beer and call it a night?" He leaned back, folding the note with Genovese's address and putting it in his shirt pocket.

Ken got up and unsteadily walked to the refrigerator. He did not notice that Simon had also risen and was just behind him.

Simon pulled a snub nosed .22 caliber revolver from his jacket pocket and, walking up behind Ken shot him in the back of the head. Ken slumped to the floor. Simon leaned over and placed the muzzle of the gun in Ken's ear and pulled the trigger a second time. Neither bullet left an exit wound. Death was instantaneous.

Simon returned to the table and sat down heavily, his hands trembling and his forehead glistening with beads of sweat.

The training camp he attended twenty years ago, where he had been taught how to kill a person a dozen different ways, did not really prepare him for actually killing another human being. They did not teach him how it would feel to kill a friend. Maybe he had been in America too long and grown soft.

He knew it had to be done. His plan was proceeding flawlessly. He could not allow emotions to get in the way now.

Simon felt good about his plans to set bombs across the country that would kill hundreds, but that was different. Just strangers, never looking into their eyes or knowing their names, not friends, just people in the wrong place at the wrong time. He took a deep breath and willed his body to relax.

Killing Ken was personal. They had been friends since Ken was a teenager living next door to him in Sacramento. Ken was a geeky kid, a nerd, and a loner, and Simon had just come to the United States from Pakistan, and didn't know anybody. They had become friends through a mutual need for companionship.

Simon's orders had always been to get the money that was so badly needed. And now his friend was out of school and working for the largest bank in the country. Planting ideas in Ken's mind wasn't too difficult, he was easily manipulated. He began planting ideas about taking a very large amount of money and travelling the world. It started as a game to see if they could devise a plan to steal a billion dollars but over time they both realized that it could actually be done.

They began talking over their different ideas, discarding some, further refining others until they had perfected a plan.

Writing a program to steal the money while it was being sent over the Wire Transfer System would be difficult but not impossible. By the time anyone had discovered the theft they would have already moved the money to many different banks all over the world, making it impossible to trace. Ken was a genius programmer and he knew it, and here was his chance to prove it.

Simon sat for a while thinking about Ken and the years they had known each other. He deeply regretted killing his friend but there was no other way.

He would call Parviz Jalili, may Allah bless him, tomorrow afternoon and let him know the plan had been carried out. He would receive the money soon.

After a few minutes, Simon began to search the cabin. Every scrap of paper, empty beer can, cell phone, magazine, or piece of clothing was thrown into a travel case. Then he began to wipe down all the surfaces that might hold his fingerprints. When he was sure that he had cleaned up thoroughly, he took an extra blanket from the closet and rolled Ken's body onto it.

Turning off the lights, he stood in the dark room until his eyes adjusted, then, opening the door, he scanned the area. By this time it was two-thirty in the morning and there did not seem to be anyone still up. The moon was just a slender crescent in the Western sky, making the night extremely dark.

It required some effort for Simon to pick up the body. Ken was tall and lanky, but still carried some solid muscle. Simon was a strong man but Ken was not as light as he appeared. As Simon carried the body out, he lurched to one side and scraped his arm on the door jamb.

Carrying Ken to the dock gave a whole new meaning to the term "dead weight." Out of breath when he reached the dock, he dumped the body into a rowboat. He rowed to what he thought was the middle of the Hood Canal. Tying the anchor chain around Ken's legs, he tried to throw Ken and the anchor overboard. Throwing a body overboard while in a small boat was difficult. The boat kept rocking as he tried to lift the body over the side. He finally had to kneel in the bottom of the boat to get enough leverage to throw the body over the side. After the body had sunk out of sight, Simon waited silently for a few minutes as he caught his breath, then he rowed back to the dock and tied up.

Before leaving the boat, Simon wiped his fingerprints from the oar handles. Back at the cabin he carried the travel case with Ken's clothing and personal items to his car then went back to the cabin for a last check. Satisfied with his work, he left the cabin, wiping off the door knob as he closed the door behind him.

He went to Ken's car and tried to remove the license plates but he needed a screwdriver. He went back to the cabin and found a knife that would serve the purpose. Working in the dark he was able to loosen the screws. He put the knife on the ground and used his fingers to finish removing the screws. He looked at his watch, it was getting late, he had to hurry. He added the license plate to the travel case.

Using Ken's car keys he started the car, looked out the rear window as he backed into the narrow driveway that circled through the fishing resort. He didn't see the flash when the headlights reflected off of the knife blade.

About a mile from the fishing resort Simon found a deserted road. Using magazines and newspapers he had found in the cabin he set the car on fire. He didn't worry about fingerprints here, he knew the fire would take care of them.

Simon ran back to the fishing resort to get to his car and drive to Bremerton, to catch the 6:00 AM ferry to Seattle. He arrived at the ferry terminal early and had time to go through the items in the travel case. When he was done he threw the travel case and its contents into a dumpster.

Simon was tired but he would nap an hour and a half on the flight to San Francisco, where he would find out how much Mr. Al Genovese knew. He removed the paper with the address from his shirt pocket and studied it, then put it back. I'll call Professor Jalili when I'm through with Mr. Genovese.

It would be a week before the bank knew they had a very serious problem.

2

Carl Lukin rolled onto one elbow, yawned, stretched, and looked down at Ann. Ann lay on her stomach with the sheets pulled up to her waist. Her auburn hair cascaded over her face and down her back. Carl looked at her tanned, well-toned back as she breathed softly, still asleep.

Carl enjoyed watching her. As he watched he felt himself becoming aroused. He leaned over and kissed the back of her neck. He ran his finger lightly up and down her spine until she slowly rolled over. Her large breasts moved up and down with each sleepy, shallow breath. He kissed her lightly on the lips, then on each breast, running his tongue lightly over her nipples until they started to become hard and erect as Ann awakened.

Without opening her eyes she reached up and pulled Carl down to her. With his elbows on each side of her body they began to move rhythmically until they both climaxed and a warm relaxed feeling swept over their bodies. They lay there a few minutes more enjoying the moment and the warmth of each other's body. Only then did Ann open her eyes and smiling, looked at Carl. In a sleepy voice she said, "Oh, it's you!"

"Are you in the habit of making love to strangers when you wake up?"

"Not since I met you." After a long and tender kiss Carl rolled onto his back. Ann rolled onto her side and slid her leg across his body. With her head on his shoulder she nuzzled and kissed his neck.

After showering, Carl entered the kitchen, and turned on the coffeemaker. It was just 7:00 A.M. and the sun was up but the house was still in the shadow of the Olympic Mountains. While the coffee was brewing he walked out onto the deck. The sun was bright and the air felt cool to his skin. Taking a deep breath, he could smell the salt water from the Hood Canal. He grabbed an old towel to wipe the morning dew from the deck furniture, and then brought out the cushions from the storage area.

The Hood Canal is a seventy-mile long waterway in the state of Washington. It begins at Puget Sound and ends near the town of Belfair on the Olympic peninsula. The canal is shaped like a backwards "J." The very end of the canal becomes a mud flat when the tide is out. The vast majority of the Hood Canal is a navigable waterway. The house where Carl and Ann were staying was just past the curve at the bottom of the "J," the canal at this point is over a mile wide, a deep blue green, and only about 200 feet deep at its deepest point.

On this day there was no wind and the surface of the canal was so smooth that the far shoreline was clearly reflected on its surface. The tide was in and the oyster bed just below the deck was under water. He thought about picking up some oysters for lunch when the tide ebbed. From the time they were picked up off the beach, shucked, breaded, and dropped into the frying pan with butter where they would turn a golden brown was just a few minutes. It just didn't get any better than that.

The red light on the coffeemaker blinked off. After pouring himself a cup, Carl sat down to enjoy what promised to be a great morning. As he did each morning, he watched for the river otters that always came swimming, playing, and diving for their breakfast. There were six otters that lived in a den on the hillside behind the house. Their morning adventures were always entertaining to watch. Their routine was to use the drainage pipe under the highway to reach the beach then swim out into the canal to get their breakfast. Once they caught a fish they would climb onto the swim float moored sixty yards from shore to enjoy their meal and play. They always left a mess of fish scraps and defecations, forcing Carl to clean the swim float daily because of the smell.

Carl had drunk about half his coffee when he spotted the six otters. As they neared the swim float one otter surfaced with a large fish in its mouth. But instead of going toward the swim float as they usually did, they swam around the float, giving it a wide berth, and headed toward the beach in front of the neighbor's house where blackberry bushes offered cover. The other otters followed closely hoping for a share of the first catch of the day.

Carl was surprised by the otters' actions in avoiding the swim float, this was not part of their morning routine. He looked at the float again and noticed something caught near one of the corners. He picked up a pair of binoculars and looked again. Whatever it was it appeared to be snagged on one of the grab ropes that hung from the sides of the float.

Curious, he went down the steps to the beach and pushed the row boat into the water. When he reached the float he could see that it was an arm that had become tangled in a loop in the grab rope, the upper half of a body just visible under the water, its arms stretched out. The lower half of the body was under the swim float. Using a rope that was normally tied to the boat's anchor, he tried to cinch a loop around the exposed arm but it was difficult to get the rope to hold because the body had been in the canal long enough to cause the skin to tear when he tried to tighten the loop. He finally moved the loop farther up the arm until he reached a point where the shirt sleeve still covered the upper arm. He then tied the rope to a cleat on the float.

Although he had been a Naval criminal investigator for five years, and had to killed in defending his life, and had seen dead and decomposing bodies, he could feel his stomach begin to become nauseous. He headed back to the house to call 911.

While he waited for the sheriff's officers, he went to the bedroom to find Ann still curled up in bed. He sat on the bed and told her he had found a body and had called the sheriff.

Ann rolled up on one elbow and said, "If there are going to be cops coming around, I guess I had better get up. I'll take my shower and be right out, would you mind pouring me a cup of coffee?"

"Coming right up. You may want to wait until the cops finish moving the body before getting anything to eat. The smell is not going to be pleasant."

Fifteen minutes later two Mason County sheriff's cars pulled up in front of the house. When Carl opened the door one of the officers said, "Are you the person who reported finding a body?"

"Yeah, I called 911 this morning about a body snagged on our swim float. Come on in and I'll show you."

When they reached the back deck Carl pointed out the swim float, saying, "I used the anchor rope to tie the body to the float."

One of the officers took the boat out to the float for a look while the other officer took a statement from Carl. They radioed the Sheriff's office and forty five minutes later the coroner and a team of divers arrived to retrieve the body.

A few minutes after the sheriff's officers had arrived Ann had finished her shower and dressed in shorts and a tee shirt. She stepped out of the house holding a coffee mug. Ann was tall with auburn hair to her shoulders, dark blue eyes, with a figure that most women only dream about. She was in her late twenties and a beautiful woman by any standard. She would draw the admiration of both men and women, although women had a tendency to step in front of the men they were with when she appeared.

The Sheriff's officers instantly stopped talking as they stared at Ann.

Carl finally turned around, saw Ann, and made introductions.

"Mr. Lukin, can you tell me again what drew your attention to the body?"

Carl recounted the story of the otters and explained the difficulty he had in tying the rope to the body. He wanted to make sure the coroner understood where the damage to the arm came from.

Carl finished answering all the officers' questions, which were not many, since from all appearances it looked like it was an accidental drowning.

They stood on the deck watching the divers put the body into a basket. They covered the body with a rubber sheet and attached restraining straps. A short time later the body was pulled to shore, loaded onto a gurney, and placed in the coroner's van. The van and the patrol cars were soon gone.

Ann said, "I'll never get used to the smell of a decomposing body. The smell seems to cling to your clothes and hair. I think I'll take another shower."

"Okay, in the meantime I'll take my swim."

"How can you swim when they just pulled a decomposing body out of there?"

As Carl turned to go put his swim suit on he said, "There are all kinds of dead things in the canal, and besides, I don't intend to swim where the body was."

Carl was used to long open ocean swims. He enjoyed the physical effort of a three or four mile swim, but today he would take only one lap, take a quick shower to rinse off the salt water, and then join Ann on the deck for some sun.

3

After her shower Ann put on a swimsuit, found a book she had been reading and pulled up a lounge chair and stretched out to enjoy the sun. Occasionally she would pick up the binoculars and watch Carl stroke cleanly through the water. After a short time she put the book down, leaned back enjoying the warmth of the sun, and closed her eyes. She thought about her life and realized that she was thoroughly contented.

Ann was not only Carl's fiancée whom he loved deeply, but she was his assistant, his partner and his best friend. She was an integral part of the investigation agency Carl owned. She was a beautiful woman of many talents.

She spoke four languages fluently. Frequently she and Carl would carry on their conversations in French, German, or Russian in order to maintain their fluency. She had degrees in linguistics and computer sciences. She was smart, capable, and in love with Carl. She was truly happy.

They had met at the beach in Southern California when Carl was in high school. The attraction between them was immediate, one could say it was love at first sight. They were both good looking, highly intelligent, had a deep interest in foreign languages, and had very compatible personalities.

Ann learned French from her parents, and growing up in Los Angeles, speaking Spanish was a necessity for getting along with the other kids in school. Her neighbors, the Bacigalluppi family, had five children who all spoke Italian so it was not long before she also spoke fluent Italian. In high school her interest was in mathematics and sciences consequently she decided to take German to meet her language requirement. When Carl came into the picture she realized that he also had a keen interest in languages, which increased her interest in him.

After high school Carl joined the Navy and Ann went to Stanford University, getting an advanced degree in computer sciences and a degree in linguistics. Carl tried to maintain contact with her but as the years went by and duties assignments took him out of the country he began to lose track of her.

Ann did not entirely forget Carl but he had faded in her memory as the workload and the challenges of her classes sapped her energy. In spite of the pressure she still managed to learn to speak Russian. She graduated at the top of her class in both majors. Just prior to graduation she was recruited by the Central Intelligence Agency and after a short vacation she moved to Washington, D.C.

When she reported for work at the CIA and had gone through her orientation she was assigned to the Russian desk to analyze documents. At first she enjoyed it but after reading market reports on wheat futures and steel production forecasts for months on end, she found the work had become boring and lacked any challenge. To give herself a break from the endless supply of reports she would bring in highly technical books on computer science to break the monotony.

Her interest in computer technology soon caught the attention of Chet Gibson, the man she had been dating. Although they dated frequently and enjoyed each other's company, Ann was not in love with him, but she was getting older and thoughts of marriage would occasionally surface at the back of her mind, only to be banished a short time later. Chet was a nice guy and he was convenient but their relationship could never seem to make the leap to a deep love with thoughts of a lifelong partnership.

Chet offered to help her get transferred to the technology office in the Special Operations Branch, which she jumped at. While there she was exposed to the latest technology and was taught all the tricks of computer espionage. Within a short time she was recognized as an expert in the field and the person to go to when a tough computer problem came up.

Ann could have been happy with her life, it certainly matched her technical curiosity, but it was less than satisfying on an emotional level. She would have probably drifted along in emotional limbo had it not be been for a fateful meeting Chet attended in the New York World Trade Center on September 11, 2001.

After Chet's death, Ann wanted to get away for a while and visit her parents in Seattle. She had been in Seattle only a short time when she decided to do a little shopping and have lunch downtown. She was wandering through the crowd at Pike's Market when she was jostled by a tall man. When he turned to apologize she recognized Carl and a flood of fond memories came rushing back.

After a few awkward seconds, recognition dawned on Carl and he simply hugged her. When he release her he said, "God, I've missed you," and hugged her again.

When he released her the second time he asked, "Can we find someplace to sit and talk, maybe have lunch? We have a lot of catching up to do."

"I'd really like that. There must be a restaurant away from the tourist crowd."

Dinners followed, sail-boating on Puget Sound, and long walks where conversation was not necessary. They simply enjoyed each other's company.

Over the following week they found that their feelings for each other had not diminished. At the end of the week Carl asked if she would be interested in working for his private investigation firm based in San Francisco. That night she called her boss at the CIA and quit her job. She joined Carl's firm and had been his partner, friend, and lover ever since. She had never regretted her decision to leave the CIA.

Carl soon returned dripping from his swim and interrupted her reminiscing about her past.

Later that afternoon a black sedan pulled up in front of the house and two men got out. They introduced themselves as homicide Detectives Murry and Davis then went on to say, "We have a few more questions concerning the body you found in the canal. Do you have a couple of minutes?"

"What did the coroner determine was the cause of death?"

"I'm sorry, Mr. Lukin, I can't discuss that, the only thing I can say is that it was an unnatural death. Are you and Ms. Curlin the only occupants of the house or do you have guests?"

"No, we are the only two staying here."

"Do you know if any of the neighbors had house guests or have you seen any strangers in the neighborhood?"

"No, we haven't spoken to any of the people in the area so I don't know the answer to your question. As far as strangers are concerned, I haven't seen any."

"I didn't think so but I had to ask. The tides could have washed that body here from anywhere but, then again, maybe not. I'll need addresses and telephone numbers for both of you in case we need to contact you.

"By the way, divers will be here shortly to search the area around the float for evidence. It's doubtful they will find anything because tidal action would have scattered any evidence over a wide area by now, but we have to look."

The following day, Carl and Ann were sitting on the deck reading when the phone rang. Carl answered and heard the voice of Alex Pribich, the President of World Bank and a personal friend. Alex was in his fifties, had a full head of graying hair, and was lean and muscular despite the fact that most of his day was spent behind a desk. He had degrees in economics and business from the best business school in the nation. The combination had allowed him to advance rapidly through the management ranks of World Bank to the top position of Bank President. Alex was tough and not prone to panic. But when he called Carl there was an edge to his voice that caught Carl's attention.

Speaking rapidly, Alex asked if Carl would come to San Francisco immediately, saying, "We have a big problem and I really need your help."

"Slow down, Alex, Ann and I are on vacation in Washington, there is no way we can get to San Francisco today. What's the problem?"

"I can't discuss it over the phone. What's the name of the nearest airport and I'll have the company jet pick you up." said Alex, in a tense voice.

"Okay, okay, the Bremerton National Airport is about thirty minutes from here, it's a small airport but I think it handles business jets."

"Be there in two hours." Without another word Alex hung up. Carl listened to the dial tone for a second or two then hung up the phone and turned to Ann. "Pack up, we're flying to San Francisco in two hours."

"What did Alex want?"

"I don't know, he didn't want to discuss it over the phone, but it must be serious because he's sending the company jet to pick us up at the Bremerton airport in two hours. He sounded nervous, which is not at all like Alex, he was really worked up."

4

It was midafternoon when Carl and Ann walked into the reception area of the office of the President of World Bank. The secretary, an attractive woman in her early forties with ash blond hair, walked around her desk, saying, "Mr. Lukin, Ms. Curlin, good to see you again, Mr. Pribich is waiting for you. Please step this way." Without waiting for a response she turned on her heel and walked to a large oak door, then opening the door she stepped aside, allowing Carl and Ann to enter.

Alex came around his desk and shook hands saying how glad he was that they could come on such short notice and apologized for interrupting their vacation.

Carl said, "Come on, Alex, you didn't interrupt our vacation and fly us down here on the corporate jet just for small talk, what's going on?"

Alex leaned forward, saying, "What I have to tell you must remain between us. If word of this should get out it could have a disastrous effect on this bank."

Pausing to think, he continued, "Two days ago we started receiving calls from a number of companies, such as Jenkins Aircraft, Armon

Shipping, and others, both small and large organizations. They all said the same thing. That money wired to them never arrived. Not just sent to the wrong address but that it had been diverted to another bank someplace in the world. As you know, World Bank has the largest wire service in the world. Billions of dollars are transferred between banks every day using our system. For instance, if China's Panda Airline buys five 747's they would be required to wire installment payments at various stages of the orders' completion. Many of these payments can be for tens or hundreds of millions of dollars.

"As of today we estimate that a little over $985 million dollars has disappeared. Each sender received a receipt from World Bank indicating that the money had been delivered. It took a couple of days for each company to realize they had not received payment as promised, research their records, and then call the sender to complain that they had not received the expected funds. The sender then had to research their records, and of course they had a World Bank confirmation that the money had been delivered. Then another couple of days of conversation back and forth until finally both companies called World Bank. We, of course, had to research the problem and another day was lost. Our best estimate is that the funds were stolen seven days ago.

"To make matters even more difficult our best system's programmer was on vacation. Today I received a call from a detective Murry in Silverdale, Washington saying that they had pulled a man out of the Hood Canal whom they believe worked for us. You guessed it, our best programmer, Ken Barkley.

"Our IT manager believes that the only way the theft could have occurred is that one or more system programs were replaced with duplicate programs containing bad code. We haven't found any bogus programs yet but that is the only way the money could have been rerouted and the dummy receipts sent out.

"Our IT manager tells me that Ken Barkley was smart enough to develop such a program but he would still have to put it into the production stream and he did not have access to that part of the system. With all the checks that have been involved in the changes to our system it would have taken a genius to pull this off, but then, Ken was a genius.

"Without the bogus programs it will be virtually impossible to trace the money to the bank account where it was sent. In any case, by now the money could be anyplace in the world."

"This appears to be a banking operations problem, where do we come in?" asked Carl.

"We want you to learn everything you can about Ken Barkley, and help us in recovering the money. We can cover the loss for a short time but if word of this gets out the bank could be ruined. You will of course be paid your usual fee and expenses plus a bonus on all recovered funds.

"And one other thing, this type of loss has to be reported to the FBI. We can probably hold them off until tomorrow afternoon because we are still in the process of conducting our internal investigation. Once the Feds get involved I don't know how much latitude you will have in your investigation, but I'll open the door for you and support your investigation as far as possible."

"If you want us to investigate of course we will. Ann will handle the investigation at the bank and I'll take on the field work."

Ann said, "Tomorrow morning I want to begin by meeting all of the DP managers, and I'll be giving them assignments. If they have any problem taking instructions from me or don't respond quickly I'm going to send them to you."

Carl continued, "You are going to have to call the Sheriff, and district attorney of Mason County, Washington, and tell them I am investigating a major crime and ask them to cooperate fully with my investigation. If they aren't willing to cooperate call the governor but get me access to all the investigative material.

"Ann will be staying here in San Francisco tonight but I need to get back to Washington as soon as possible. Can your plane fly me back to Washington tonight and bring me back tomorrow afternoon? I'll need to speak to detective Murry as soon as possible.

"Lastly, both Ann and I will need to be in on the meeting with the FBI. If they have a problem with our involvement we'll want to know what it is."

"The plane will be ready for you within the hour and I'll call the Washington authorities right now."

5

Alex looked at the two men sitting in front of his desk and said. "As you two know we have had a serious theft. I've hired the Lukin Investigation Agency to help us. Ann Curling will be in charge of the investigation here at the bank until they are done. You will follow all instructions she may have with respect to the investigation. If you have any serious concerns with following her instructions see me. Any instruction she issues will have the highest priority, is that clear?"

Vice President for Security, Jim Gordon, and the Vice President for Information Technology, Phillip Wise both nodded their understanding.

"Ann, do you have any comments?"

"Not at this time."

Alex continued by making it clear that the theft was not to be discussed with anyone. They had less than twenty-four hours before the theft had to be reported to the FBI and he wanted answers before then.

After the meeting with Alex, Ann met with Philip Wise and Jim Gordon to get a briefing on the banks operation. Ann was a world class computer systems analyst who could quickly grasp the essential elements of a complex computer system and devise a plan to find a problem. Phillip Wise outlined the operation of the banking network and suggested that the problem most likely occurred in the modules of the production stream that handled wire transfers.

Ann said, "I agree, the problem is in programs supporting the Wire Transfer. We need to isolate that section of the system. Do you have a backup available?"

Phillip said "We take a backup of the entire system once each week. More often if we are going to make significant changes."

Ann said, "Ok, let's go back about five weeks. It's doubtful that the phony program was introduced that far back, there would be too much risk that a Trojan Horse program would be discovered."

Philip said, "It'll take about an hour to update the system with the back-up tape."

"We'll also use the backup tape to do a bit by bit comparison against the existing system. Once we have identified the bad code have two of your best system programmers begin to backward engineer the phony code."

Ann said "Jim, can you get me a roster of all employees who had access to the production and testing systems?"

"Sure, there are very few employees that have the authority to access the production system and special authority is also required to use the testing system. It's only used for testing changes to the production system. Development work is done on a totally different computer in another part of the building and it's not connected to the testing or production system."

"Okay, tell me how you control access to the production system?"

"The process requires that after a new program has been developed or any changes made to the existing system, the new program, or modified program must undergo weeks of testing. Testing uses a set of specifically developed test data as well as live production data. After the testing is complete, Department managers must approve the changes and test results before any changes are placed in the production stream.

Development programmers are not allowed to do final testing. All testing is done by a special team on a separate computer. After all the approvals have been received only one production manager has the authority and password to update the production stream.

The production and testing are even in a separate part of the building behind locked doors. Development people are not allowed to enter this area, violation of this rule is sufficient reason for dismissal.

"Which production manager has the authority to make changes to the production system?"

"Al Genovese has had the authority for the past few years but he is on vacation. While Al is gone John Cary has the authorization to make any necessary changes."

"By the way, the managers' passwords are changed every sixty days. When Al gets back it will be changed again even though it will not have been sixty days."

6

"Are all four managers available for an interview?" asked Ann.

"No. One is on vacation but the rest are working or can be called in. The manager who is on vacation, Al Genovese, is planning a few local area hiking trips and might be at home."

Within two hours all the production managers had been questioned, with the exception of Al Genovese, who could not be reached. Both Ann and Jim felt it was necessary to talk to Genovese immediately and the place to start was at his apartment. They tried to reach Genovese by phone again but received no answer.

When Ann and Jim arrived at the Genovese apartment they knocked on the door but there was no answer. There was a faint odor that seemed to be coming from the apartment. Ann stepped back, she had smelled that odor only two days ago and it made her nauseous. "I hope this is not what I think it is. We need to find the apartment manager and get him to open the door, there's something dead in there."

Five minutes later the apartment manager was inserting a key into the door lock. When the door opened a wave of the foul odor came floating out. The shocked manager put a hand over his mouth and nose saying, "Oh my God!"

Ann grabbed the apartment manager by the arm and said, "Call 911, tell them we have a dead body." With that, Jim and Ann cautiously entered the apartment.

The front room had obviously been ransacked, desk drawers had been pulled open and dumped, books pulled from the bookshelves and dropped, pictures pulled from the walls and smashed.

The kitchen was also a mess, all the cabinets were open and the contents strewn about the room, drawers had been dumped on the floor.

There were two bedrooms, one of which was apparently used as an office. It had been thoroughly searched, the desk that once held a computer had been ransacked and the computer taken, all that was left was the dust imprint where it once sat.

The door to the other bedroom stood open. What they saw sickened both of them. Al Genovese was tied to a chair and had obviously been tortured then killed. The chair he was seated on was turned to face the bed on which there was a woman whose hands had been tied to the head of the bed and her legs spread and tied to the corners at the foot of the bed. She had tape over her mouth and her clothes had been ripped off. She had also been tortured and it appeared as if she had been raped. She was obviously dead.

Ann heard Jim say, "Oh shit."

They carefully backed out of the apartment and waited for the police to arrive. While they waited Ann called Carl and told him in detail about what they had found and what they were doing at the bank to find how the money had been stolen. She told him that they expected to have some answers by that afternoon.

The police arrived within a few minutes. Both Ann and Jim were asked to give statements.

They overheard the forensic team tell one of the detectives it appeared that the cause of death for both bodies was a gunshot wound to the head from a small caliber weapon, probably a .22, revolver since no shell casings were found.

7

Carl approached the front desk of the Sheriff's Office in Silverdale, a town about twenty minutes north of Bremerton, Washington. He asked for Detective Murry.

"May I say who wants to see him?" asked the middle-age receptionist, as she pushed a visitor's logbook toward him.

Carl told her his name and signed the log book, then sat down to wait.

A few minutes later the Detective who Carl had met at the Hood Canal house came through the door, said hello and shook hands with him. "We'll use one of the interview rooms, that way we won't be disturbed."

They entered a small interview room and Detective Murry gestured for Carl to sit in a chair across the table from him. He said, "I don't know who you know in this state but I received a call from both the Sheriff and the District Attorney, and they each received a call from the State Attorney General with orders to fill you in on everything we know about the body you found in the Hood Canal."

"I'm investigating a large scale robbery for a major bank in San Francisco and the dead man appears to have played a key role in the robbery. We're trying to find out as much information as we can about Ken Barkley and hopefully recover the money."

"How much was taken?"

"The bank has requested that I not disclose that figure. The only thing I am permitted to say is that it was substantial. I suggest that you talk to Detective Jomblonski of the San Francisco Police Department."

There were a few seconds of silence as Detective Murry thought about Carl's answer, obviously not happy with it, he shrugged, and said, "Okay, I'll tell you all I know, which isn't a whole hell of a lot at this time.

"When we fished the body out of the canal we thought it was another drunk who had been fishing, fell out of a boat, and drowned. We had a hard time identifying him because of the damage from the crabs that had fed on him so it was not evident that he had been murdered until he was examined by the coroner, who found a small bullet hole in the back of the head. He had also been shot in the right ear. The bullets were recovered. The killer used a .22 caliber gun, from the groves on the bullet it was determined to be a Smith and Wesson, snub nose, revolver, which explains why we didn't find any shell casings. The bullet in the back of the head went through the brain stem then rattled around inside the skull, turning his brain to mush. The second shot wasn't really necessary, but it too just rattled around in the Vic's head, further damaging the brain. We haven't found the gun yet. The killer probably dumped it in the canal or took it with him.

"There was a tattooing around the entry wounds on the back of the head as well as singed hair from the muzzle blast. There was also tattooing on the ear as well indicating that the gun was held very close to the victims head. There was too much narcosis and damage to the brain to provide any directionality information about the bullet path. But from the position of the entry wound I would guess that the victim was bending over for the first shot and prone on the floor for the second shot.

"The first shot damaged the brain stem so much that all bodily movement would have stopped instantly. The heart would also have stopped pumping blood immediately. That's probably why we didn't find much blood at the crime scene. He would have simply fallen to the floor after the first shot.

"It took us a while to identify him because the crabs had pretty much destroyed his face and fingerprints but there was enough on the right hand thumb to get a six-point match for an ID, which as you know is not enough to take to court but it pointed us to a DMV record. Hair color, weight, and height matched the body we found so we're pretty sure we have the right ID.

"How did you find the crime scene?"

"A couple of days earlier we received a call from a fishing resort manager who was concerned about one of their guests. A resort housekeeper had reported that when she went to clean up his cabin she didn't see any personal items or clothes. She noticed that a pillowcase, blanket, and some towels were missing. She also found what looked like blood on the door jamb. The housekeeper reported her findings to the manager who called the sheriff's office. Since Mr. Barkley hadn't checked out he was concerned. DNA tests show the blood didn't belong to Mr. Barkley.

"We didn't think much about it at the time, just another guest who skipped out without paying his bill.

"At about the same time a patrol officer found a burned out car about a mile from the resort. The license plates were gone but we found ID numbers on the motor block and chassis that led to a car rental company at the SEA/TAC airport. The reading on the odometer matched the distance from the airport to the fishing resort. The car had been rented to a Ken Barkley from San Francisco. A check with the airlines indicated that Mr. Barkley had arrived early the previous morning. It turns out it's the same guy that skipped out on the resort.

"That's about all I can tell you, if we find anything else I'll give you a call."

"Did your divers find any evidence in the canal?"

"No, either there wasn't any or the tides washed it away.

"We did find a kitchen knife on the ground where cars are usually parked. And it had a fingerprint on it that we ran through AFIS. It came back as belonging to a Simon Rossman of Sacramento, California. We checked with the manager and there has never been a Simon Rossman registered there. Rossman probably used it to take off the license plates and forgot it. Of course we have the blood on the door jamb, it didn't belong to Barkley, and it doesn't show up on the Criminal Justice DNA File. We'll check it against Rossman when we find him.

"It looks like the killer took the time to clean up. That's probably why the towels are gone. The cabin had been wiped down, we didn't find any fingerprints in any of the normal places that you would expect to find them, Ken Barkley's, or anyone else's. It was a little too clean, if you know what I mean.

"There was a complaint from one of the other people staying at the resort that someone had stolen the anchor from their boat that had been tied up at the dock. It looks as if the body might have been carried to the boat, rowed out and thrown overboard tied to an anchor. Which makes me think the killer was a man. A woman would have had a hard time carrying the body. We checked the oars for fingerprints, there weren't any, they had been wiped clean.

"That about covers it, I don't know what else I can tell you."

"Thanks, I guess that's it for now. I have to get back to San Francisco in the morning but I would like to look around the cabin before I go."

"I'll meet you at the cabin in the morning. We intend to release it back to the resort sometime tomorrow unless you find something that we missed."

Carl arrived at the Ferguson fishing resort a few minutes early. While he waited for Detective Murry he looked around the resort grounds. He found that someone could have carried a body to the dock without being seen, particularly if it was late at night and dark. Nothing else caught his attention.

When Detective Murry arrived they examined the inside of the cabin, found nothing, and were standing outside when Carl asked, "Do you know if there was a full moon when Barkley disappeared?"

"I don't know, why do you ask?"

"The cabin is at the back side of the resort. If the moon was dark it would have been almost impossible to see the killer, but if it was full it might be worthwhile to check with the other guests."

"Good point. I'll check it out."

Carl said he had to return to San Francisco. He thanked Detective Murry for his help and left